NOT WHAT YOU EXPECTED

NOT WHAT YOU EXPECTED

A Collection of Short Stories by

Joan Aiken

DOUBLEDAY & COMPANY, INC.
Garden City, New York

The following stories in this collection first appeared in *A
Small Pinch of Weather:* The Cost of Night, A Leg Full of
Rubies, The Boy Who Read Aloud. *All and More:* More
Than You Bargained For, Dolls' House to Let, Mod. Con.,
The People in the Castle, Don't Pay the Postman, The Third
Wish, Pigeon Cake for Miss Samphire, Nutshells, Seashells,
Some Music for the Wicked Countess, A Room Full of
Leaves. *A Harp of Fishbones:* The Boy with a Wolf's Foot,
A Harp of Fishbones, The Lost Five Minutes, The Rose of
Puddle Fratrum, Humblepuppy, A Long Day Without Wa-
ter, The Dark Streets of Kimball's Green, Mrs Nutti's Fire-
place, Hope. All published by Jonathan Cape Ltd.

Library of Congress Cataloging in Publication Data

Aiken, Joan, 1924–
   Not what you expected.

    CONTENTS: A harp of fishbones.—The boy with a
wolf's foot.—The lost five minutes. [etc.]
    [1. Short stories] I. Title.
PZ7.A2695No   [Fic]
ISBN 0-385-07518-9 Trade
      0-385-08516-8 Prebound
Library of Congress Catalog Card Number 73–81121

Contents

Foreword

For me, looking through these stories is like a trip back over half my life, since they have been written during a span of nearly twenty-five years. Some of the places in them—for instance, the garden in *More Than You Bargained For,* the castle in *The People in the Castle*—are real places. The house called Troy, in *A Room Full of Leaves,* was based on Knole House, in Kent.

Some of the stories, like *Doll's House to Let, Mod. Con.,* were written so long ago that I think, if I were to write them now, I would probably do it in a different way. In fact I considered rewriting a few, to make them all more uniform. But a story, once written, takes on a life of its own. Trying to change it is like trying to change somebody's character. In the end I decided that rewriting them would be wrong—almost a kind of cheating—and so I left them alone.

J.A.

NOT WHAT YOU EXPECTED

A Harp of Fishbones

Little Nerryn lived in the half-ruined mill at the upper end of the village, where the stream ran out of the forest. The old miller's name was Timorash, but she called him uncle. Her own father and mother were dead, long before she could remember. Timorash was no real kin, nor was he particularly kind to her; he was a lazy old man. He never troubled to grow corn as the other people in the village did, little patches in the clearing below the village before the forest began again. When people brought him corn to grind he took one-fifth of it as his fee and this, with wild plums which Nerryn gathered and dried, and carp from the deep millpool, kept him and the child fed through the short bright summers and the long silent winters.

Nerryn learned to do the cooking when she was seven or eight; she toasted fish on sticks over the fire and baked cakes of bread on a flat stone; Timorash beat her if the food was burnt, but it mostly was, just the same, because so often half her mind would be elsewhere, listening to the bell-like call of a bird or pondering about what made the difference between the stream's voice in winter and in summer. When she was a little older Timorash taught her how to work the mill, opening the sluice-gate so that the green, clear mountain water could hurl down against the great wooden paddle-wheel. Nerryn liked this much better, since she had already spent hours watching the stream endlessly pouring and plaiting down its narrow passage. Old Timorash had hoped that now he would be able to give up work altogether and lie in the sun all day, or crouch by the fire, slowly adding one stick after another and dreaming about barley wine. But Nerryn forgot to take flour in payment from the villagers, who were in no hurry to remind her, so the old man angrily decided that this plan would not answer, and sent her out to work.

First she worked for one household, then for another.

The people of the village had come from the plains; they were surly, big-boned, and lank, with tow-coloured hair and pale eyes; even the children seldom spoke. Little Nerryn sometimes wondered, looking at her reflection in the millpool, how it was that she should be so different from them, small and brown-skinned, with dark hair like a bird's feathers and hazelnut eyes. But it was no use asking questions of old Timorash, who never answered except by grunting or throwing a clod of earth at her. Another difference was that she loved to chatter, and this was perhaps the main reason why the people she worked for soon sent her packing.

There were other reasons too, for, though Nerryn was willing enough to work, things often distracted her.

"She let the bread burn while she ran outside to listen to a curlew," said one.

"When she was helping me cut the hay she asked so many questions that my ears have ached for three days," complained another.

"Instead of scaring off the birds from my corn-patch she sat with her chin on her fists, watching them gobble down half a winter's supply and whistling to them!" grumbled a third.

Nobody would keep her more than a few days, and she had plenty of beatings, especially from Timorash, who had hoped that her earnings would pay for a keg of barley wine. Once in his life he had had a whole keg, and he still felt angry when he remembered that it was finished.

At last Nerryn went to work for an old woman who lived in a tumbledown hut at the bottom of the street. Her name was Saroon and she was by far the oldest in the village, so withered and wrinkled that most people thought she was a witch; besides, she knew when it was going to rain and was the only person in the place who did not fear to venture a little way into the forest. But she was growing weak now, and stiff, and wanted somebody to help dig her corn-patch and cut wood. Nevertheless she hardly seemed to welcome help when it came. As Nerryn moved about at the tasks she was set, the old woman's little red-rimmed eyes followed her suspiciously; she hobbled round the hut watching through cracks, grumbling and chuntering to herself, never losing sight of the girl for a moment, like some cross-grained old animal that sees a stranger near its burrow.

On the fourth day she said,

"You're singing, girl."

"I—I'm sorry," Nerryn stammered. "I didn't mean to—I wasn't thinking. Don't beat me, please."

"Humph," said the old woman, but she did not beat Nerryn that time. And next day, watching through the window-hole while Nerryn chopped wood, she said,

"You're not singing."

Nerryn jumped. She had not known the old woman was so near.

"I thought you didn't like me to," she faltered.

"I didn't say so, did I?"

Muttering, the old woman stumped off to the back of the hut and began to sort through a box of mildewy nuts. "As if I should care," Nerryn heard her grumble, "whether the girl sings or not!" But next day she put her head out of the door, while Nerryn hoed the corn-patch, and said,

"Sing, child!"

Nerryn looked at her, doubtful and timid, to see if she really meant it, but she nodded her head energetically, till

the tangled grey locks jounced on her shoulders, and repeated,

"Sing!"

So presently the clear, tiny thread of Nerryn's song began
again as she sliced off the weeds; and old Saroon came out and
sat on an upturned log beside the door, pounding roots for
soup and mumbling to herself in time to the sound. And at
the end of the week she did not dismiss the girl, as everyone
else had done, though what she paid was so little that Timorash grumbled every time Nerryn brought it home. At this
rate twenty years would go by before he had saved enough for
a keg of barley wine.

One day Saroon said,

"Your father used to sing."

This was the first time anyone had spoken of him.

"Oh," Nerryn cried, forgetting her fear of the old woman.
"Tell me about him."

"Why should I?" old Saroon said sourly. "He never did
anything for *me*." And she hobbled off to fetch a pot of water.
But later she relented and said,

"His hair was the colour of ash buds, like yours. And he
carried a harp."

"A harp, what is a harp?"

"Oh, don't pester, child. I'm busy."

But another day she said, "A harp is a thing to make music.
His was a gold one, but it was broken."

"Gold, what is gold?"

"This," said the old woman, and she pulled out a small,
thin disc which she wore on a cord of plaited grass round her
neck.

"Why!" Nerryn exclaimed. "Everybody in the village has
one of those except Timorash and me. I've often asked what
they were but no one would answer."

"They are gold. When your father went off and left you
and the harp with Timorash, the old man ground up the harp

between the millstones. And he melted down the gold powder and made it into these little circles and sold them to everybody in the village, and bought a keg of barley wine. He told us they would bring good luck. But I have never had any good luck and that was a long time ago. And Timorash has long since drunk all his barley wine."

"Where did my father go?" asked Nerryn.

"Into the forest," the old woman snapped. "I could have told him he was in for trouble. I could have warned him. But he never asked *my* advice."

She sniffed, and set a pot of herbs boiling on the fire. And Nerryn could get no more out of her that day.

But little by little, as time passed, more came out.

"Your father came from over the mountains. High up yonder, he said, there was a great city, with houses and palaces and temples, and as many rich people as there are fish in the millpool. Best of all, there was always music playing in the streets and houses and in the temples. But then the goddess of the mountain became angry, and fire burst out of a crack in the hillside. And then a great cold came, so that people froze where they stood. Your father said he only just managed to escape with you by running very fast. Your mother had died in the fire."

"Where was he going?"

"The king of the city had ordered him to go for help."

"What sort of help?"

"Don't ask *me,*" the old woman grumbled. "You'd think he'd have settled down here like a person of sense, and mended his harp. But no, on he must go, leaving you behind so that he could travel faster. He said he'd fetch you again on his way back. But of course he never did come back—one day I found his bones in the forest. The birds must have killed him."

"How do you *know* they were my father's bones?"

"Because of the tablet he carried. See, here it is, with his name on it, Heramon the harper."

"Tell me more about the harp!"

"It was shaped like this," the old woman said. They were washing clothes by the stream, and she drew with her finger in the mud. "Like this, and it had golden strings across, so. All but one of the strings had melted in the fire from the mountain. Even on just one string he could make very beautiful music, that would force you to stop whatever you were doing and listen. It is a pity he had to leave the harp behind. Timorash wanted it as payment for looking after you. If your father had taken the harp with him, perhaps he would have been able to reach the other side of the forest."

Nerryn thought about this story a great deal. For the next few weeks she did even less work than usual and was mostly to be found squatting with her chin on her fists by the side of the stream. Saroon beat her, but not very hard. Then one day Nerryn said,

"I shall make a harp."

"Hah!" sniffed the old woman. "You! What do you know of such things?"

After a few minutes she asked,

"What will you make it from?"

Nerryn said, "I shall make it of fishbones. Some of the biggest carp in the millpool have bones as thick as my wrist, and they are very strong."

"Timorash will never allow it."

"I shall wait till he is asleep, then."

So Nerryn waited till night, and then she took a chunk of rotten wood, which glows in the dark, and dived into the deep millpool, swimming down and down to the depths where the biggest carp lurk, among the mud and weeds and old sunken logs.

When they saw the glimmer of the wood through the water, all the fish came nosing and nibbling and swimming round

Nerryn, curious to find if this thing which shone so strangely was good to eat. She waited as long as she could bear it, holding her breath, till a great barrel-shaped monster slid nudging right up against her; then, quick as a flash, she wrapped her arms round his slippery sides and fled up with a bursting heart to the surface.

Much to her surprise, old Saroon was there, waiting in the dark on the bank. But the old woman only said,

"You had better bring the carp to my hut. After all, you want no more than the bones, and it would be a pity to waste all the good meat. I can live on it for a week." So she cut the meat off the bones, which were coal-black but had a sheen on them like mother-of-pearl. Nerryn dried them by the fire, and then she joined together the three biggest, notching them to fit, and cementing them with a glue which she made by boiling some of the smaller bones together. She used long, thin, strong bones for strings, joining them to the frame in the same manner.

All the time old Saroon watched closely. Sometimes she would say,

"That was not the way of it. Heramon's harp was wider," or "You are putting the strings too far apart. There should be more of them, and they should be tighter."

When at last it was done, she said,

"Now you must hang it in the sun to dry."

So for three days the harp hung drying in the sun and wind. At night Saroon took it into her hut and covered it with a cloth. On the fourth day she said,

"Now, play!"

Nerryn rubbed her finger across the strings, and they gave out a liquid murmur, like that of a stream running over pebbles, under a bridge. She plucked a string, and the noise was like that a drop of water makes, falling in a hollow place.

"That will be music," old Saroon said, nodding her head, satisfied. "It is not quite the same as the sound from your father's harp, but it is music. Now you shall play me tunes every day, and I shall sit in the sun and listen."

"No," said Nerryn, "for if Timorash hears me playing he will take the harp away and break it or sell it. I shall go to my father's city and see if I can find any of his kin there."

At this old Saroon was very angry. "Here have I taken all these pains to help you, and what reward do I get for it? How much pleasure do you think I have, living among dolts in this dismal place? I was not born here, any more than you were. You could at least play to me at night, when Timorash is asleep."

"Well, I will play to you for seven nights," Nerryn said.

Each night old Saroon tried to persuade her not to go, and she tried harder as Nerryn became more skilful in playing, and drew from the fishbone harp a curious watery music, like the songs that birds sing when it is raining. But Nerryn would not be persuaded to stay, and when she saw this, on the seventh night, Saroon said,

"I suppose I shall have to tell you how to go through the forest. Otherwise you will certainly die, as your father did. When you go among the trees you will find that the grass underfoot is thick and strong and hairy, and the farther you go, the higher it grows, as high as your waist. And it is sticky and clings to you, so that you can only go forward slowly, one step at a time. Then, in the middle of the forest, perched in the branches, are vultures who will drop on you and peck you to death if you stand still for more than a minute."

"How do you know all this?" Nerryn said.

"I have tried many times to go through the forest, but it is too far for me; I grow tired and have to turn back. The vultures take no notice of me, I am too old and withered, but a tender young piece like you would be just what they fancy."

"Then what must I do?" Nerryn asked.

"You must play music on your harp till they fall asleep;

then, while they sleep, cut the grass with your knife and go forward as fast as you can."

Nerryn said, "If I cut you enough fuel for a month, and
catch you another carp, and gather you a bushel of nuts, will
you give me your little gold circle, or my father's tablet?"

But this Saroon would not do. She did, though, break off
the corner of the tablet which had Heramon the harper's
name on it, and give that to Nerryn.

"But don't blame me," she said sourly, "if you find the city
all burnt and frozen, with not a living soul to walk its streets."

"Oh, it will all have been rebuilt by this time," Nerryn
said. "I shall find my father's people, or my mother's, and I
shall come back for you, riding a white mule and leading another."

"Fairy tales!" old Saroon said angrily. "Be off with you,
then. If you don't wish to stay I'm sure *I* don't want you
idling about the place. All the work you've done this last week
I could have done better myself in half an hour. Drat the
woodsmoke! It gets in a body's eyes till they can't see a thing."
And she hobbled into the hut, working her mouth sourly and
rubbing her eyes with the back of her hand.

Nerryn ran into the forest, going cornerways up the mountain, so as not to pass too close to the mill where old Timorash
lay sleeping in the sun.

Soon she had to slow down because the way was so steep.
And the grass grew thicker and thicker, hairy, sticky, all
twined and matted together, as high as her waist. Presently, as
she hacked and cut at it with her bone knife, she heard a
harsh croaking and flapping above her. She looked up, and
saw two grey vultures perched on a branch, leaning forward to peer down at her. Their wings were twice the length
of a man's arm and they had long, wrinkled, black, leathery
necks and little fierce yellow eyes. As she stood, two more,
then five, ten, twenty others came rousting through the
branches, and all perched round about, craning down their

long black necks, swaying back and forth, keeping balanced by the way they opened and shut their wings.

Nerryn felt very much afraid of them, but she unslung the harp from her back and began to play a soft, trickling tune, like rain falling on a deep pool. Very soon the vultures sank their necks down between their shoulders and closed their eyes. They sat perfectly still.

When she was certain they were asleep, Nerryn made haste to cut and slash at the grass. She was several hundred yards on her way before the vultures woke and came cawing and jostling through the branches to cluster again just overhead. Quickly she pulled the harp round and strummed on its fishbone strings until once again, lulled by the music, the vultures sank their heads between their grey wings and slept. Then she went back to cutting the grass, as fast as she could.

It was a long, tiring way. Soon she grew so weary that she could hardly push one foot ahead of the other, and it was hard to keep awake; once she only just roused in time when a vulture, swooping down, missed her with his beak and instead struck the harp on her back with a loud strange twang that set echoes scampering through the trees.

At last the forest began to thin and dwindle; here the tree-trunks and branches were all draped about with grey-green moss, like long dangling hanks of sheepswool. Moss grew on the rocky ground, too, in a thick carpet. When she reached this part, Nerryn could go on safely; the vultures rose in an angry flock and flew back with harsh croaks of disappointment, for they feared the trailing moss would wind round their wings and trap them.

As soon as she reached the edge of the trees Nerryn lay down in a deep tussock of moss and fell fast asleep.

She was so tired that she slept almost till nightfall, but then the cold woke her. It was bitter on the bare mountain-side; the ground was all crisp with white frost, and when Nerryn started walking uphill she crunched through it, leaving deep black footprints. Unless she kept moving she knew that she would probably die of cold, so she climbed on, higher and higher; the stars came out, showing more frost-covered slopes ahead and all round, while the forest far below curled round the flank of the mountain like black fur.

Through the night she went on climbing and by sunrise she had reached the foot of a steep slope of ice-covered boulders. When she tried to climb over these she only slipped back again.

What shall I do now? Nerryn wondered. She stood blowing on her frozen fingers and thought, "I must go on or I shall die here of cold. I will play a tune on the harp to warm my fingers and my wits."

She unslung the harp. It was hard to play, for her fingers were almost numb and at first refused to obey but, while she had climbed the hill, a very sweet, lively tune had come into her head, and she struggled and struggled until her stubborn fingers found the right notes to play it. Once she played the tune—twice—and the stones on the slope above began to roll and shift. She played a third time and, with a thunderous roar, the whole pile broke loose and went sliding down the mountain-side. Nerryn was only just able to dart aside out of the way before the frozen mass careered past, sending up a smoking dust of ice.

Trembling a little, she went on up the hill, and now she came to a gate in a great wall, set about with towers. The gate stood open, and so she walked through.

"Surely this must be my father's city," she thought.

But when she stood inside the gate, her heart sank, and she remembered old Saroon's words. For the city that must once have been bright with gold and coloured stone and gay with music was all silent; not a soul walked the streets and the houses, under their thick covering of frost, were burnt and blackened by fire.

And, what was still more frightening, when Nerryn looked

through the doorways into the houses, she could see people standing or sitting or lying, frozen still like statues, as the cold had caught them while they worked, or slept, or sat at dinner.

"Where shall I go now?" she thought. "It would have been better to stay with Saroon in the forest. When night comes I shall only freeze to death in this place."

But still she went on, almost tiptoeing in the frosty silence of the city, looking into doorways and through gates, until she came to a building that was larger than any other, built with a high roof and many pillars of white marble. The fire had not touched it.

"This must be the temple," she thought, remembering the tale Saroon had told, and she walked between the pillars, which glittered like white candles in the light from the rising sun. Inside there was a vast hall, and many people standing frozen, just as they had been when they came to pray for deliverance from their trouble. They had offerings with them, honey and cakes and white doves and lambs and precious ointment. At the back of the hall the people wore rough clothes of homespun cloth, but farther forward Nerryn saw wonderful robes, embroidered with gold and copper thread, made of rich materials, trimmed with fur and sparkling stones. And up in the very front, kneeling on the steps of the altar, was a man who was finer than all the rest and Nerryn thought he must have been the king himself. His hair and long beard were white, his cloak was purple, and on his head were three crowns, one gold, one copper, and one of ivory. Nerryn stole up to him and touched the fingers that held a gold staff, but they were ice-cold and still as marble, like all the rest.

A sadness came over her as she looked at the people and she thought, "What use to them are their fine robes now? Why did the goddess punish them? What did they do wrong?"

But there was no answer to her question.

"I had better leave this place before I am frozen as well,"

she thought. "The goddess may be angry with me too, for coming here. But first I will play for her on my harp, as I have not brought any offering."

So she took her harp and began to play. She played all the tunes she could remember, and last of all she played the one that had come into her head as she climbed the mountain.

At the noise of her playing, frost began to fall in white showers from the roof of the temple, and from the rafters and pillars and the clothes of the motionless people. Then the king sneezed. Then there was a stirring noise, like the sound of a winter stream when the ice begins to melt. Then someone laughed—a loud, clear laugh. And, just as, outside the town, the pile of frozen rocks had started to move and topple when Nerryn played, so now the whole gathering of people began to stretch themselves, and turn round, and look at one another, and smile. And as she went on playing they began to dance.

The dancing spread, out of the temple and down the streets. People in the houses stood up and danced. Still dancing, they fetched brooms and swept away the heaps of frost that kept falling from the rooftops with the sound of the music. They fetched old wooden pipes and tabors out of cellars that had escaped the fire, so that when Nerryn stopped playing at last, quite tired out, the music still went on. All day and all night, for thirty days, the music lasted, until the houses were rebuilt, the streets clean, and not a speck of frost remained in the city.

But the king beckoned Nerryn aside when she stopped playing and they sat down on the steps of the temple.

"My child," he said, "where did you get that harp?"

"Sir, I made it out of fishbones after a picture of my father's harp that an old woman made for me."

"And what was your father's name, child, and where is he now?"

"Sir, he is dead in the forest, but here is a piece of a tablet with his name on it."

And Nerryn held out the little fragment with Heramon the harper's name written. When he saw it, great tears formed in the king's eyes and began to roll down his cheeks.

"Sir," Nerryn said, "what is the matter? Why do you weep?"

"I weep for my son Heramon, who is lost, and I weep for joy because my grandchild has returned to me."

Then the king embraced Nerryn and took her to his palace and had robes of fur and velvet put on her, and there was great happiness and much feasting. And the king told Nerryn how, many years ago, the goddess was angered because the people had grown so greedy for gold from her mountain that they spent their lives in digging and mining, day and night, and forgot to honour her with music, in her temple and in the streets, as they had been used to do. They made tools of gold, and plates and dishes and musical instruments; everything that could be was made of gold. So at last the goddess appeared among them, terrible with rage, and put a curse on them, of burning and freezing.

"Since you prefer gold, got by burrowing in the earth, to the music that should honour me," she said, "you may keep your golden toys and little good may they do you! Let your golden harps and trumpets be silent, your flutes and pipes be dumb! I shall not come among you again until I am summoned by notes from a harp that is not made of gold, nor of silver, nor any precious metal, a harp that has never touched the earth but came from deep water, a harp that no man has ever played."

Then fire burst out of the mountain, destroying houses and killing many people. The king ordered his son Heramon, who was the bravest man in the city, to cross the dangerous forest and seek far and wide until he should find the harp of which the goddess spoke. Before Heramon could depart a great cold had struck, freezing people where they stood; only just in time he caught up his little daughter from her cradle and carried her away with him.

"But now you are come back," the old king said, "you shall be queen after me, and we shall take care that the goddess is honoured with music every day, in the temple and in the streets. And we will order everything that is made of gold to be thrown into the mountain torrent, so that nobody ever again shall be tempted to worship gold before the goddess."

So this was done, the king himself being the first to throw away his golden crown and staff. The river carried all the golden things down through the forest until they came to rest in Timorash's millpool, and one day, when he was fishing for carp, he pulled out the crown. Overjoyed, he ground it to powder and sold it to his neighbours for barley wine. Then he returned to the pool, hoping for more gold, but by now he was so drunk that he fell in and was drowned among a clutter of golden spades and trumpets and goblets and pickaxes.

But long before this Nerryn, with her harp on her back and astride of a white mule with knives bound to its hoofs, had ridden down the mountain to fetch Saroon as she had promised. She passed the forest safely, playing music for the vultures while the mule cut its way through the long grass. Nobody in the village recognized her, so splendidly was she dressed in fur and scarlet.

But when she came to where Saroon's hut had stood, the ground was bare, nor was there any trace that a dwelling had ever been there. And when she asked for Saroon, nobody knew the name, and the whole village declared that such a person had never been there.

Amazed and sorrowful, Nerryn returned to her grandfather. But one day, not long after, when she was alone, praying in the temple of the goddess, she heard a voice that said,

"Sing, child!"

And Nerryn was greatly astonished, for she felt she had heard the voice before, though she could not think where.

While she looked about her, wondering, the voice said again, "Sing!"

And then Nerryn understood, and she laughed, and, taking her harp, sang a song about chopping wood, and about digging, and fishing, and the birds of the forest, and how the stream's voice changes in summer and in winter. For now she knew who had helped her to make her harp of fishbones.

The Boy With a Wolf's Foot

Once when I was travelling on a train from Waterloo to Guildford I looked out of the window and saw a boy and a great Alsatian dog running through the fields. Just for a few moments they seemed to be able to run faster than the train.

This is that boy's story.

The night of Will Wilder's birth was one of rain and gale; the wind went hunting along the railway embankment between Worplesdon and Woking like something that has been shut in a cave for twenty years.

Have you ever noticed what a lot of place names begin with a W in that part of the world? There's Wandsworth and Wimbledon, Walton and Weybridge and Worcester Park; there's Witley and Wanborough and West Byfleet; then, farther east, Waddon and Wallington, Woodmansterne, Woodside, Westerham, Warlingham, and Woldingham; it's as if ancient Surrey and Kent had been full of the wailing of wild things in the woods.

Maybe it was the wind that caused the train derailment; anyway, whatever the cause, young Doctor Talisman, who, tired out, had fallen asleep in his non-smoking carriage after coming off duty at the Waterloo Hospital, was woken by a violent grinding jerk and at the same moment found himself flung clean through the train window to land, unhurt but somewhat dazed, in a clump of brambles that luckily broke his fall.

He scrambled through the prickles, trying to rub rain and darkness from his eyes, and discovered that he was standing, as it were, in a loop of train. The middle section had been derailed and sagged down the embankment, almost upside down; the two ends were still on the track. People were running and shouting; lights flared; the rain splashed and hissed on hot metal; the wind howled over all.

Pulling himself together the doctor made his way to the nearest group.

"I'm a medical man," he said. "Is anybody in need of help?"

People were glad to turn to him; there were plenty of cuts and bruises and he was kept busy till the ambulances managed to make their way to the spot—which took time, for the crash had happened quite a long way from the nearest road, and they had to come bumping over grass and round bushes and past stacks of timber and bricks, through a bit of dark countryside that was half heath, half waste land, with the River Wey running through it.

"Any seriously hurt?" an ambulance attendant asked, finding the young doctor working among the injured.

"One broken leg; several concussions; and there's one man killed outright," said the doctor sadly. "What makes it worse is that he had a young baby with him—born today I'd guess. The child's all right—was thrown clear in his carry-cot. Hasn't even woken."

At that moment the baby did wake and begin to cry—a faint thread of sound in the roaring of the wind.

"He'd best come along with us," said the ambulance man, "till we find someone to claim him. Hear the wind—hark to it blow! You'd think there was a pack of wolves chasing along the embankment."

Police and firemen arrived on the scene; the doctor was given a lift back to his home in Worplesdon. Next day he went along to the hospital where the injured people had been taken, and inquired after the baby.

"It's a sad thing," the matron said. "We've found out his father had just fetched him from the London hospital where he was born; his mother died there yesterday. Now the father's dead too the child has no relations at all; seems to be alone in the world. They'd just come from Canada, but had no family there. So the baby will have to go to the orphanage. And there's another queer thing: one of his feet is an odd shape, and has fur growing on it; as if the poor child hadn't enough bad luck already."

Young Doctor Talisman sighed, looking at the dark-haired baby sleeping so peacefully in his hospital cot, still unaware of the troubles he had inherited.

"I'll call in at the orphanage from time to time and see how he goes on," he promised. "What's his name?"

"Wilder. Will Wilder. Luckily we found his birth certificate in the father's suitcase. What are you looking for, doctor?"

"I was just wondering what I had done with my watch," Dr Talisman said. "But I remember now: I took it off when I was helping to pull hurt people out of the wreckage last night and buckled it on to the branch of a tree growing on the embankment; I'll go back and find it sometime."

True to his word, the doctor called at Worplesdon Orphanage to see young Will Wilder and, having formed the habit, he went on doing it year after year; became a kind of adopted uncle and, as there was nobody else to do it, took Will for trips to the zoo and the pantomime, days at the beach, and weekends canoeing on the river. No real relatives ever turned up to claim the boy. Nor did the doctor ever marry and have children of his own; somehow he was always too busy looking after his patients to have time for courtship; so a closeness grew between the two of them as year followed year.

Young Will never made friends at school. He was a silent,

inturned boy, and kept himself to himself. For one thing his odd foot made, him lame, so he could not run fast; he was no good at football or sports, which helped separate him from the others. But though he could not run he loved speed, and went for long rides on a bicycle the doctor gave him; also he loved books and would sit reading for hours on end while everyone else was running and fighting in the playground. And, from being a silent, solitary boy he became a thoughtful, solitary young man. He did well at his exams, but seemed to find it hard to decide on a career. While he was thinking, he took a job in the public library, and lived on his own in a bedsitter. But he still called in on the doctor once or twice a week.

One time when he called in he said, "I've been reading up the old history of this neighbourhood. And I found that way back, centuries back, there was a whole tribe of Wilders living in these parts."

"Is that so?" said the doctor with interest. "Maybe they were your ancestors. Maybe that was why your parents were travelling here, from Canada, to find the place their forefathers had come from. What did they do, those Wilders? Where did they live?"

"They were gypsies and tinkers and charcoal burners," Will said. "They lived in tents and carts on a piece of land known as Worplesdon Wilderness. I haven't been able to discover exactly where it was. It seems the Wilders had lived there so long—since Saxon times or before—that they had a sort of squatters' right to the land, although they never built houses on it."

"You ought to try and find an ancient map of the neighbourhood," the doctor said, "and discover where it could have been." He glanced at his watch—not the watch he had buckled on a tree on the railway embankment, for somehow he had never found time to go back and reclaim that one, but another, given him by a grateful patient. Patients were always giving him presents, because he was a good doctor, and kind as well. "Dear me, how late it's getting. I must be off to the hospital; I promised to look in on old Mrs Jones."

They walked to the gate together, Will limping; then Will mounted the bike and pedalled swiftly away. "I wish something could be done about that foot of his," the doctor thought, sighing over the contrast between Will's slow, limping walk and his speedy skilful progress on the bike. During the years since Will's babyhood the doctor had read up all the cases of foot troubles he could find, from fallen arches to ingrowing toenails, but he had never come across any case exactly like Will's. "But there's that new bone specialist just come to the Wimbledon Hospital; I'll ask his opinion about it."

"I've found out a bit more about those Wilders," Will said, next time he called on the doctor. "They had a kind of a spooky reputation in the villages round about."

"Gypsies and people living rough often did in the old days," said the doctor. "What were they supposed to do?"

"Anything from stealing chickens to hobnobbing with the devil! People were scared to go past Worplesdon Wilderness at night."

"I wish we knew where it had been exactly," said the doctor. "Maybe where the football fields are now. Oh, by the way, there's a new consultant, Dr Moberley, at the Wimbledon Hospital, who'd very much like to have a look at your foot, if you'd agree to go along there sometime."

Will's face closed up, as it always did when his foot was mentioned.

"What's the good?" he said. "No one can do anything about it. Oh, very well—" as the doctor began to protest. "To please you I'll go. But it won't be any use."

"That certainly is a most unusual case," the consultant said to Dr Talisman when they met at the hospital the following week. "The only thing at all similar that I've ever come across was a case in India, years ago."

"Could you do anything for him?"

"I'm not sure. I'll have to consider, and read up some old histories. I'll talk to you again about him."

But in the meantime Will came to the doctor one evening and said,

"I've decided to go to Canada."

"Why go there?" Dr Talisman was astonished. For, privately, he thought that in such an outdoor kind of place the boy with his lame foot would be at even more of a disadvantage. But Will surprised him still further by saying,

"The museum has given me a small grant to do some research into legends about wolves."

"Wolves? I didn't know you were interested in wolves."

"Oh yes, I am," said Will. "I've been interested in wolves for a long time. Ever since I was a child and you used to take me to the zoo, remember?"

Dr Talisman did remember then that Will always stopped for a long time by the wolves' enclosure and seemed as if he would rather stay watching them than look at anything else in the zoo; as if he felt he could learn something important from them.

"You won't be going to Canada for good?" he said. "I shall miss you, Will."

"Oh no, I'll be back. I just want to go to a place where there are still wolves wild in the woods. And while I'm over there I'll see if I can find out anything about my parents. Do you remember, among my father's things there was a little book with a couple of addresses in a town called Wilderness, Manitoba? A Mrs Smith and a man called Barney Davies. Of course they may be dead by now but I shall go there and see."

"When are you off?"

"Tomorrow."

"But what about Dr Moberley? He was going to think about your case."

"He wouldn't have been able to do anything," said Will, and limped down the garden to where his bike leaned against the fence.

"What about the Worplesdon Wilders? Did you find out any more about them?"

Will paused, his foot on the pedal.

"Yes," he said, "there was a tale in the Middle Ages that some of them practised something called lycanthropy."

"Lycanthropy? But that's—"

"And there was one who lived in Saxon times—he was known as Wandering Will. He was supposed to come back every twenty years to see how his descendants were getting on. And when he came back—"

"Oh dear, there's my phone," said the doctor. "Just a minute. Don't go yet, Will."

But when the doctor returned from answering the phone, Will had cycled away.

"I wonder if he'll take his bike to Canada?" the doctor thought, looking after him.

* * *

Will did; the great plains of northern Canada are wide and flat, endless pine forest and corn prairie, corn prairie and pine forest, through which the roads, straight as knives, run on seemingly for ever; wonderful roads they are for cycling, though you seldom see a cyclist on them. People stared in amazement to see the little dot that was Will come pedalling over the horizon, on and on across that huge flatness, sometimes under the broiling sun, sometimes in a fierce wind that had swept straight down from the North Pole.

Will was so quiet and serious, so straightforward and eager after knowledge, that people everywhere were ready to answer his questions. Yes, there were still wolves in the woods; yes, the Indians still believed that if you trod on a wolf's footprint you were drawn after him and must follow him helplessly day and night through the forest. And there were wolves in the prairie too, the Indians thought; when a wave of wind passed over those great inland seas of maize or wheat they would say, "Look, a wolf is running through the corn!" and they believed that when the last sheaf was harvested, the wolf who was hiding in it must be caught, or there would be no grain harvest next year.

Did the wolves ever attack people? Will asked. Opinions were divided on that; some said yes, wolves would follow a sleigh all day, and pounce on the travellers when dark came; others said no, wolves seldom or never harmed a man but preyed only on small game, rabbits, chipmunks, or woodmice.

So Will went on, and at last he came to the town of Wilderness, which stood beyond the forest, on the edge of a great frozen swamp. Its wooden frame houses were so old, so grey, that they looked more like piles of lichen than human dwellings; not many people lived here now, and all the ones who did were old; they sat on their weathered porches in the sun all summer long, and in rocking-chairs by large log fires through the winter.

Will asked if Mrs Smith lived here still. No, somebody said, she died last winter. But, yes, old Barney Davies was still alive; he lived in the last house on the left, before the forest began.

So Will went to call on old Barney Davies; a little shrunken wisp of a man, as weathered and grey as his house. He sat by a pine-knot fire, over which Will heated a can of beans that he took from his pack.

"Yes," said old Barney, eating his share of the beans, "your grandfather used to live here. A quiet fellow he was, come from farther east. And his son, your father, yes, he lived here too, married Mary Smith and they went off saying they'd be back. But they never came back. Your grandfather died a couple of years after they left. Friend of mine, he was. I've a few of his things still, if you'd like to see them."

"I'd like to very much," said Will, making coffee in an old kerosene tin. So Barney Davies rummaged in a wooden chest and presently brought out a rope of Indian beads and a tobacco pouch and a mildewed leather belt and a small oilskin bag which held a wad of old, yellowed linen folded so damp and flat that Will had trouble prising it apart.

"Did my grandfather come from England?" he asked, holding the wad near the fire to dry it.

"Never said. Maybe he did. Never let on. Used to talk about England some. Made a living mending folks' pots and pans. A rare clever hand he was at that."

"What else did he do?"

"Used to spend a lot of time in the woods. Whole days, weeks together he'd be away. Not hunting or trapping. Never brought anything back. Seemed as if he was searching for something he never found."

By now Will had got the linen a bit dried and, very slowly, with infinite care, he unfolded it.

"Kind of an old map?" said Barney Davies, taking the pipe from his mouth. "Nowhere round here, though, I reckon."

"No," Will said, "it's an English map."

Ye Wildernesse of Whorplesdene, said the aged script across the top of the mildewed sheet. A river ran across the middle, the River Wey. Pine forests were drawn in one corner, ash forests in another. Camp, it said, between the pine forest and the ash. Norman Village, in another corner. Pitch kettles, charcoal fire. And, crossways, a path seemed to be marked. By straining his eyes, Will thought he could just make out the inscription along the path—which seemed, as far as he could judge, to follow the track now taken by the main line from Woking to Guildford: he read the name aloud.

"Wandering Will's Way."

"Wandering Will," said old Barney. "I mind your grandfather talking about him."

"What did he say?"

"The Indians believe in something called the Wendigo," old Davies said. "Half man, half wolf. Runs through the forest. When you hear him, you have to follow. Or if you tread on his footprint, or if he crosses your track. Wandering Will was the same sort of critter, I reckon, only back in England. When he takes hold of you, he gives you a kind of longing for places where folk have never been, for things nobody knows."

"Yes I see."

"Want to keep the map?"

"May I?"

"Sure. It's properly yours. Well," said old Barney, "guess it's time for me to have my nap. Nice meeting you. So long, young fellow. Be going back to England now, I reckon?"

"Quite soon," said Will. He put the map carefully in his pocket, mounted his bike, and rode away along the road that skirted between forest and swamp.

He reckoned that before nightfall he ought to be able to reach the next town, Moose Neck, forty miles farther on.

But he reckoned without the weather.

In mid afternoon a few flakes of snow began to fall, and by dusk they had increased to a blizzard. Will did not dare continue cycling, he could not see ahead; there was nothing to prevent his going straight into the swamp, or into the river that crossed it.

He dismounted, tightened the strings of his Parka, wrapped his waterproof cape round him, and huddled under the shelter of a spruce tree. Colder and colder it grew, darker and darker. The wind wailed through the forest like a banshee, like a mourning dragon, like a pack of starved dinosaurs. But in spite of the wind's roar, Will found it hard to keep his eyes open.

"I mustn't go to sleep," he thought. "To sleep in this

would be certain death. But I'm so tired—so tired . . . I shall have to go to sleep . . ."

His eyes closed . . .

It seemed to him that he was not alone. All about him he could feel the nearness of live creatures, feel movement and stirring and warm breath. It seemed to him that he opened his eyes and saw many pairs of green lights, shining luminous in the dark; he knew they were the eyes of wolves. He could feel fur, and the warmth of bodies pressed tight against him.

"Don't be afraid," their voices were telling him. "Don't be afraid, we are your friends."

"I'm not afraid," Will said truly. "But why are you my friends? Most men are afraid of you."

"We are your friends because you are part of our family. You are the boy with a wolf's foot."

"Yes, that is true," said Will in his dream.

"You do not belong here, though. You must go back to the place you came from; you will not get what you are seeking here."

"What am I seeking?" Will asked.

"You will know when you find it."

"Where shall I find it?"

"In your own place, where the wolves hunt no longer, save in dreams, or in memory, or in thought, or in fear. In your own corner of your own land, where your forefathers were friends to wolves, where your cradle lay across the wolf's path. You must go back. You must go back."

"Yes," said Will in his sleep. "I must go back."

He sank deeper into warmth and darkness.

When he next opened his eyes, a dazzling sun was rising over the swamp. No wolves were to be seen; but all round the spruce tree were the prints of paws like dogs' paws, only bigger; a tuft of grey fur had lodged under a flap of Will's Parka. He tucked it between the folds of his map of Worplesdon Wilderness.

Then, through the loose, soft new snow he bicycled on to Moose Neck.

* * *

When Will returned to England, he caught the 18.06 stopping train from Waterloo to Guildford. He got out at Worplesdon, left the station, climbed over a fence, and limped back along beside the track until he came to a piece of waste land, dotted all over with clumps of bramble, and with piles of bricks and stacks of old timber.

Then he sat himself down on the embankment beside a clump of willow, and waited.

It was dark. The wind was rising.

Presently he felt a puff of cold air on his cheek, and heard a voice in his ear.

"Well, my child? Finding me took you long enough, and far enough! Now you have found me at last, what do you want?"

"I'm not certain," said Will. "When I was younger I always wanted one thing—to be able to run faster than a train. But now—I'm not sure. I seem to want so many different things."

"Well, think carefully! If you wanted it, I could take away your wolf's foot; I could help you run faster than a train. Do you want to try?"

It seemed to Will that the cold wind caught him by the arms; he was running along the grassy embankment—fast, faster—black air and signal lights streamed past him, there was a black-and-gold ribbon ahead of him; he caught up and overtook the 22.50 from Waterloo and raced into Guildford ahead of it. Then the wind swung him round and took him back to where he had been before.

"That was wonderful!" Will gasped, grabbing the old willow to steady himself. "But I know now that it's not what

I want. I want to learn, I want to find out hundreds of things. Can you help me do that?"

"Yes, I can help you! Goodbye then, my child. You won't see me again, but I shall be with you very often."

"Goodbye, great-grandfather," said Will.

*   *   *

Dr Talisman was sitting late in his study, writing up his notes on the day's cases, when he heard his bell ring. He went to the door.

"Will! So you're back from Canada! It's good to see you— come and have some coffee."

"It's good to be back." Will limped into the doctor's study.

"So—did you hear many legends about wolves?"

"Yes I did," said Will. "And some true tales too."

"And did you find the town where your father had lived?"

"Yes, I found it."

"By the way," Dr Talisman said, "Moberley thinks he can operate on that foot of yours and cure your lameness; make you the same as everybody else."

"That's kind of him," said Will, "but I've decided I don't want an operation. I'd rather keep my foot the way it is."

"Are you quite sure?" said the doctor, somewhat astonished. "Well—you know your own mind, I can see. And have you decided on a career?"

"Yes," Will said. "I'm going to be a doctor, like you— Oh, I think this is yours: I found it tonight."

And he handed the doctor a tarnished old watch that looked as if it had been buckled round the branch of a tree for twenty years.

The Lost Five Minutes

There was once a dragon who kept a museum and did quite well from it. He had become (at some point during the several thousand years of his life) rather bored with just eating people, and the museum made a nice change and a new interest. He charged ten pence entry fee and instead of requests to the public not to smoke and climb over the guard ropes and touch the exhibits, there were simply signs saying, "If you do not behave yourself properly the dragon will eat you."

You'd think such signs might have stopped people from being very keen to visit the museum. Not a bit of it; there was a kind of daredevil fascination about going there. People simply flocked. Maybe it was from the excitement of not knowing quite what the dragon would consider proper behaviour, maybe—human nature being what it is—because everyone had a sneaking hope of seeing somebody else misbehave and get swallowed. But quite apart from these reasons, the museum was a particularly nice and unusual one, everything in it being made of glass. In the main hall stood Cinderella's glass coach and slippers, on the first floor was a glass doll's house all complete with furniture, lovely music was played all day long on a glass harmonica, and in smaller rooms there were collections of glass fruit from Venice (every colour of the rainbow), glass animals, and a whole aviary full of birds with spun-glass tails.

For that matter the dragon himself was made of glass: stretched out in the sun or coiled round the great ilex tree in front of his museum he made a stunning spectacle, each feather and scale flashing like a frozen waterfall, his three heads keeping a sharp lookout for customers in every direction. It was due to his three heads, in fact, that the dragon had given up his regular habit of eating people, since, either because of old age or greed or just general cantankerousness, the heads could never come to an agreement over whose turn it was to swallow the next victim. And all this fuss before meals gave the dragon indigestion and hiccups, so, on the whole, he had found it simpler not to swallow anybody. Of course the public did not know this.

In every museum there has to be somebody to dust the exhibits and take the entry money, unlock the doors in the morning, and tell people where to find the ladies' room. The dragon had occasionally encountered difficulty in hiring assistants, but at present he was very well suited: the post was filled by a blind girl called Anthea, who was extremely careful and conscientious, besides being very pretty; she never broke anything when she dusted, having that extra sixth radar-sense of where objects are that blind people often possess; she wasn't a bit frightened of the dragon, since she had never seen how huge and dazzling he was; and because she was blind, people never tried to cheat her out of the tenpence entry fees. And in the evenings she told fairy tales to the dragon, which also made a pleasant change for him. Nobody had ever done such a thing before.

One day, however, Anthea came to grief.

The dragon had recently come by a new treasure for his museum: a very beautiful clock, every single part made of glass, hands, face, chimes, pendulum, mainspring, and all. It stood under a glass dome and when you looked at it you felt that you could see time itself in motion. The clock was more than five hundred years old and had neither lost nor gained a minute, nor stopped, since the day it was first wound up.

Well! Anthea had been showing the clock to the editor of the local paper, the *Wormley Observer*. He was a fat little fellow, all smiles, called Sam Inkfellow. She was just replacing the glass dome when somebody jogged her elbow. Instinctively Anthea clasped both hands round the dome to steady it, and set it carefully down, but as she did so she tipped it—*very* slightly—against the works of the clock, shaking loose five minutes from the mainspring. And before she could push the dome straight, the five minutes had slipped out from underneath and darted away through the museum window, like a handful of bees escaped from the hive.

The museum had a very efficient alarm system. Bells began to clang, doors automatically slammed, two carloads of police came whizzing round from headquarters, and the dragon cascaded off his ilex tree like a glacier from an erupting volcano. But the mischief was done: the five minutes could not be recovered.

"It was my fault," poor Anthea said to the police. "Please let everyone go, nobody has stolen anything. It was entirely my fault."

The police could only agree. All the members of the public who had been shut in by the automatic doors were allowed to go.

"You realize this means I shall have to swallow you?" the dragon said very crossly to Anthea.

"Yes I know; I really am sorry; please go ahead and get it over with."

"Certainly not; things must be done in due order," the dragon said hurriedly. "I shall swallow you a week today, next Thursday, at eight a.m." For he was not at all pleased at the troublesome prospect of having to find a new assistant, nor at the likelihood of hiccups and indigestion. "After all, somebody may return the five minutes before then."

He stuck up a sign saying LOST: FIVE MINUTES. FINDER PLEASE RETURN TO WORMLEY MUSEUM. REWARD.

Meantime the *Wormley Observer* came out with huge headlines: DRAGON TO SWALLOW ANTHEA NEXT THURSDAY A.M.

Special excursion buses were to be run to the town from as far away as Brighton, the *Observer* published a timetable of events, and wooden seats were hastily erected in the main square facing the museum. Extra police were fetched in and a one-way traffic system organized; the shops sold little dragon flags, a commemorative stamp was issued, and a public holiday was proclaimed.

"All this publicity is very distasteful," said the dragon.

"I really am sorry," said Anthea.

But Sam Inkfellow, editor of the *Wormley Observer,* was rubbing his hands. He had a guaranteed sale of eighty thousand copies for next week's issue (in full colour), the Press Association had paid him large sums for the story with pictures, and he was charging ten guineas a head standing room in the *Observer* offices, which overlooked the square.

Anthea's family were very upset. Her brother Bill came and tried to reason with the dragon.

"Can't you substitute some other penalty?" he asked.

"Sorry," said the dragon. "I regret the necessity quite as much as you. But rules are rules. You produce the lost five minutes, I'll cancel the swallowing."

"Would any five minutes do?"

"Oh, certainly, just so long as they are a *spare* five minutes."

When he heard this, Bill became slightly more cheerful. Surely, he thought, someone about the town must have five minutes to spare. Or even three, or two; it shouldn't be impossible to collect a few minutes together.

Elderly people seemed likelier to have time to spare, so he called on the old lady who lived next door to his mother.

She was working in her garden, picking up scattered rose petals and brushing all the grass blades straight, so that they pointed in one direction.

"Mrs Pentecost, could you possibly spare five minutes for my sister Anthea? Or even two, or one?"

"Oh, good gracious, no, my dear boy! Why, when you get to my age, there's so little time left that you have to hoard every minute like gold. Sorry, but no, no indeed!"

Perhaps it would be better to try somebody young, Bill thought, so he went to a schoolmate of Anthea's.

"Sally, could you possibly spare me a minute or two for Anthea?"

"Oh, honestly, Bill darling, I'm so rushed I haven't a *second* to spare, let alone a minute, what with getting my hairpiece set, and my false lashes stuck on, and my nail varnish dried, and reading my horoscope in *Seventeen,* and looking for a new leather jacket—"

Bill saw that he would get no help there.

Nobody, anywhere, had any time to spare, not just at that moment.

"If you were to come back next week—" they said. "Now next week I'll have *plenty* of spare time. Or next month, even better. But just *now,* I do seem to be so terribly short of time—"

So it went on, all week. On Wednesday evening Bill went to see the dragon.

"Can't you suggest anybody, sir?"

The dragon scratched one of his glass chins, with a sound like icicles tinkling together.

"What about the town genius?" he suggested after a while.

"That's a good idea!" said Bill. "Why didn't I think of it? I'll go directly."

And he got on his bicycle and set out.

The town genius, whose name was Marcantonio Smith-to-the-power-Nine, did not live in the town nowadays; he had done so, but found he got little work done because people constantly came to him asking him to solve their problems. So now he lived in a tower with a studio in the nearby forest, where he painted, and sculpted, and wrote poetry, and conceived new kinds of mathematics, and invented perpetual motion, and did everything a genius ought.

Bill found him in the studio, standing in front of a huge slab of marble. On the marble he had a football-sized lump of colourless, shining material, like nothing so much in the world as a good big bit of glass putty, and he was squeezing it, and kneading it, and thumping it, and palming it into a ball, and then flattening it out, and then rolling it into a sausage, and then tearing it into thin strips, and those into small nuggets, shaping them all into different things, animals, stars, flowers, figures, faces, and then flinging the whole mass together and beginning again.

He smiled kindly at Bill, who came hesitating over and stood by the slab.

"Well, my boy? What can I do for you?"

All this time Smith never stopped playing with the lump of stuff.

Bill told the sad tale of Anthea and the lost five minutes.

"I was wondering if you could possibly help us," he said. "The dragon's due to swallow her tomorrow at eight sharp unless I can find somebody to give me five minutes."

"Five minutes? Is that all?" said Marcantonio Smith-to-the-power-Nine, and he pinched off a bit of his glass putty. "Do you want them marked out?" He flattened the small lump he had pinched off, shaped it into an oblong, and marked five divisions on it as if he were scoring fudge.

Bill gaped, watching him, and he laughed.

"No need to look so astonished, my boy!"

"It seems so easy for you!"

"It's always easy to be kind."

"It didn't seem so for the other people in the town," Bill said. "How is it you have so much time when nobody else has any at all?"

"That's because I only do the things that interest me. Do you want your five minutes in a bag?"

"Oh, please don't trouble, sir. I wish I could do something for you!"

"Bring your sister to visit me sometime. I like fairy tales too."

Bill promised he would, and hurried off with his precious little slab of minutes.

But on the way home he met a man mending a puncture in his motor bike tyre.

"Oh, my dear boy! Is that five minutes you have there? Do, do give me just a couple of them—*please!* I'm on my way with a pardon for my son, who is to be shot for a crime he didn't commit, and I got this puncture—I shall be too late—do, please help me!"

Bill was very upset. I can't let the poor man's son be shot for a crime he didn't commit, though, he thought, maybe the dragon will let me off two of the minutes.

Very carefully he broke two off his little cake of five.

"Heaven bless you, my boy. You're a real friend in need!"

Bill went on his way. Near the town harbour he met a man running downhill, hell-for-leather.

"Help!" he called. "Is that three minutes you've got there? Give me two of them, like a good lad! Do you see that ship, that's just casting off anchor? If only I can get to her before she sails, I've got a bit of paper to deliver on board that will stop two great countries going to war against each other, but I'm going to be too late—for heaven's sake help me!"

Very unwillingly, Bill gave him a couple of minutes— maybe, after all, the dragon will be satisfied with just one, he thought—and the man rushed away down the hill.

Now there was only one minute left. And as Bill **was** passing the school, a teacher put his head out of the window and said,

"Please, my dear boy! I see that is a spare minute you have in your hand. Be a good lad and give it here—if I had just *one* minute more, before the end-of-period bell went, I could teach this class of thickheads how to save the world!"

Well, you can't refuse a request like that, can you? So Bill handed over his last minute. By now it was seven o'clock Thursday morning.

So Bill went along to the dragon and explained that, although Mr Smith had given him five minutes, due to one reason or another he had been obliged to part with them.

"Since it's now my fault the five minutes are lost," he said, "will you please swallow me instead of Anthea?"

The dragon considered. He saw the benefits of this arrangement, because at least Anthea would then still be available to dust the exhibits and tell him fairy tales at night.

"Very well," he said at length grudgingly. "But you are both putting me to a lot of trouble."

By now huge crowds of people were gathered in Wormley Square, all anxious to watch the swallowing.

"Ma," said a child to his mother, "shall we be able to see the young lady go all the way down inside the dragon?"

"D'you think he'll chew her?" said a man to his wife.

"I am excited, Henry!" said a girl to her boyfriend. "Which head will he swallow with, d'you think?"

This remark was overheard by the dragon's heads, who instantly began arguing.

"Belial had the last swallow, it's my turn!"

"No it isn't, Thammuz, it's mine!"

"Shut up, Dagon and Belial it's neither of you, it's my turn!"

The dragon retired behind his ilex to sort the matter out. Eight o'clock struck and people began to grumble because nothing had happened.

"What's the crowd waiting for?" asked a traveller in false teeth who happened to be passing through the town.

"Don't you know? Our dragon's going to swallow the young lady because she let five minutes escape from the clock last Thursday."

"No, she didn't, it was five hours!"

"Anyway it isn't her, it's the young gentleman he's going to swallow."

"It wasn't from the clock they escaped."

"They didn't escape, he ran over them on his motor bike and squashed them flat."

"No he didn't, they rolled down the hill and fell on to a ship!"

"That's a lie! My hubby told me the teacher at the school gave them to his physics class and they dissolved them in sulphuric acid!"

Everybody began arguing. People came to blows.

But the traveller pushed his way to the ilex tree and said to the dragon,

"If you are really about to swallow that young lady for losing five minutes, you are being unfair! I happened to be in your museum last Thursday and I saw that man there jog her elbow. He did it on purpose. *He's* the one you ought to swallow!"

"Really?" said the dragon, and he turned to the man the traveller had indicated and swallowed him down without more ado (Belial happened to be the nearest head and did the job). Everybody saw fat little Sam Inkfellow travel slowly and spirally down through all the glass coils. It took a long time, gave the dragon frightful indigestion and hiccups, and he was sorry for himself for three days after, but all the townspeople were delighted, as Inkfellow had published unpleasant, and mostly untrue, stories about them all in his paper at one time or another.

"No hard feelings, I hope?" said the dragon to Anthea when his hiccups had died down and he was feeling better.

"You'll come back and start helping in the museum again, won't you?"

"I'm afraid not," said Anthea. "No hard feelings, but Bill and I are going to go and work for the town genius. So goodbye."

And that is what they did. The dragon had terrible trouble finding another assistant. And in the end, Anthea married Marcantonio Smith-to-the-power-Nine.

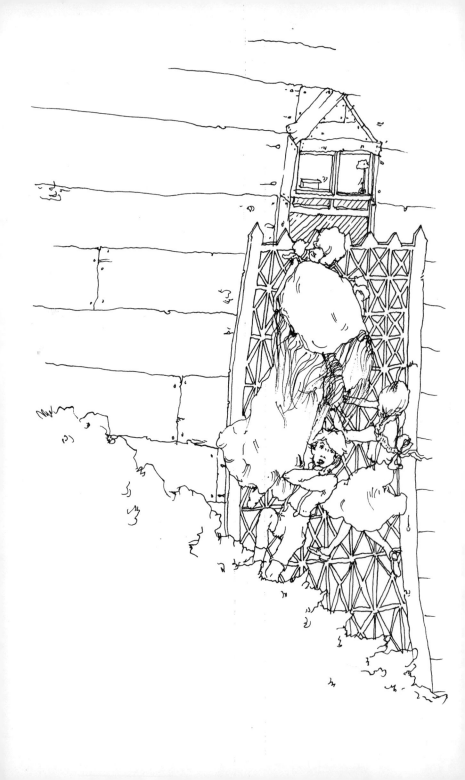

Dolls' House to Let, Mod. Con.

The family were at breakfast when the front door bell rang, and Harriet went to see who it was.

"It's old Mrs. Perrow," she said returning. "She says can she speak to you, Mother?"

"Oh dear," said Mrs. Armitage sadly. "What can she want?"

She left her bacon and went into the front hall. The rest of the family watched the bacon sympathetically as it gradually went cold on her plate while they listened to a shrill stream of complaints going on and on, punctuated occasionally by a soothing murmur from Mrs. Armitage.

"Wretched woman," said Mr. Armitage crossly. "She must be telling all her family troubles back to Adam, by the sound of it. Mark, put your mother's plate in the hot-cupboard."

Mark had just done this when his mother came back looking indignant.

"It really is too bad, poor things," she said sitting down. "That miserable Mr. Beezeley has turned them out of Rose Cottage on some flimsy excuse—the real reason is that he wants to do it up and let it to a rich American. So the Perrows have nowhere to live."

"What an old scoundrel," exclaimed Mr. Armitage. "All the same, I don't see that there's much we can do about it."

"I said they could live in our loft till they found somewhere else."

"You did *what?*"

"Said they could live in the loft. I don't know if they'll be able to climb in, though. Children, you'd better go and see if you can rig up a ladder for them."

Mark and Harriet ran off, leaving their father to fume and simmer while his wife placidly went on with her breakfast.

The loft was over the kitchen, but it was approached from outside, by a door over the kitchen window. Harriet and Mark used it as a playroom and always climbed up by means of the toolshed roof, but grown-ups used a ladder when they entered it.

"Will the Perrows be able to use the ladder?" said Harriet doubtfully. "The rungs are rather far apart."

"No, I've had a better idea—Father's new trellis. We'll take a length of that. It's still all stacked by the back door."

The trellis was ideal for the job, being made of strong metal criss-crossed in two-inch squares. They leaned a section over the kitchen window, fastened the top securely with staples to the doorsill of the loft, and jammed the bottom firmly with stones.

"That should take their weight," said Mark. "After all they're not heavy. Here they come."

The Perrow family were peculiar in that none of them was more than six inches high. Ernie Perrow and his wife were cousins and lived with his old mother and their nine children. There had always been some Perrows in the village, but no one knew exactly why they were so small. There were various theories about it. Some people thought that a Perrow ancestor had been frightened by Stevenson's Rocket when he was young, and had never grown any more. Others said that it was a curse laid on the family by someone who had suffered from their bad temper, or that the Perrows always gave their children juniper wine instead of milk to keep them small.

Whatever the cause of their small size, they were very proud of it, and seldom married outside the family. They were a hard-working, self-respecting clan, rather dour and surly, earning their living mostly by rat-catching, chimney-sweeping, drain-clearing and other occupations in which their smallness was useful. The women did marvellous embroidery.

They had always owned Rose Cottage, portioning it off, one or two rooms to each family. But Ernie's father, old Mrs. Perrow's husband, had been a waster and had been obliged to sell the cottage to Farmer Beezeley's father, who had let him stay on in it and pay rent. The present Beezeley was not so accommodating, and had been trying to get them out for a long time.

Harriet and Mark watched with interest as the Perrows made their way up the path to the loft. Lily and Ernie were each pushing barrows loaded with household belongings, and a trail of minute children followed, some of them only an inch or so high. Harriet began to wonder how the children would manage to climb up the trellis, but they scrambled up like monkeys, while Ernie was rigging a pulley to take the furniture. At the end of the procession came old Mrs. Perrow carrying a bluebottle in a cage and keeping up a shrill incessant grumble.

"What I mean to say, fine place to expect us to live, I'm sure. Full of cobwebs, no chimney—where's Lily going to put her oil stove. We shall all be stunk out with paraffin."

Harriet was enraptured with the oil stove, which the resourceful Ernie had made out of biscuit tins and medicine glasses. She rushed off to call her father to come and see it.

Unfortunately he arrived just as the stove, dangling at the end of the rope, swung inward and cracked a pane of the kitchen window. Mr. Armitage growled and retired again. He decided to soothe himself by watering his tomatoes, but had only just begun when he was startled by tiny, but piercing shrieks; he found a small Perrow in a pram the size of an eggshell (and in fact made from one) in the shade of one of his tomato plants. He had just copiously sprinkled it with Liquifert. He hurried off in a rage, tripped over a long line of washing which had been strung between two hollyhocks and had to replace twenty nappies the size of postage stamps fastened with clothes pegs made from split matches bound with fuse wire.

He strode indoors to find his wife.

"This arrangement won't do," he thundered. "I'll go and see that miserable Beezeley myself. I cannot have my garden used in this manner. I'm sure to tread on one of those children sooner or later."

Mrs. Armitage ruefully looked at a little Perrow sobbing over the fragments of a doll's tea-set made from corn husks which she had trodden on before she saw it.

"They do seem to spread," she agreed.

They heard frantic yells from the garden and saw two more children slide down from a cloche and run off, pursued by Ernie with a hairbrush.

"You touch any of these things and I'll tan you," he shouted.

"It's no use, though," Mrs. Armitage said. "Ernie and Lily do their best, but they can't be in nine places at once."

Her husband clapped on his hat and rushed off to Beezeley's farm. He met Mr. Beezeley himself, just outside the gate of Rose Cottage.

"Now look here, Beezeley," he shouted. "What right have you to turn those Perrows out of Rose Cottage? They paid their rent, didn't they? You can't do things like that."

"Oh yes, I can, Mr. Armitage," Beezeley replied smoothly. "Rose Cottage belongs to me, and it's supposed to be an agricultural labourer's cottage intended for men working on my farm. Perrow never did a hand's turn for me, he was all over the village."

"Indeed," said Mr. Armitage dangerously, "and who is the agricultural labourer that you have put in, may I ask?"

He turned to look at a huge Packard which stood outside the gate of Rose Cottage.

"Here he comes now," replied Mr. Beezeley agreeably. "Meet my new farm worker, Mr. Dunk R. Spoggin."

"Well, well!" said that gentleman, strolling towards them. He wore a silk check shirt, diamond tiepin and red and white saddle shoes. "I sure am pleased to meet another new neighbour. Quaint little rural spot you live in here, Mr. Er. I aim to wake it up a little."

"Mr. Spoggin is going to work on my farm for a year," explained Mr. Beezeley. "He has invented a new all-purpose agricultural machine which he wishes to try out, and my farm is going to be the testing ground. You can see them putting it up over there."

Indeed a small army of men in blue jeans were putting together something the size of a factory on the big meadow behind Beezeley's Farm.

"It ploughs, harrows, sows, manures, hoes, applies artificial heat, sprinkles with D.D.T., reaps, threshes, and grinds," Mr. Spoggin informed them. "It raises a crop in three days and has it harvested and out of the way in another three. Three days later the field is ready for a second crop. We should get sixty crops off that field of yours, Mr. Beezeley, in the course of the next year."

Mr. Armitage looked incredulous. Dunk R. Spoggin drew himself up.

"You don't believe me, eh? Let me tell you I am *the* Dunk R. Spoggin, maker of the Spoggin Combine, the Spoggin Diesel Dam Dredger, the Spoggin Potato Clamper, the Spoggin Gloucester Old Spot Scratcher and the Spoggin Gilt-Edged Pig Palace. I could buy out Henry Ford any time, *if* I wanted to. Have a cigar." He held out a two-foot one.

Mr. Armitage accepted, and turned to find that Mr. Beezeley had strolled away to inspect the new machine.

"Won't you find it rather confined in Rose Cottage? Surely it is smaller than the sort of thing you are used to?" he asked. Mr. Spoggin smiled expansively.

"Why no, I just love your quaint little old houses. This one is genuine Tooder, I understand. Mr. Beezeley wanted to lease it to me but I said straight out 'No, Mr. Beezeley, I'm a buying man. I'll give you twenty thousand for it, take it or leave it.' "

"Twenty thousand *pounds?*"

"Pounds, yes sir."

"And did he take it?"

"He did, and a cheaper property I've never bought. I felt downright mean, and nearly clapped another twenty on top of the first."

Mr. Armitage came home to lunch very thoughtful, and told his wife about their new neighbour.

"No hope of getting the Perrows back if he's bought the place," he said. "I'm afraid we're fixed with them for life."

After lunch Mrs. Armitage said: "Children, if you're going into Bunstable this afternoon, could you get me some embroidery silks? I don't seem to have as many as I thought I had."

"I know where they are," thought Harriet, who had seen all the little Perrow girls with beautiful new hair ribbons and sashes.

"And some napkin rings in Woolworth's, please. All those seem to have gone too."

A loud cry outside the window startled them, and Mark got there in time to see the butcher's boy trip on the path and scatter chops all over the pansies. The object that had tripped him appeared to be a napkin ring, which was being bowled by a small Perrow boy.

"Right, napkin rings and embroidery silks," he said. "That all? Coming, Harriet?"

Harriet always preferred the right-hand side of Bunstable High Street, because the left side was all taken up with banks, house agents, coal merchants and building societies, none of which have interesting shop windows. Today, however, her eye was caught as she cycled slowly along by a notice in a house agent's window, and giving a shout to Mark, who was in front, she jumped off and went to investigate.

TO LET: DOLLS' HOUSE 4FT. HIGH. MOD. CON.

DESIRABLE RESIDENCE, NEWLY DECORATED

SEEN BY ARRANGEMENT   INQUIRE WITHIN

Harriet and Mark ran inside and saw a shady, seedy, young man picking his nails behind a deal desk. On a table at the back of the room was an elegant Queen Anne house with steps up to a pillared porch, and bow windows.

"Oh," breathed Harriet, all eyes. Mark was brisker.

"We wish to inquire about the dolls' house," he said.

"Yes, sir. A delightful family residence. Two recep., three bed, kitchen, bath, usual offices. Calor gas lighting and heating installed by last tenant, who vacated suddenly. Do you wish to have an order to view?"

"Can't we just *view* it?" asked Harriet, gazing covetously through a bow window at one of the two recep.

"Oh dear, no, Madam. It's all locked up. The keys are obtainable from the owner."

"Where does the owner live?"

"The address is Mrs. Maria Nightshade, Cobweb Corner, Dead Man's Lane, Blackwood."

Harriet and Mark burst in to tea full of enthusiasm.

"We've found a house for the Perrows," they cried. Their parents looked sceptical.

"Old Mrs. Nightshade? I seem to know the name. Isn't she a witch?"

"Very likely," Harriet said. "She lives in a dark little den full of pots and jars with a black cat and an owl. But the dolls' house is *lovely,* just think how pleased the Perrows will be."

They were having their tea in the kitchen, and at that moment an outburst of thuds and angry screeches reminded them that the Perrows were just overhead.

"It will certainly be nice for them to have a separate room

for old Mrs. Perrow," Mrs. Armitage agreed. "I always think it's a mistake to live with your mother-in-law."

She took the lid off the jam-jar and found a small Perrow girl inside, having a peaceful feast and coated from head to foot in raspberry.

"Oh dear. Harriet, put Elsie on this saucer—I should pick her up with the sugar tongs—and take her to her mother. Really it's just like the evacuees all over again."

Harriet did as she was requested, holding Elsie under the tap on the way in spite of howls.

"*There* she is, the wicked little thing," exclaimed Lily. "I'm sorry, Miss, I'm sure, but really they're that active it's a job to keep up with them all."

She was putting them to bed, so Harriet postponed telling her about the house and ran back to the tea-table where Mark was explaining that they had paid a quarter's rent in advance.

"And they are bringing the house out tomorrow."

"Where are they going to put it? Not in my garden I beg."

"No, no, Miss Rogers said it could go at the end of her field."

"What's the rent?"

Harriet and Mark looked a little guilty.

"It's three packets of birthday candles a week—the pink, white and blues ones."

"Funny sort of rent," remarked her father suspiciously.

"Well you see she can't get them herself. People won't sell them to her in case she makes wax images, you know, and sticks pins in them."

"She'll be able to make plenty now," Mr. Armitage said drily. "However, far be it from me to interfere in any arrangement which rids us of the Perrows."

An aniseed ball thudded against the window and cracked it. The Perrow boys were playing hockey with pencil hockey sticks from Woolworth's which Mark had generously but thoughtlessly given them.

"That's the eighth window," said Mrs. Armitage resignedly.

Next day the Perrows moved out amidst universal rejoicing. Harriet and Mark went along to Miss Rogers's field hoping to hear cries of delight at the sight of the beautiful house, but the Perrow enthusiasm was very lukewarm.

"Just look at all those big windows to clean," said Lily gloomily. "And Calor gas. Where am I going to put my oil stove? These old-fashioned houses are draughty too."

"Don't you take any notice of her, Miss. She's pining for the cottage and that's the truth," Ernie apologized.

They seemed to settle in comfortably enough though, old Mrs. Perrow taking the best front room, and Harriet and Mark presently strolled away to see how Mr. Beezeley's new cultivator was getting on. It now covered the entire hundred-acre field and looked like the Crystal Palace. Through the glass walls nothing could be seen but machinery, with Mr. Dunk R. Spoggin darting among the cogs and belts.

They saw Mr. Beezeley and said good morning to him rather coldly.

"Morning, morning young people," he replied. "Bitter weather for the time of year, isn't it. My rheumaticks are terrible bad."

Indeed he was walking with great difficulty, almost doubled up.

"You'll be glad to hear that the Perrows have found a suitable house," Harriet said shortly. "They've rented Mrs. Nightshade's dolls' house."

"Old Mrs. Nightshade over at Blackwood?" said Mr. Beezeley, bursting into hearty laughter. "I sold her a couple of hens that had the henbane once. She's never forgiven me; I bet she'd do me a bad turn if she could. But all's fair in love and farming, *I* say. Ugh, this rheumatism is fairly crippling me."

The children left him and went home.

"Gosh," said Harriet, "do you suppose Mrs. Nightshade is giving him rheumatism?"

"Well he jolly well deserves it. I hope she ties him in knots."

When they arrived home they were dismayed to hear Mrs. Perrow's shrill, complaining voice in the kitchen.

"What I mean to say, it's a fine thing, first to turn us out of our house, then have to live in a loft, all cobwebs though kindly meant I daresay, not what we're used to, and then when we move into the new house what do we find?"

"Well, what *do* you find?" said Mrs. Armitage patiently.

"Nothing won't stay put!" cried Mrs. Perrow. She had climbed on to a chair and was standing on it, quivering with indignation. "You put down the kettle and it flies across and sticks on the wall. There's all Lily's bottled elderberries fallen down and broken and the daisy wine full of ashes that blew out of the fire by themselves, and young Sid's got a black eye from the mustard, and the bedroom door slammed and knocked baby down the stairs, and the dishes fall off the dresser all the time, it won't do, Mrs. Armitage, it really won't do."

"Oh dear," Mrs. Armitage said sympathetically, "it sounds as if you have a poltergeist."

"Can't say about that, Mum, but it's not good enough for me and Ernie and Lily, and that's a fact. We'd sooner live in your loft, though it's not what we're used to, but stay in that house we cannot and will not."

Mrs. Armitage gazed at her in despair.

Just at that moment they all heard an extraordinary noise from the direction of Beezeley's farm, a sort of whistling which rose to a roar.

"What can be going on?" exclaimed Harriet. "Let's go and see. I bet it's the new cultivator."

They all ran out, leaving Mrs. Perrow to continue her complaints to an empty kitchen. A strange sight met their eyes as they reached the new cultivator. It was swaying from side to side, shuddering and groaning as if at any moment it might leave the ground and take off into the air. Mr. Spoggin was rushing about in great agitation with an oilcan. Mr. Beezeley was there too, but did not seem to be taking much notice; he was standing hunched up looking very miserable and groaning from time to time.

"Look!" said Mark, "there's corn sprouting through the walls."

Wheat ears of an enormous size were pushing their way out between the panes of glass, and through the windows they could see that the whole inside was a tangled mass of stalks which continuously writhed and pushed upwards.

"It's cursed," cried poor Mr. Spoggin frantically. "None of my other machines has done this. Someone's put a hoodoo on it."

As he spoke there was a shattering explosion. Bits of broken glass and ears of corn the size of vegetable marrows filled the air. Fortunately the spectators were all blown backwards across several fields by the blast, and came to rest, breathless but un- hurt, in Miss Rogers's field outside the dolls' house.

"Well that certainly is the end," said Mr. Spoggin, strug- gling to his feet. "Never again do I try any experiments in your country. There must be something peculiar about the soil. I'm going straight back to the U.S.A. by the next boat." He paused, with his mouth open and his eyes bulging.

"That dolls' house! Am I dreaming, or is it real?"

"Oh, it's real right enough," they assured him gloomily as a saucepan and two little Perrows, inextricably entangled, rolled screaming and kicking down the front steps.

"I must add it to my collection. I have the largest collection of dolls' houses in five continents, including a real Eskimo child's dolls' igloo, made out of genuine snow. I definitely must have that house."

"That's a fine thing," shrieked Mrs. Perrow, who had come

up behind him in time to hear this. "And where do we live, I should like to know?"

Mr. Spoggin was visibly startled but recovered himself quickly and bowed to her.

"I'll make you a present of my place, Ma'am," he said. "It's a poky little hole, I only paid twenty thousand pounds for it, but such as it is, it's yours. Just up the road, Rose Cottage is the name. Here are the title deeds." He pulled them out of his pocket.

"We'll take you to see the agent," Harriet said quickly. "The dolls' house doesn't belong to the Perrows, and I don't know if the owner will want to sell. I fancy she prefers letting it."

"She'll sell," said Mr. Spoggin confidently. "Where's Tin Lizzie?"

He found his Packard roosting in a nearby hawthorn tree and whirled them off to the agent who received them warily. He was evidently used to complaints from tenants.

"If you want your quarter's rent back, I'm afraid it's out of the question," he said at once. "It's been used already."

"I want to buy that dolls' house," shouted Mr. Spoggin. "Name your figure."

"I should warn you that it's haunted," Harriet muttered. "There's a poltergeist in it."

"Haunted?" said Mr. Spoggin, his eyes like stars. "A haunted dolls' house! It'll be the gem of the whole collection." He was in ecstasies.

"I don't know if my client wishes to sell," said the agent repressively.

"I'll give you forty thousand pounds for it, not a penny more, so it's no use acting cagey in the hope that I'll put my price up, I shan't," said Mr. Spoggin. "You can take it or leave it."

The agent took it.

Mr. Spoggin took them home and carried off the dolls'

house then and there in Tin Lizzie, having telephoned the *Queen Mary* to wait for him. He left the remains of the cultivator.

Mr. Beezeley was not seen for some hours after the explosion, but finally turned up in a bed of stinging-nettles, which had cured his rheumatism but left him much chastened. He spent a lot of time wandering round the deep hole which was all that was left of the hundred-acre field, and finally sold his farm and left the neighbourhood.

As the children came down to breakfast next morning they heard the grumbling voice of old Mrs. Perrow in the porch:

"It's all very well, Mrs. Armitage, but what I mean to say is, Rose Cottage is not what we've been used to. Cooking on that old oil stove of Lily's after Calor gas and a bathroom and all, say what you like, it's not the same thing, and what I mean to say—"

The Rose of Puddle Fratrum

Right, then: imagine this little village, not far back from the sea, in the chalk country, Puddle Fratrum is its name. One dusty, narrow street, winding along from the Haymakers' Arms to Mrs Sherborne's Bed and Breakfast (with french marigolds and bachelors' buttons in the front garden): half-way between these two, at an acute bend, an old old grey stone house, right on the pavement, but with a garden behind hidden from the prying eyes of strangers by a ten-foot wall. And the house itself—now here's a queer thing—the house itself covered all over *thick*, doors, windows, and all, by a great climbing rose, fingering its way up to the gutters and over the stone-slabbed roof, sending out tendrils this way and that, round corners, over sills, through crevices, till the place looks not so much like a house, more like a mound of vegetation, a great green thorny thicket.

In front of it, a B.B.C. man, standing and scratching his head.

Presently the B.B.C. man, whose name was Rodney Cushing, walked along to the next building, which was a forge.

TOBIAS PROUT, BLACKSMITH AND FARRIER, said the sign, and there he was, white-haired, leather-aproned, with a pony's bent knee gripped under his elbow, trying on a red-hot shoe for size.

Rodney waited until the fizzling and sizzling and smell of burnt coconut had died down, and then he asked,

"Can you tell me if that was the ballerina's house?"—pointing at the rose-covered clump.

B.B.C. men are used to anything, but Rodney was a bit startled when the blacksmith, never even answering, hurled the red-hot pony shoe at the stone wall of his forge (where it buckled into a figure-eight and sizzled some more), turned his back, and stomped to an inner room where he began angrily working his bellows and blowing up his forge fire.

Rodney, seeing no good was to be had from the blacksmith, walked along to the Haymakers' Arms.

"Can you tell me," he said to Mr Donn the landlord over a pint of old and mild, "can you tell me anything about the house with the rose growing over it?"

"Arr," said the landlord.

"Did it belong to a ballet dancer?"

"Maybe so."

"Famous thirty years back?"

"Arr."

"By name Rose Collard?"

"Arr," said the landlord. "The Rose of Puddle Fratrum, they did use to call her. And known as far afield as Axminster and Poole."

"She was known all over the world."

"That may be. I can only speak for these parts."

"I'm trying to make a film about her life, for the B.B.C. I daresay plenty of people in the village remember her?"

"Arr. Maybe."

"I was asking the blacksmith, but he didn't answer."

"Deaf. Deaf as an adder."

"He didn't seem deaf," Rodney said doubtfully.

"None so deaf as them what won't hear. All he hears is nightingales."

"Oh. How very curious. Which reminds me, can you put me up for the night?"

"Not I," said the landlord gladly. "Old Mrs Sherborne's fule enough for that, though; she'll have ye."

Mrs Sherborne, wrinkled and tart as a dried apricot, was slightly more prepared to be communicative about the Rose of Puddle Fratrum.

"My second cousin by marriage, poor thing," she said, clapping down a plate with a meagre slice of Spam, two lettuce leaves, and half a tomato. "Slipped on a banana-peel, she did ('twas said one of the scene-shifters dropped it on the stage); mortification set in, they had to take her leg off, that was the end of her career."

"Did she die? Did she retire? What happened to her?"

In his excitement and interest, Rodney swallowed Spam, lettuce, tomato, and all, at one gulp. Mrs Sherborne pressed her lips together and carried away his plate.

"Came back home, went into a decline, never smiled again," she said, returning with two prunes and half a dollop of junket so thickly powdered over with nutmeg that it looked like sandstone. "Let the rose grow all over the front of her house, wouldn't answer the door, wouldn't see a soul. Some say she died. Some say she went abroad. Some say she's still there and the nightingales fetch her food. (Wonderful lot of nightingales we do have hereabouts, all the year round.) But one thing they're all agreed on."

"What's that?" The prunes and junket had gone the way of the Spam in one mouthful; shaking her head, Mrs Sherborne replaced them with two dry biscuits and a square centimetre of processed cheese wrapped in a seamless piece of foil that defied all attempts to discover its opening.

"When she hurt her leg she was a-dancing in a ballet that was writ for her special. About a rose and a nightingale, it was. They say that for one scene they had to have the stage knee-deep in rose-petals—fresh every night, too! Dear dear! Think of the cost?"

Mrs Sherborne looked sadly at the mangled remains of the

cheese (Rodney had managed to haggle his way through the foil somehow) and carried it away.

"Well, and so?" Rodney asked, when she came back into the dark, damp little parlour with a small cup of warm water into which a minute quantity of Dark Tan shoe-polish had almost certainly been dissolved. "What about this ballet?"

" 'Twas under all the rose-petals the banana-peel had been dropped. That was how she came to slip on it. So when Rose Collard retired she laid a curse on the ballet—she came of a witch family, there's always been a-plenty witches in these parts, as well as nightingales," Mrs Sherborne said, nodding dourly, and Rodney thought she might easily qualify for membership of the Puddle Fratrum and District Witches' Institute herself—"laid a curse on the ballet. 'Let no company ever put it on again,' says she, a-sitting in her wheel-chair, 'or, sure as I sit here—' "

"Sure as I sit here, what?" asked Rodney eagerly.

"I disremember exactly. The dancer as took Rose's part would break *her* leg, or the stage'd collapse, or there'd be some other desprat mischance. Anyway, from that day to this, no one's ever dared to do that ballet, not nowhere in the world."

Rodney nodded gloomily. He already knew this. It had been extremely difficult even to get hold of a copy of the score and choreographic script. *The Nightingale and the Rose* had been based on a version of a story by Oscar Wilde. Music had been specially written by Augustus Irish, choreography by Danny Pashkinski, costumes and scenery designed by Rory el Moro. The original costumes were still laid away in mothballs in the Royal Museum of Ballet. Rodney was having nylon copies made for his film.

"Well, you won't be wanting nothing *more,* I don't suppose," Mrs Sherborne said, as if Rod might be expected to demand steak tartare and praline ice. "Here's the bath plug, I daresay you will wish to retire as the TV's out of order. Put the plug back in the kitchen after you've had your bath."

This was presumably to discourage Rodney from the sin of taking two baths in quick succession, but he had no wish to do so. The water was hardly warmer than the coffee. When he ran it into the tiny bath, a sideways trickle from the base of the tap flowed on to the floor, alarming an enormous spider so much that all the time Rodney was in the bath he could hear it scurrying agitatedly about the linoleum. A notice beside a huge canister of scouring powder said PLEASE LEAVE THIS BATH CLEAN, after which some guest with spirit still unbroken had added WHY USE IT OTHERWISE?

Shivering, Rodney dropped the bath plug in the kitchen sink and went to his room. But the bed had only one thin, damp blanket; he got dressed again, and leaned out of the window. Some nightingales were beginning to tune up in the distance. The summer night was cool and misty, with a great vague moon sailing over the dim silvered roofs of Puddle Fratrum. Due to the extreme curve in the village street, the corner of Mrs Sherborne's back garden touched on another, enclosed by a high wall, which Rod was almost sure was that of the legendary Rose Collard.

He began to ponder. He scratched his head.

Then, going to his suitcase, he extracted a smallish piece of machinery, unfolded it, and set it up. It stood on one leg, with a tripod foot.

Rodney pulled out a kind of drawer on one side of this gadget, revealing a bank of lettered keys. On these he typed the message,

"Hullo, Fred."

The machine clicked, rumbled, let out one or two long experimental rasping chirrs, not at all unlike the nightingales warming up, and then replied in a loud creaking voice,

"Friday evening June twelve nineteen seventy eight thirty p.m. Good evening, Rodney."

The door shot open. Mrs Sherborne came boiling in.

"What's this?" she cried indignantly. "I let the room to *one,* no more. Entertaining visitors in bedrooms is strictly against the—" She stopped, her mouth open. "What's *that?*"

"My travelling computer," Rodney replied.

Mrs Sherborne gave the computer a long, doubtful, suspicious glare. But at last she retired, saying, "Well, all right. But if there's any noise, or bangs, mind, or if neighbours complain, you'll have to leave, immediate!"

"I have problems, Fred," Rodney typed rapidly as soon as the door closed. "Data up to the present about Rose Collard are as follows": and he added a summary of all that he had learned, adding, "People in the village are unhelpful. What do you advise?"

Fred brooded, digesting the information that had been fed in.

"You should climb over the garden wall," he said at length.

"I was afraid you'd suggest that," Rodney typed resignedly. Then he closed Fred's drawer and folded his leg, took a length of rope from a small canvas holdall, and went downstairs. Mrs Sherborne poked her head out of the kitchen when she heard Rodney open the front door.

"I lock up at ten sharp," she snapped.

"I hope you have fun," Rodney said amiably, and went out.

He walked a short way, found a narrow alley to his left, and turned down it, finding, as he had hoped, that it circled round behind the walled garden of the rose-covered house. The wall, too, was covered by a climbing rose, very prickly, and although there was a door at the back it was locked, and plainly had not been opened for many years.

Rodney tossed up one end of his rope, which had a grappling-hook attached, and flicked it about until it gripped fast among the gnarled knuckles of the roses.

Inside the wall half a dozen nightingales were singing at the tops of their voices.

"The place sounds like a clock factory," Rodney thought, pulling himself up and getting badly scratched. Squatting on top of the wall, he noticed that all the nightingales had fallen silent. He presumed that they were staring at him but he could not see them; the garden was full of rose-bushes run riot into twenty-foot clumps; no doubt the nightingales were sitting in these. But between the rose thickets were stretches of silvery grass; first freeing and winding up his rope, Rodney jumped down and began to wander quietly about. The nightingales started tuning up once more.

Rodney had not gone very far when something tapped him on the shoulder.

He almost fell over, so quickly did he spin around.

He had heard nothing, but there was a person behind him, sitting in a wheel-chair. Uncommon sight she was, to be sure, the whole of her bundled up in a shawl, with a great bush of moon-silvered white hair (he could see the drops of mist on it) and a long thin black stick (which was what she had tapped him with), ash-white face, thinner than the prow of a Viking ship, and a pair of eyes as dark as holes, steadily regarding him.

"And what do *you* want?" she said coldly.

"I—I'm sorry miss—ma'am," Rodney stammered. "I did knock, but nobody answered the door. Are you—could you be —Miss Rose Collard?"

"If I am," said she, "I don't see *that's* a cause for any ex-Boy Scout with a rope and an extra share of impertinence to come climbing into my garden."

"I'm from the B.B.C. I—we did write—care of Covent Garden. The letter was returned."

"Well? I never answer letters. Now you *are* here, what do you want?"

"We are making a film about your life. Childhood in Puddle Fratrum. Career. And scenes from the ballet that was written for you."

"So?"

"Well, Miss Collard, it's this curse you laid on it. I—" He hesitated, jabbed his foot into a dew-sodden silvery tussock of grass, and at last said persuasively, "I don't suppose you could see your way to take the curse *off* again?"

"Why?" she asked with interest. "Is it working?"

"Working! We've had one electricians' strike, two musicians', three studio fires, two cameras exploded, five dancers sprained their ankles. It's getting to be almost impossible to find anyone to take the part now."

"My part? Who have you got at present?"

"A young dancer called Tessa Porutska. She's pretty inexperienced but—well, no one else would volunteer."

Rose Collard smiled.

"So—well—couldn't you take the curse off? It's such a long time since it all happened."

"Why should I take it off? What do I care about your studio fires or your sprained ankles?"

"If I brought Tess to see you? She's so keen to dance the part."

"So was I keen once," Rose Collard said, and she quoted dreamily, " 'One red rose is all I want,' cried the Nightingale."

"It's such a beautiful ballet," pleaded Rodney, "or at least it *would* be, if only the stage didn't keep collapsing, and the props going astray, and the clarinettist getting hiccups—"

"Really? Did all those things happen? I never thought it would work half so well," Rose Collard said wistfully, as if she rather hoped he would ask her to a rehearsal.

"What exactly were the terms of the curse?"

"Oh, just that some doom or misfortune should prevent the ballet ever being performed right through till Puddle church clock ran backwards, and the man who dropped the banana-peel said he was sorry, and somebody put on the ballet with a company of one-legged dancers."

Rodney, who had looked moderately hopeful at the beginning of this sentence, let out a yelp of despair.

"We could probably fix the church clock. And surely we could get the chap to say he was sorry—where is he now, by the way?"

"How should I know?"

"But *one-legged* dancers! Have a heart, Miss Collard!"

"*I've* only got one leg!" she snapped. "And I get along. Anyway it's not so simple to take off a curse."

"But wouldn't you like to?" he urged her. "Wouldn't you enjoy seeing the ballet? Doesn't it get a bit boring, sitting in this garden year after year, listening to all those jabbering nightingales?"

There was an indignant silence for a moment, then a chorus of loud, rude jug-jugs.

"Well—" she said at last, looking half convinced, "I'll think about it. Won't promise anything. At least—I tell you what. I'll make a bargain. You fix about the church clock and the apology, I'll see what I can do about remitting the last bit of the curse."

"Miss Collard," said Rodney, "you're a prime gun!" and he was so pleased that he gave her a hug. The wheel-chair shot backwards, Miss Collard looked very much surprised, and the nightingales all exclaimed,

"Phyooo—jug-jug-jug, tereu, tereu!"

Rodney climbed back over the wall with the aid of his rope. Mrs Sherborne had locked him out, so he spent the night more comfortably than he would have in her guest-room, curled up on a bed of hassocks in the church. The clock woke him by striking every quarter, so he rose at six forty-five and spent an hour and a half tinkering with the works, which hung down like a sporran inside the bell tower and could be reached by means of his rope.

"No breakfasts served after eight-fifteen!" snapped Mrs Sherborne, when Rodney appeared in her chilly parlour. Outside the windows mist lay thick as old-man's-beard.

"It's only quarter to," he pointed out mildly. "Hark!"

"That's funny," she said, listening to the church clock chime. "Has that thing gone bewitched, or have I?"

Rodney sat down quietly and ate his dollop of cold porridge, bantam's egg, shred of marmalade and thimbleful of tea. Then he went off to the public call-box to telephone his fiancée Miss Tessa Prout (Porutska for professional purposes) who was staying at the White Lion Hotel in Bridport along with some other dancers and a camera team.

"Things aren't going too badly, love," he told her. "I think it might be worth your while to come over to Puddle. Tell the others."

So presently in the Puddle High Street, where the natives were all scratching their heads and wondering what ailed their church clock, two large trucks pulled up and let loose a company of cameramen, prop hands, ballet chorus, and four dancers who were respectively to take the parts of the Student, the Girl, the Nightingale, and the Rose. Miss Tessa Porutska (née Prout) who was dancing the Nightingale, left her friends doing battements against the church wall and strolled along to Mrs Sherborne's, where she found Rodney having a conversation with Fred.

"But Fred," he was typing, "I have passed on to you every fact in my possession. Surely from what you have had you ought to be able to locate this banana-peel dropper?"

"Very sorry," creaked Fred, "the programming is inadequate," and he retired into an affronted silence.

"What's all this about banana-peel?" asked Tess, who was a very pretty girl, thin as a ribbon, with her brown hair tied in a knot.

Rodney explained that they needed to find a stage-hand who had dropped a banana-peel on the stage at Covent Garden thirty years before.

"We'll have to advertise," he said gloomily, "and it may take months. It's not going to be as simple as I'd hoped."

"Simple as pie," corrected Tess. "That'll be my Great-Uncle Toby. It was on account of him going on all the time about ballet when I was little that I took to a dancer's career."

"Where does your Uncle Toby live?"

"Just up the street."

Grabbing Rodney's hand she whisked him along the street to the forge where the surly Mr Prout, ignoring the ballet chorus who were rehearsing a Dorset schottische in the road just outside his forge and holding up the traffic to an uncommon degree, was fettling a set of shoes the size of barrel-hoops for a great grey brewer's drayhorse.

"Uncle Toby!" she said, and planted a kiss among his white whiskers.

"Well, Tess? What brings you back to Puddle, so grand and upstage as you are these days?"

"Uncle Toby, weren't you sorry about the banana-peel you dropped that was the cause of poor Rose Collard breaking her leg?"

"Sorry?" he growled. "Sorry? Dang it, o' *course* I was sorry. Sorrier about that than anything else I did in my whole life! Followed her up to' London parts, I did, seeing she was sot to be a dancer; got a job shifting scenery so's to be near her; ate nowt but a banana for me dinner every day, so's not to miss watching her rehearse; and then the drabbited peel had to goo and fall out through a strent in me britches pocket when we was unloading all they unket rose-leaves on the stage, and the poor mawther had to goo and tread on it and bust her leg. Worst day's job I ever did, that were. Never had the heart to get wed, on account o' that gal, I didn't."

"Well, but, Uncle Toby, did you ever *tell* her how sorry you were?"

"How could I, when she shut herself up a-grieving and a-laying curses right, left, and rat's ramble?"

"You could have written her a note?"

"Can't write. Never got no schooling," said Mr Prout, and

slammed down with his hammer on the horseshoe, scattering sparks all over.

"Here, leave that shoe, Uncle Toby, do, for goodness' sake, and come next door."

Very unwilling and suspicious, Mr Prout allowed himself to be dragged, hammer and all, to the back of Rose Collard's garden wall. Here he flatly refused to climb over on Rodney's rope.

"Dang me if I goo over that willocky way," he objected. "I'll goo through the door, fittingly, or not at all."

"But the door's stuck fast; hasn't been opened for thirty years."

"Hammer'll soon take care o' that," said Uncle Toby, and burst it open with one powerful thump.

Inside the garden the nightingales were all asleep; sea-mist and silence lay among the thickets. But Uncle Toby soon broke the silence.

"Rose!" he bawled. "Rosie! I be come to say I'm sorry."

No answer.

"Rose! Are you in here, gal?"

Rodney and Tess looked at one another doubtfully. She held up a hand. Not far off, among the thickets, they heard a faint sound; it could have been somebody crying.

"Rosie!" shouted Uncle Toby. "Said I was sorry, didn't I? Can't do more'n that, can I?"

Silence.

"*Rosie?* Confound it gal, where are you?" And Uncle Toby stumped purposefully off among the thickets.

"Suppose we go and wait at the pub?" suggested Tess. "Look, the sun's coming out."

An hour later Mr Prout came pushing Miss Pollard's wheel-chair along Puddle Fratrum's main street.

"We're a-going to get wed," he told Rodney and Tess, who were drinking cider in the little front garden of the Hay-makers' Arms. (It was not yet opening hours, but since the church clock now registered five a.m. and nobody could be sure of the correct time there had been a general agreement to waive all such fiddling rules for the moment.) "A-going to get wed we are, Saturday's a fortnight. And now we're a-going to celebrate in cowslip wine and huckle-my-buff, and then my intended would like to watch a rehearsal."

"What's huckle-my-buff?"

Huckle-my-buff, it seemed, was beer, eggs, and brandy, all beaten together; Tess helped Mr Donn (who was another uncle) to prepare it.

The rehearsal was not so easily managed. When the chorus of village maidens and haymakers were halfway through their schottische, a runaway hay-truck, suffering from brake-fade, came careering down the steep hill from Puddle Porcorum and ran slap against the post office, spilling its load all the way up the village street. The dancers only escaped being buried in hay because of their uncommon agility, leaping out of the way in a variety of jetés, caprioles, and pas de chamois, and it was plain that no filming was going to be possible until the hay had somehow been swept, dusted, or vacuumed away from the cobbles, front gardens, door-steps, and window-sills.

"Perhaps we could do a bit of filming in your garden, Miss Collard?" Rodney suggested hopefully. "That would make a wonderful setting for the scene where the Nightingale sings all night with the thorn against her heart, while the Rose slowly becomes crimson."

"I don't wish to seem disobliging," said Miss Collard (who had watched the episode of the hay-truck with considerable interest and not a little pride; *"Well,"* she had murmured to her fiancé, "just fancy my curse working as well as that, after all this time!") "but I should be really upset if anything—well, troublesome, was to happen in my garden."

"But surely in that case—couldn't you just be so kind as to remove the curse?"

"Oh," said Rose Collard, "I'm afraid there's a bit of a difficulty there."

"What's that, Auntie Rose?" said Tess.

"As soon as you get engaged to be married you stop being a witch. Soon as you stop being a witch you lose the power to lift the curse."

They gawped at her.

"That's awkward," said Rodney at length. He turned to Tess. "I don't suppose you have any talents in the witchcraft line, have you lovey, by any chance?"

"Well, I did just have the rudiments," she said sadly, "but of course I lost them the minute I got engaged to you. How about Mrs Sherborne?"

"The curse has to be taken off by the one who put it on," said Rose.

"Oh." There was another long silence. "Well," said Rodney at length, "maybe Fred will have some suggestion as to what's the best way to put on a ballet with a company of one-legged dancers."

They drank down the last of their huckle-my-buff and went along to Mrs Sherborne's.

"Hullo, Fred? Are you paying attention? We have a little problem for you."

*   *   *

And that is why, when *The Nightingale and the Rose* was revived last year, it ran for a very successful season at Covent Garden danced by a company of one-legged computers, with Fred taking the part of the Nightingale.

A Long Day Without Water

This story is all about tears—tears locked inside a heart, heart lost in a river, river shut inside a house, house in a village that didn't want it. Better get out your handkerchiefs, then, for it sounds like a whole sky full of cloud coming along, doesn't it? And yet the ending, when we get there, isn't solid sad.

So listen.

Our village is called Appleby under Scar, and there's a river, the Skirwith Beck, that runs through the middle of it. Or did. Ran down the middle of the village green, chuckling and muttering among its rocks; clean-washed gravel-beds in summer on either side; in winter, of course, it was up to chest high, brown and foamy like the best oatmeal stout. In summer, days together, the children would be playing there, with dams, and stepping-stones, making castles on the sandbanks, picking up quartz stones, white, purple, and pink, all sparkling. A beautiful stream, the Skirwith Beck, the best kind. You can keep your willowy, muddy, winding rivers.

And the village green, on either side, was common land, villagers used to pasture their geese and donkeys there; lots of people used to have an old moke for when they wanted to go up on the fell and bring down a load of peat.

Summer evenings, half the village would be out on the green, enjoying the sunshine. There was a young fellow, Johnny Rigby, who had a little farm; hardly more than a smallholding, but he worked it hard and made a living from it; he was one of three brothers. Anyway this Johnny **Rigby** was a rare lad for playing the fiddle and composing **songs**; he used to play his fiddle on the green, and the girls used to dance. Or everybody would gather round to listen if he'd made up a new song.

I can remember one of his to this day; kind of a catch, or round, it was:

> Standing corn, running river
> Singing wind, laughing plover
> Running fox, standing grain
> Leaping salmon, weeping·rain
> Shining sun, singing lark
> Running roe, listening dark
> Laughing river, standing corn
> Happy village where I was born.

You see? It went round and round; pretty tune it had, still goes round and round in my head.

Johnny Rigby was friendly with a girl called Martha; nothing definite yet, but when he'd made up a new song, Martha would generally be the one that sat nearest to hear him sing it, and the first to get it by heart: Martha Dyson, pink cheeks and black hair, and bright dark eyes that saw further than most. Folks were pretty certain they'd get wed by and by.

Well, somewhere in among those long summer evenings of singing and chat on the Skirwith bank, some little chaps in glasses drove up to the village in a big Bentley car, and they were busy for days together, pottering about, taking samples of soil, poking instruments into the ground, weighing and measuring, peering about them through spyglasses, even getting down into the Skirwith Beck and taking samples of gravel from underneath *that*.

Nobody bothered about them. We're peaceable folk in these parts; if chaps don't worry us, we won't worry them. They used to eat their dinners in the Falcon pub, and we'd give them a civil good-day, but no more; we don't get thick with strangers all in a hurry round here; we give ourselves time to look them over first. And we had hardly given ourselves more than a couple of weeks to do that, when they were gone again, and then time went by and we forgot them.

But two or three months later—the hay was in and the harvest was half through—we heard what they'd been up to, and it was this.

It seems some big chemical firm—United Kingdom Alloys, the name was—had got wind there was a layer of mineral right under our village green, something quite uncommon and out of the way. Demetrium, it was called; a kind of nickel, Tom Thorpe told me it was, but that's as may be. And the long and the short of it was, they wanted permission to dig up the green, or, in their language, opencast mine it, to a depth of fifteen feet.

Well! You can guess that stirred up a lot of talk in the village.

A few folk were dead against it, old Thunders Barstow for one. He was the sexton, and got his nickname from his habit of shouting "The Lord shall send his thunders upon you," when he didn't approve of something.

"What'll happen?" he said. "They'll come here, wi' all their load of heavy digging equipment, they'll wreck the road from here to Paxton, carting yon stuff away, they'll make a right shambles o' the green; I shouldn't wonder if half the houses didn't tumble down because they'll undermine the foundations; they'll spoil the beck wi' their gravel and refuse, tha can say goodbye to t'trout and salmon, and then what? When they've got what they came for, they'll be off, leaving the place a fair wilderness."

Of course United Kingdom Alloys promised and swore they would do no such thing. Every care would be taken of amenities, they said, in a letter on stiff crackly paper, the dug-out area would be filled in again and landscaped, all debris taken away, any damage made good, and so forth.

"Landscaped!" snorted old Thunders. "What about our chestnuts? Tha cannot tweak up a two-hundred-year-old chestnut tree and set it back again as if it was a snowdrop bulb, sithee!"

Well, United Kingdom Alloys did admit they'd have to chop down the chestnuts—twenty of them, there were, all round the edge of the green—but they said they'd plant others, *mature trees,* they said, in another letter on even stiffer, cracklier paper, as soon as the work was completed.

"After all," said Sam Oakroyd, "there's no brass wi'out muck. And tha can see they mean to play fair by us."

Brass, of course, was the nub of the business. U.K.A. were offering a right handsome sum for the use of our land—a figure that made most folk's eyes pop out on stalks when they heard it, though of course you had to remember it was going to be split up among the twenty people who owned the grazing rights on the green. And that was the hitch—everyone whose cottage faced on to the green had a say in the matter, and the firm couldn't so much as set a trowel into the ground till the whole twenty had agreed, as well as the Ministry of Town and Country Planning.

Well, the Ministry agreed—no argument there—and bit by bit everyone else did, as they realized what advantage it would bring them. Tom Thorpe could get a new farm truck, the Oakroyds would be able to send their daughter to music college, widow Kirby could get a modern stove put in her cottage, young Sally Gateshead could buy herself a hunter, the Bateses would be able to achieve their dearest wish, which was a colour telly, and the Sidebothams had set their heart on a holiday in Madeira. One person who didn't agree was old Thunders Barstow, but his cottage didn't front on the green, so he had no say in the matter. And a lot of people thought old Thunders was a bit touched, anyway.

But just when everything seemed swimming along merrily and in a fair way to be fixed up, the whole scheme came to a stop because of one person.

That person was Johnny Rigby.

His two brothers had signed on the dotted line quick enough. Old man Rigby had died without making a will, and his farm had been split in three; there was just enough land for each brother, but you had to work hard to make it pay, and the two elder Rigbys, who shared the old man's house, though they weren't bone idle, weren't all that keen on work; they were fair tickled at the prospect of a nest egg from United Kingdom Alloys. Each brother owned grazing rights on the green, as Johnny had his own cottage, left him by his gran, and each had to agree before the company started work.

But Johnny wouldn't, and he was the last person in the village to make a stand.

He said it would spoil the place. He said no matter what was done afterwards, in the way of landscaping, Appleby would never be the same again. I think there was quite a few others agreed with him in their hearts, but they were overborne by their husbands—or wives—or children—who could see the benefits of hard cash, and were happy to let the future take care of itself.

Everybody argued with Johnny and tried to persuade him to change his mind. And as he wouldn't, the arguments grew more and more hot-tempered. People don't mince words in our parts.

"Tha stupid young milksop!" shouted old Sam Oakroyd. "Tha'rt holding up progress and keeping good brass out o' folk's pockets, all for the sake of a moonshiny notion. A few trees and a bit o' rough pasture! Grass can be sown again, can't it?"

"And what about the river?" said Johnny. "Can they put that back the way it was, after it's been taken out of its bed and run through a concrete pipeline?"

Johnny had fished and paddled and swum in the beck since he was out of his pram; he knew every rock and rowan tree along it, from Skipley to Paxton-le-Pool.

"Aye, they'll put it back—they said so, didn't they? Come on lad, don't be daft—just stop fussing and sign." Old Oakroyd had the letter of acceptance, with everybody's names on it.

But Johnny wouldn't.

So there was a lot of ill-feeling against him. The Sidebothams said flat out that he must be mental, to refuse good cash, and ought to be committed to Skipley Home for Defectives. Tom Thorpe threatened to punch his head, several times his front windows were smashed, and I even heard someone let fly at him with a shotgun one night, as he came home on his motorbike from Paxton. There was no legal way he could be forced to change to his mind, see; he had a right to his own point of view. The only person who stood by him was Martha Dyson.

"How are we going to get that thick-skulled brother of yours to change his mind?" Tom Thorpe said to Wilfred and Michael Rigby in the pub one night.

"I daresay he'll come round in time," Wilfred said.

"Time! The firm won't keep their offer open for ever. There's big deposits of demetrium in Brazil, I read in the paper."

"Then why the devil can't they *go* to Brazil for the stuff, 'stead o' scraping up our green to get tuppence-haporth out of it?" grumbled old Thunders.

"This is cheaper and handier for them, you silly old man."

"Cheaper! Cheaper! The Lord shall call his thunders down on this penny-pinching generation—aye, he shall give their flocks to hot thunderbolts," declared the old man, who loved every stone of Appleby, and hated the thought of change.

Taking no notice of old Thunders, Wilfred Rigby said,

"The only way to get John to change his mind is by public boycott. He's always been a kind of a friendly, popular chap, with his fiddling and his songs; he'd feel it hard if nobody spoke to him, if nobody listened to his songs any more. That'd bring him round, I reckon."

"Bring him round? It'd break his heart," said old Thunders angrily. But no one took any notice of *him*.

So that was what they did. Nobody in the village would speak to Johnny. If he went into the pub, or the post office, folk turned their backs; if he strolled up to a group on the green, they all walked away.

Well, it's bitter hard for anybody in the world to have a thing like that happen to them—to be thrust out and given the cut by your own kin and neighbours—but for a song-writer it's worst of all. See, if you think about it, a song-writer needs folk to sing his songs *to,* he doesn't just make them up to sing into the empty air. It's like electricity: no connection, no current. Without friends to listen to his songs, and dance to his tunes, Johnny was like a fish without water to swim in, a bird without air to fly in; there just wasn't any point to him.

When it got too cold, in autumn-time, for musical evenings on the village green, Johnny'd been in the habit of holding a kind of open-house every Thursday evening. He hadn't much furniture in his cottage, for all the spare cash he had went on fertilizer and stuff for his land, but that made all the more room for friends. He had an old piano that had been his gran's, and anyone who liked could drop in for a bit of singing. If they brought a bottle of beer with them, all the better. Past winters, the house used to be chock full every Thursday, and people dancing in his patch of front garden too. He'd leave the door open, so the light would shine across the green, and you could hear the sound of fiddle and singing clear over the chuckle of the Skirwith Beck.

But not this autumn.

The first Thursday when it was too rainy and dark to linger

outside, Johnny left his door open. It was pouring wet, and the sound of the beck was like a train running over points in the distance. The light from the door shone out, yellow on the rain. Martha was away, staying with her auntie in London, expected back next day. So Johnny was alone. He'd written a new song, and he played the tune over softly on the piano, and louder on the fiddle; but nobody came. An hour went by, still nobody came. Johnny went outside in the wet and looked this way and that; no sign of anybody coming. But there was a light, and noise, from the Falcon pub, across the green, so he walked over. As he got closer he could hear voices singing and someone bashing the old pub piano; Mrs Ellie Sidebotham, it was, he saw when he got outside the window; her playing was enough to give you sinus trouble. But all the village seemed to be in there, singing and enjoying themselves.

Johnny pushed open the door and went in.

A dead silence fell.

Johnny nodded to Mr Baker, who kept the pub, and said he'd have a pint of bitter. Mr Baker couldn't refuse to serve him, so he did, but he didn't speak. Then Johnny took his drink and went over to the piano and pulled a bit of sheet music out of his pocket.

"I've written a new song, Mrs Sidebotham," he said. "Like to play it for me?"

Ellie Sidebotham was a silly, flustered kind of woman; put you in mind of a moulting pullet. She didn't know how to refuse, so she started to play the tune, making a right botch of it.

And Johnny turned and faced the room, and began to sing.

It's a long walk in the dark
On the blind side of the moon
And it's a long day without water
When the river's gone—

But before he had sung any more than that, the bar had emptied. Folk just put down their drinks and left.

Ellie Sidebotham shuffled her way off the piano stool. "I—I must be going too," she said, and scuttled off.

Johnny looked round at the emptiness. He said, "It seems I'm not welcome here," and he walked out.

Wherever he went from the pub, he didn't go home till daylight; some folk said he just walked up and down the village green all night, thinking. In the morning he did go home, but that night's tramping up and down in the wet had done for him; big, strong chap as he was, he came down with a raging pneumonia, and when Martha got back from her auntie's in London and went along to see how he was, she found him tossing and turning on his bed with a temperature of a hundred and six. She ran to the pub and phoned for an ambulance to take him to hospital, but the Skirwith Beck was flooded and they had to take the long way round, and by the time they got there, Johnny was in a coma from which he didn't recover.

Folk felt pretty bad after his death, as you can guess.

There was a big turn-out for the funeral; the whole village came along, done up in black, looking respectful.

Appleby church stands on a kind of knoll above the village, opposite Martha's cottage. The knoll is an island when the beck's in spate, and it was in spate that day; it had rained solid ever since Johnny died. The footbridge was under water, so the only way to get to the graveyard was to row across. The vicar, Mr Haxley, was waiting on the other side. When all the mourners got to the river-bank, Martha Dyson came out from her cottage and faced them.

"You lot can just go home again," she said. "You didn't want my Johnny, and *you're* not wanted here. And if you want my opinion of you, you can have it—you're a lot of cowardly murderers, and you broke Johnny's heart among you, and I hope you're proud of yourselves."

Not a soul had owt to say. They turned round, looking as shamed as dogs that have been caught sheep-worrying, and walked away through the rain. Martha Dyson and old Thunders began rowing the coffin across to the church. But the current was fierce, he was an old man and she only a bit of a lass; a huge eddy of flood water and branches came down on them and capsized the boat. Martha was a good swimmer, but she had her hands full with getting the old man to the bank; the vicar helped pull him out and the first thing was to get the pair of them dry and tended. By the time folk came to look for the boat and the coffin, neither could be found. The boat finally turned up, stove-in, down at Paxton-le-Pool. But the coffin with Johnny's body in it they never found, though the police dragged the Skirwith Beck clear down to where it joins the Ouse.

Well, you know how tales start up; it wasn't long before folk were saying the heart in Johnny's body had been so heavy with grief that it sank the boat.

But that wasn't the end of the matter, as you shall hear.

Of course, even if they pulled long faces, there were plenty of folk in the village who were relieved at Johnny's death, because now there was nothing to stand in the way of the United Kingdom Alloy scheme. His land went to his two brothers, and they had already signed the form. So within two weeks the green was covered with bulldozers and those big grabbing machines that look like nought in the world but prehistoric monsters, and they'd cut down the chestnuts, and the grass on Appleby Green was a thing of the past.

Some folk were even mean enough to say, Wasn't it a good thing that Johnny and Martha hadn't got wed yet—they'd fixed to get married at Christmas, it came out—because if she'd been his widow, instead of only his intended, she'd have owned the grazing rights and been able to withhold her permission. And there's no doubt she would have. She was very bitter against the village. Very bitter indeed, she was.

Those Rigby brothers must have felt guilty right down to their socks for, believe it or not, when the U.K.A. paid over the fee for use of land—which, fair play, they did pretty promptly, though it turned out to be only half what they'd said; the other half, they explained, would be paid on completion of the operation—Wilfred Rigby went along to see Martha Dyson. They hadn't spoken since the funeral.

Martha's cottage, up the dale, opposite the church, had been her family home from way back. Martha's grandmother had been a celebrated witch, or wise woman, in her day, could charm warts and lay curses and make prophecies; some folk said that Martha could too. Her mother and father had died in the bad flood of '68, and she lived on her own, kept bees, and sold the honey in Paxton; did quite well out of it. She was feeding her bees with sugar syrup when Wilfred came along. The beck ran right past her gate, and there were two queer old carved swans on the gateposts, asleep with their heads under their wings—at least they were said to be swans, but you could make them into pretty well anything you chose.

Wilfred had to clear his throat several times and finally shout quite loud to attract Martha's attention; the beck was brawling away, still extra-high, and from the village there was a continuous grinding and roaring from the earth-moving machinery, and every now and then the ground would tremble as they dumped a big load of topsoil, or split a rock. By now, naturally, the whole village was a sea of slurry, and the road down to Paxton just a rutted, muddy watercourse.

"Well," said Martha, hearing at last and turning round, "what do *you* want?"

Wilfred—awkward and fumbling enough—went into an explanation of how—if by this time Martha had been married to Johnny—and if Johnny hadn't died—and if he'd agreed to the U.K.A. scheme—Martha would have come in for a bit of the brass. At last she understood him.

"You're offering me money?"

Wilfred shuffled his feet and brought out that, yes, he was.
"Why?"

He looked more uncomfortable still. He didn't like to admit that he was scared stiff of Martha's anger and wanted to soothe her down. He shuffled his feet again in the wet grass and said,

"We thought—Mike and I—that you might like to go on a bit of a holiday. Or—or the vicar was suggesting that as poor Johnny hasn't got a grave, we might wish to put up a memorial tablet to him. Maybe you'd like to use some of the money for that?"

Martha's eyes fairly blazed at him.

"You can just take your dirty money away from here, Wilfred Rigby, back to the mucky hole you've made of Appleby," she said. "I've got some brass of my own, that my gran left me, and I intend to put up my own memorial to Johnny. And I'd advise you not to try—there's some hypocrisy that even the wind and weather can't abide. Any tablet *you* put up would crack in the first frost, it would get struck by lightning or washed away by a flood."

"You're a hard, unforgiving woman, Martha Dyson," said Wilfred.

"I've cause," she snapped.

At that moment there was an extra-loud crashing rumble from the village. And then Wilfred and Martha saw a queer and frightening thing. The Skirwith Beck, rushing down its rocky way, did a kind of sudden lurch sideways in its bed— just as a startled horse will shy at something ahead of it—the water lurched and rocked, and then, quick as I'm speaking, sank away out of sight, down into the ground.

"My lord! The beck! What's come to it?" Wilfred gasped.

"It's gone," Martha said sombrely. "Due to you and your money-grabbing mates it's gone. And I can tell you this, Wilfred Rigby—I shan't forgive you or anybody else in Appleby till it comes back again."

And with that she turned her back on him and wouldn't speak any more and he was glad enough to hurry away.

Well, you can guess there was plenty more talk in the village about the lost beck. Some said it was due to natural causes—the vibrations from the heavy digging had likely cracked open an underground cavern, and the water had sunk through into it. But there were plenty believed it was the weight of Johnny Rigby's heavy heart that had sunk the river, as it had sunk the rowboat. And there were a few that thought Martha Dyson had done it, out of revenge against the village that had killed her Johnny. Martha never spoke to a soul in Appleby these days—except old Thunders—she bought her groceries in Paxton when she went with the honey.

Meanwhile the digging went on. Appleby looked like some place in a war-zone that's had half a dozen battles fought in it, back and forth. And the beck never came back. Trees in gardens began to die, because their roots weren't getting enough water.

And Martha built her memorial to Johnny Rigby. She had a grand architect from London come down for the job, and a builder from York. It was a queer-looking thing enough when it was done—a little house in the churchyard, made of stone, with carvings on the outside all over—ears of wheat, birds, foxes, deer, fish, leaves, and what looked like ripples of water twining in and among and through all these things. It had a right unchancy feel about it—when you looked at it close enough you could swear the stone was moving, like grass waving or water running. There was a door at one end, and over the lintel Martha got the architect to put the two swans from her gateposts, with their heads under their wings.

On the side was carved the name John Rigby, and underneath some words:

. . . thou art cast out of thy grave like an abominable branch . . .

For the waters of Nimrim shall be desolate: for the hay is withered away, the grass faileth, there is no green thing . . .

Woe to the multitude of many people, which make a noise like the noise of the seas . . .

And behold at eveningtide trouble; and before the morning he is not. This the portion of them that spoil us, and the lot of them that rob us. (Isaiah XIV, XV, XVII.)

The vicar wasn't best pleased when he saw the words that had been carved, but Martha said they were Bible words, and by that time the architect and the builders had left, so in the end they were allowed to stay. There were a lot of complaints in the village about the tomb itself—folk said it was an outrage, and should be taken away. But the vicar put a stop to that.

Pretty soon there was a new tale in the village about this tomb.

The Bates family had a boy who wasn't quite right in the head. Simple Steve, or Silly Steve, he was called; the other children wouldn't play with him because he hardly ever spoke, but only made patterns on the ground with leaves and twigs and stones. It was a queer tale enough about him, and a sad one. Mrs Bates had had two boys, and was set on a girl for her next; when Steve was born, another boy, she wouldn't speak to him, kept him shut away in a back bedroom, and fed him only slops till he was six or seven. Lots of folk didn't even know he existed till the school attendance officer, doing a check, discovered that Steve ought to have been going to school for a couple of years and couldn't even speak. There was a fuss, threats of prosecution, but in the end it died down. Steve was sent to school, but he didn't learn much. The teacher was very angry about it all, and said he wasn't really simple; if he'd been cared for and spoken to properly from the start it would have been all right; but it was too late now. Well, there you are; that's the kind of thing you find even in families that seem quite normal and aboveboard.

Simple Steve used to spend quite a lot of time in the graveyard, playing his pattern-games on the flat tombstones. Old
Thunders didn't mind him; in fact the two got on quite well;
they could make themselves understood to each other in a kind
of sign language. Steve used to help cut the grass and clip the
hedges. The old man would whistle as he worked and Steve,
though he could hardly talk, could hum a tune; old Thunders
taught him some of Johnny Rigby's tunes. But there was one
corner of the graveyard Steve would never go near, and that
was where Johnny Rigby's memorial stood; he explained to
the old man that he was afraid of the tomb because the beck
was all shut up inside that little house, and one day it was going to break out and flood all over the village. By and by
somehow this tale got round, and although they knew it was
nonsense, a lot of folk half believed it, specially the children.

Nobody could get inside; Martha kept the key of the locked
door; she said, if ever Johnny's coffin was found, it should be
put in. On a bright sunshiny afternoon it used to be a dare
game for the braver kids to go and listen at the keyhole.
They'd come away quaking and giggling, declaring they could
hear the beck running inside—like when you put your ear to
a shell. Not one of them would have had the nerve to go near
the place at night.

By this time the winter was nearly over. Frost and snow
hadn't stopped the U.K.A.—they'd been digging away like
badgers all through. There had been one or two mishaps—a
few people fell into the diggings at night and broke legs or
arms; the works were taken a bit too near the Rigby
brothers' house and it collapsed, but they weren't killed, and
the U.K.A. swore they'd pay compensation. Also they cut
through the village water-supply and sewage system, but the
Public Health lot made them put the sewer right pretty quick,
before they had a typhoid epidemic on their hands. The
Rigbys weren't so lucky; they hadn't got their compensation
by the time the U.K.A. people left, nor had Thorpe, for his

collapsed barn, nor the Bateses for their garden which had sunk down ten feet, nor widow Kirby, who'd had twelve ton of subsoil accidentally dumped on hers. And there were various other troubles of the kind, but people reckoned the company would pay for these things at the same time as they paid the second half of the fee for use of land.

Well, the excavators left, and took their machinery with them, leaving the place like the crater of a volcano; and folk were beginning to wonder when the landscapers would be along with their turf, and mature trees, and whatnot, to make good the devastation, fill in the excavated area, and carry out all their promises.

It was at this point that we read in the papers about the United Kingdom Alloy Company going bankrupt.

Over-extended its resources, was the phrase used in court when the case was heard.

They'd had irons in too many fires, borrowed cash here to pay for operations there which turned out less successful than they'd hoped; and the outcome of the matter was they'd gone into liquidation, paid sixpence in the pound to their creditors, and the head of the firm had disappeared, thought to have absconded to Brazil to escape all the trouble he'd left behind him.

And as for our mature trees, topsoil, turf, compensation, and the Skirwith Beck, we could whistle for them.

You'd hardly believe what happened next.

Martha Dyson still wasn't speaking to anyone in the village. People said she was so bitter, even the birds and the wild animals kept away from her garden. But one day a deputation from the village went to call on her: Mrs Kirby, Mrs Bates, Tom Thorpe, and the Sidebothams. They stood inside Martha's gate looking nervous till she came out and asked them what they wanted. They all hummed and ha'd and looked at one another, until at last Ellie Sidebotham burst out with it.

"We've come to ask you to take the curse off!"

"Curse, what curse?" Martha says.

"The curse you put on the village! We've no water-supply, the trees and plants are all dying, the green's just a hole full of shingle—there's no end to the trouble. Oh, Miss Dyson, do please take it off. We're scared to think what might happen if it gets any worse!"

At that Martha laughed, a short, scornful laugh.

"You poor fools, *I* didn't put any curse on you," she said. "It was your own short-sighted greed put you in this mess, and you'll just have to get yourselves out of it as best you can."

"But you said to Will Rigby that until the Skirwith Beck came back—"

"I said I shouldn't forgive you till then, and it's true, I shan't. Now go away and leave me in peace," Martha said.

"Then you're a hard, heartless woman, Martha Dyson!" squeaked Ellie Sidebotham. "And with all your memorials and show of mourning Johnny Rigby I don't believe you've ever shed a tear for him!"

White-faced and dry-eyed Martha glared at her. Then she said,

"Get out of my garden. And you can tell the rest of them, down in the village, that if anyone else comes here without being asked, I *shall* get out my grandmother's book of curses."

They cleared out pretty quick at that, and went back to the village muttering. As for Martha, she sat down on her doorstep, sick with sadness, and shivering, shivering cold. For it was true, since Johnny's death, she hadn't been able to cry; not a tear.

Well, the people of Appleby saw they'd get no help from Martha, and they found they'd get none, either, from the Ministry of Town and Country Planning, which said it might be able to do something for them in a couple of years but not sooner. So they realized they'd have to help themselves, and they clubbed together and started a fund for Village Beauti-

fication. The Bateses reckoned they could do without their
colour TV another year, Sally Gateshead sold the new hunter,
the Sidebothams fixed to go to Blackpool instead of Madeira.
And so on. Furthermore they arranged a rota of working par-
ties to start getting the green back into shape. The trouble
was fetching down enough topsoil from the fells to fill in the
hole; that was going to take a lot of men a lot of time. However they'd hardly got started when the cold came on, very
severe.

Up to then it had been an unusually mild winter, for our
parts. But in late March, after a specially warm spell, there
was a sudden real blizzard. First it thundered, then it hailed,
then the snow came down solid white, out of a black sky. And
the snow went right on for twenty-four hours, till all you could
see of Appleby were a few humps, the roofs of houses, and the
church spire on its knoll. The shallow crater in the middle of
the village was filled with snow, and looked decenter than it
had for many a week. There were no trees above the snow;
what hadn't been chopped had all fallen during the winter.

We're well used to snow, of course; so folk who hadn't
beasts to tend stayed in and kept snug. At least there was
plenty of firewood: chestnut wood. But in the middle of the
night following the storm, all of a sudden there came the
loudest noise you can imagine; some thought it was the H-
bomb, others that the top of Skipley Fell had come loose and
slid down in an avalanche.

Well, it was a kind of avalanche, they discovered in the
morning. The bottom of the crater that had been Appleby
Green had fallen in, due to the weight of snow piled in it,
and the crater was now a whole lot deeper; but before they
had time to discover how much deeper, it filled up with
water. For the sudden cold had turned to a sudden thaw; the
snow melting as fast as it had come.

That morning Martha was looking over her bee-hives, to
make sure they'd taken no hurt in the snow, when she saw a

black procession of men going up to the church, carrying something shoulder-high.

Mr Haxley the vicar came over and tapped on Martha's gate. His face was solemn, and he looked as if he didn't know how to begin what he had to say. But she got there first.

"They've found him?"

"Yes, my dear. I've come to ask for the key."

Seemingly all that rock and snow and rubble, crashing down through the bottom of the crater, must have filled up the underground chamber again, or blocked the entrance, and in doing so it had floated up Johnny Rigby's coffin, on the melted snow-water, from where it had been lodged underground. It was found beached on the edge of the pool that had been Appleby Green.

Martha gave the key to Mr Haxley. But the men found they didn't need it, for the end of the empty tomb, and the tree that stood nearest to it, had both been struck by lightning in the storm the night before. The end wall of the tomb had fallen away, and the door was all charred.

The men of the village, who had carried Johnny's coffin up, laid it inside the tomb while the vicar read the funeral service, and then they rebuilt the wall and set in a new door. But they couldn't find the two stone swans, which seemed to have been clean destroyed. All that time, Martha watched them from her garden gateway. When they were leaving she made them a kind of bow, to signify she was grateful for what they'd done. And when they'd gone, she sat down on her doorstep, threw her apron over her head, and cried as if a dam had burst inside her.

But that day wasn't over for Martha yet. After a while, as she sat there grieving, but more gently now, she heard a sound by her. She pulled the apron off her face, and found the little Bates lad, Simple Steve, sitting on the step next to her, quiet-like, making one of his patterns with sticks and leaves.

"Hallo!" she said, fair astonished, for no kid from the village ever set foot inside her garden.

He gave her a nod, and the kind of grunt that was all he'd do for hallo. And went on with his pattern. It was a peaceful kind of thing to watch, and presently she got to helping him, handing him bits of stuff, and showing him where he could make the pattern better.

Steve began humming to himself as he often did.

"Where did you learn that?" asked Martha, startled. For the tune was one of Johnny's.

Steve nodded his head sideways, towards the churchyard over the way, meaning, probably, that old Thunders had taught it him.

Martha took up the tune with him, singing the words.

> It's a long walk in the dark
> On the blind side of the moon
> And it's a long day without water
> When the river's gone
> And it's hard listening to no voice
> When you're all alone.

Steve learned the words from her, after his fashion, and he began singing them too.

"You sing well, Steven," she told him.

At that, Steve's face did a thing it had never done before. It smiled. Then he pointed past Martha. She turned, and saw that an old tail-less black cat, Mrs Kirby's Tib, had come into the garden. And that wasn't all. There were rabbits, and a stray ewe, a young fox, even a roe-deer, had all pushed their way through the hedge.

"Mercy, what's come over the creatures?" said Martha, more and more amazed.

"They know the beck's coming," said Steve nodding. "I did, too."

She understood what he meant, then. In the bad flood of '68, only Martha's cottage and the church knoll stood above water level.

"I'd best warn them," she said. "You stay here, Steve."

And she walked quickly down to Appleby, where half the village was out, gazing at the pool that had been Appleby Green. They gawped when they saw Martha, as you can guess.

"I've come to tell you the beck's coming down," she said. "You'd best—you'd best come up to my place."

They didn't hang about. In our parts we know how, when the snow melts up on the high fells, a little trickle of water can turn to a raging torrent in ten minutes. Tom Thorpe went round, shouting them out of their houses, and they were up at Martha's carrying all they could, almost as quick as I'm telling it. And only just in time, too, for the Skirwith Beck came thundering down the dale only a few minutes after, as if it were carrying the troubles and quarrels of the whole village on its back.

They had to stay up at Martha's for three hours, while the water raged through the village. She made them cups of tea, and so forth, while the women helped, and they all shared out what food they'd brought with them. Then the water went down—it's fast come, fast go, up here—and they went back to look at the damage.

Well, it wasn't too bad. The houses are solid-built, they were all right; of course there was a lot of mud and wet that would want cleaning out. Everybody set to, right off, scrubbing and lighting fires and airing. But the wonderful thing was that in its wild spate the beck had fetched down enough peat and loam and topsoil from the high fell to cover the ugly stony crater the United Kingdom Alloy Company had left behind them. There was still a small, deep round pool in the middle; the beck had made a new course for itself, ran in one side and out the other.

Two swans were swimming about on the pool. No one knew where they had come from.

It was all hard work, after that, for months. Getting the dirt evenly spread, making a new pathway round the green, paving it with flat stones, and sowing grass. Whatever was done, Martha Dyson was there, helping. With the Beautification Fund they bought young chestnut trees from a nursery and set them round the way the others had been.

"Reckon they ought to see our grandchildren's grandchildren out," Tom Thorpe said.

Young Steve Bates went to live with Martha. He just wouldn't leave her house, when the others went back after the flood. Mrs Bates raised no objections and Martha said she'd like to adopt him. He did better with his book-learning, after, though he'd never make Skipley Grammar. But he started learning the fiddle, and he was handy at that.

Well, Johnny Rigby was right in one thing he said. He'd said that, no matter what happened afterwards, Appleby would never be the same again. And it isn't. But maybe in some ways it's better.

> So carry a thousand candles in your pocket
> When you walk on the moon
> And swiftly swiftly tie a knot in the river
> Before all the water's gone
> And listen for my voice, if for no other
> When you're all alone.

The Dark Streets of Kimball's Green

"Em! You, Em! Where has that dratted child got to? Em! Wait till I lay hold of you, I won't half tan you!"

Mrs Bella Vaughan looked furiously up and down the short street. She was a stocky woman, with short, thick, straight grey hair, parted on one side and clamped back by a grip; a cigarette always dangled from one corner of her mouth and, as soon as it dwindled down, another grew there. "Em! Where have you got to?" she yelled again.

"Here I am, Mrs Vaughan!" Emmeline dashed anxiously round the corner.

"Took long enough about it! The Welfare Lady's here, wants to know how you're getting on. Here, let's tidy you up."

Mrs Vaughan pulled a comb and handkerchief out of her tight-stretched apron pocket, dragged her comb sharply through Emmeline's hair, damped the handkerchief with spit and scrubbed it over Emmeline's flinching face.

"Hullo, Emmeline. Been out playing?" said the Welfare Lady, indoors. "That's right. Fresh air's the best thing for them, isn't it, Mrs Vaughan?"

"She's always out," grunted Mrs Vaughan. "Morning, noon and night. I don't hold with kids frowsting about indoors. Not much traffic round here."

"Well, Emmeline, how are you getting on? Settling down with Mrs Vaughan, quite happy, are you?"

Emmeline looked at her feet and muttered something. She was thin and small for her age, dark-haired and pale-cheeked.

"She's a mopey kid," Mrs Vaughan pronounced. "Always want to be reading, if I didn't tell her to run out of doors."

"Fond of reading, are you?" the Welfare Lady said kindly. "And what do you read, then?"

"Books," muttered Emmeline. The Welfare Lady's glance strayed to the huge, untidy pile of magazines on the telly.

"Kid'll read anything she could lay hands on, if I let her," Mrs Vaughan said. "I don't though. What good does reading do you? None that I know of."

"Well, I'm glad you're getting on all right, Emmeline. Be a good girl and do what Mrs Vaughan tells you. And I'll see you next month again." She got into her tiny car and drove off to the next of her endless list of calls.

"Right," said Mrs Vaughan. "I'm off too, down to the town hall to play bingo. So you hop it, and mind you're here on the doorstep at eleven sharp or I'll skin you."

Emmeline murmured something.

"Stay indoors? Not on your nelly! And have them saying, if the house burnt down, that I oughtn't to have left you on your own?"

"It's so cold out." A chilly September wind scuffled the bits of paper in the street. Emmeline shivered in her thin coat.

"Well, run about then, and keep warm! Fresh air's good for you, like that interfering old busybody said. Anyway she's come and gone for the month, that's something. Go on, hop it now."

So Emmeline hopped it.

Kimball's Green, where Mrs Vaughan had her home, was a curious, desolate little corner of London. It lay round the top of a hill, which was crowned with a crumbling, blackened church, St Chad's. The four or five streets of tiny, aged houses were also crumbling and blackened, all due for demolition, and most of them empty. The houses were so old that they seemed shrunk and wrinkled, like old apples or old faces, and they were immeasurably, unbelievably dirty, with the dirt of hundreds of years. Around the little hill was a flat, desolate tract of land, Wansea Marshes, which nobody had even tried to use until the nineteenth century; then it became covered with railway goods yards and brick-works and gas-works and an electric power station, all of which belched their black smoke over the little island of Kimball's Green on the hill-top.

You could hardly think anybody would *choose* to live in such a cut-off part; but Mrs Vaughan had been born in Sylvan Street, near the top of the hill, and she declared she wasn't going to shift until they came after her with a bull-dozer. She took in foster children when they grew too old for the Wansea Orphanage, and, though it wasn't a very healthy neighbourhood, what with the smoke and the damp from the marshes, there were so many orphans, and so few homes for them to go to, that Emmeline was the latest of a large number who had stayed with Mrs Vaughan. But there were very few other children in the district now; very few inhabit-ants at all, except old and queer ones who camped secretly in the condemned houses. Most people found it too far to go to the shops: an eightpenny bus-ride, all the way past the goods yards and the gas-works, to Wansea High Street.

So far as anyone knew, Emmeline belonged in the neigh-bourhood; she had been found on the step of St Chad's one windy March night; but in spite of this, or because of it, she was rather frightened by the nest of little dark empty streets. She was frightened by many things, among which were Mrs Vaughan and her son Colin. And she particularly hated the nights, five out of seven, when Mrs Vaughan went off to play bingo, leaving Emmeline outside in the street. Indeed, if it hadn't been for two friends, Emmeline really didn't know how she could have borne those evenings.

As Mrs Vaughan's clumping steps died away down the

hill, one of the friends appeared: his thin form twined out from between some old black railings and he rubbed encouragingly against Emmeline's ankles, sticking up his tail in welcome.

"Oh, Scrawny! There you are," she said with relief. "Here, I've saved you a piece of cheese-rind from tea."

Old Scrawny was a tattered, battered tabby, with ragged whiskers, crumpled ears, and much fur missing from his tail; he had no owner and lived on what he could find; he ate the cheese-rind with a lot of loud, vulgar, guzzling noise, and hardly washed at all afterwards; but Emmeline loved him dearly, and he loved her back. Every night she left her window open and old Scrawny climbed in, by various gutters, drain-pipes, and the wash-house roof. Mrs Vaughan wouldn't have allowed such a thing for a minute if she had known, but Emmeline always took care that old Scrawny had left long before she was called in the morning.

When the rind was finished Scrawny jumped into Emmeline's arms and she tucked her hands for warmth under his scanty fur; they went up to the end of the street by the church, where there was a telephone booth. Like the houses around it was old and dirty, and it had been out of order for so many years that now nobody even bothered to thump its box for coins. The only person who used it was Emmeline, and she used it almost every night, unless gangs were roaming the streets and throwing stones, in which case she hid behind a dustbin or under a flight of area steps. But when the gangs had gone elsewhere the call-box made a very convenient shelter; best of all, it was even light enough to read there, because although the bulb in the call-box had been broken long ago, a street lamp shone right overhead.

"No book tonight, Scrawny, unless Mr Yakkymo comes and brings me another," said Emmeline, "so what shall we do? Shall we phone somebody, or shall I tell you a story?"

Scrawny purred, dangling round her neck like a striped scarf.

"We'll ring somebody up, shall we? All right."

She let the heavy door close behind her. Inside it was not exactly warm, but at least they were out of the wind. Scrawny climbed from Emmeline's shoulder into the compartment where the telephone books would have been if somebody hadn't made off with them; Emmeline picked up the broken receiver and dialled.

"Hullo, can I speak to King Cunobel? Hullo, King Cunobel, I am calling to warn you. A great army is approaching your fort—the Tribe of the Children of Darkness. Under their wicked queen Belavaun they are coming to attack your stronghold with spears and chariots. You must tell your men to be extra brave; each man must arm himself with his bow and a sheaf of arrows, two spears and a sword. Each man must have his faithful wolfhound by his side." She stroked old Scrawny, who seemed to be listening intently. "Your men are far outnumbered by the Children of Dark, King Cunobel, so you must tell your Chief Druid to prepare a magic drink, made from vetch and mallow and succory, to give them courage. The leaves must be steeped in mead and left to gather dew for two nights, until you have enough to wet each man's tongue. Then they will be brave enough to beat off the Children of Dark and save your camp."

She listened for a moment or two with her ear pressed against the silent receiver, and then said to old Scrawny,

"King Cunobel wants to know what will happen if the Children of Dark get to the fort before the magic drink is prepared?"

"Morow," said Scrawny. He jumped down from the bookshelf and settled himself on Emmeline's feet, where there was more room to stretch out.

"My faithful wolfhound says you must order your men to

make high barricades of brambles and thorns," Emmeline told King Cunobel. "Build them in three rings round the encampment, and place one-third of your men inside each ring. King Cunobel and the Druids will be in the middle ring. Each party must fight to the death in order to delay the Children of Dark until the magic drink is ready. Do you understand? Then goodbye and good luck."

She listened again.

"He wants to know who *I* am," she told Scrawny, and she said into the telephone, "I am a friend, the Lady Emmeline, advised by her faithful enchanted wolfhound Catuscraun. I wish you well."

Then she rang off and said to Scrawny, "Do you think I had better call the Chief Druid and tell him to hurry up with that magic drink?"

Old Scrawny shut his eyes.

"No," she agreed, "you're right, it would only distract him. I know, I'll ring up the wicked Queen of Dark."

She dialled again and said,

"Hullo, is that the wicked Queen Belavaun? This is your greatest enemy, ringing up to tell you that you will never, never capture the stronghold of King Cunobel. Not if you besiege it for three thousand years! King Cunobel has a strong magic that will defeat you. All your tribes, the Trinovans and the Votadins and the Damnons and the Bingonii will be eaten by wolves and wild boars. Not a man will remain! And you will lose your wealth and power and your purple robes and fur cloaks, you will have nothing left but a miserable old mud cabin outside King Cunobel's stronghold, and every day his men will look over the walls and laugh at you. Goodbye, and bad luck to you forever!"

She rang off and said to Scrawny, "That frightened her."

Scrawny was nine-tenths asleep, but at this moment footsteps coming along the street made him open his eyes warily.

Emmeline was alert too. The call-box made a good look-out point, but it would be a dangerous place in which to be trapped.

"It's all right," she said to Scrawny, then. "It's only Mr Yakkymo."

She opened the door and they went to meet their other friend.

Mr Yakkymo (he spelt his name Iachimo, but Yakkymo was the way it sounded) came limping slightly up the street until he reached them; then he rubbed the head of old Scrawny (who stuck his tail up) and handed Emmeline a book. It was old and small, with a mottled binding and gilt-edged leaves; it was called *The Ancient History of Kimball's Green and Wansea Marshes,* and it came from Wansea Borough Library.

Emmeline's eyes opened wide with delight. She began reading the book at once, skipping from page to page.

"Why, this tells all about King Cunobel! It's even better than the one you brought about ancient London. Have you read this, Mr Yakkymo?"

He nodded, smiling. He was a thin, bent old man with rather long white hair; as well as the book he carried a leather case, which contained a flute, and when he was not speaking he would often open this case and run his fingers absently up and down the instrument.

"I thought you would find it of interest," he said. "It's a pity Mrs Vaughan won't let you go to the public library yourself."

"She says reading only puts useless stuck-up notions in people's heads," Emmeline said dreamily, her eyes darting up and down the pages of the book. "Listen! It tells what King Cunobel wore—a short kilt with a gold belt. His chest was painted blue with woad, and he had a gold collar round his neck and a white cloak with gold embroidery. He carried a shield of beaten brass and a short sword. On his head he wore a fillet of gold, and on his arm gold armlets. His house was built of mud and stone, with a thatched roof; the walls were hung with skins and the floor strewn with rushes."

They had turned and were walking slowly along the street; old Scrawny, after the manner of cats, sometimes loitered behind investigating doorsteps and dark crannies, sometimes darted ahead and then waited for them to come up with him.

"Do you think any of King Cunobel's descendants still live here?" Emmeline said.

"It is just possible."

"Tell me some more about what it was like here then."

"All the marshes—the part where the brick-works and the goods yards are now—would have been covered by forest and threaded by slow-flowing streams."

"Threaded by slow-flowing streams," Emmeline murmured to herself.

"All this part would be Cunobel's village. Little mud huts, each with a door and a chimney hole, thatched with reeds."

Emmeline looked at the pavements and rows of houses, trying to imagine them away, trying to imagine forest trees and little thatched huts.

"There would be a stockade of logs and thorns all round. A bigger hall for the King, and one for the Druids near the sacred grove."

"Where was that?"

"Up at the top of the hill, probably. With a specially sacred oak in the middle. There is an oak tree, still, in St Chad's churchyard; maybe it's sprung from an acorn of the Druids' oak."

"Maybe it's the same one? Oaks live a long time, don't they?"

"Hark!" he said checking. "What's that?"

The three of them were by the churchyard wall; they kept still and listened. Next moment they all acted independently, with the speed of long practice: Mr Iachimo, murmuring, "Good night, my child," slipped away round a corner; Emmeline wrapped her precious book in a polythene bag and poked it into a hole in the wall behind a loose stone; then she and old Scrawny raced downhill, back to Mrs Vaughan's house. She crouched panting on the doorstep, old Scrawny leapt up on to a shed roof and out of reach, just as a group of half a dozen people came swaggering and singing along the street.

"What was that?" one of them called.

"A cat."

"Let's go after it!"

"No good. It's gone."

When they got to Mrs Vaughan's their chief left the others and came over to Emmeline.

"It's you, is it, Misery?" he said. "Where's Ma?"

"Out at bingo."

"She would be. I wanted to get a bit of the old girl's pension off her before she spent it all."

He gave Emmeline's hair a yank and flipped her nose, hard and painfully, with his thumbnail. She looked at him in stony silence, biting her lip.

"Who's *she,* Col?" a new gang-member asked. "Shall we chivvy her?"

"She's one of my Ma's orphanage brats—just a little drip. Ma won't let me tease her, so long as she's indoors, or on the step. But watch it, you, if we catch you in the street." Colin flipped Emmeline's nose again and they drifted off, kicking at anything that lay on the pavement.

At half-past eleven Mrs Vaughan came home from her bingo and let in the shivering Emmeline, who went silently up to her bed in the attic. At eleven thirty-five old Scrawny jumped with equal silence on to her stomach, and the two friends curled round each other for warmth.

* * *

Colin was not at breakfast next morning. Often he spent nights on end away from home; his mother never bothered to ask where.

Emmeline had to run errands and do housework in the morning but in the afternoon Mrs Vaughan, who wanted a nap, told her to clear off and not show her face a minute before six. That gave her five whole hours for reading; she dragged on her old coat and flew up to the churchyard.

The door in the high black wall was always kept locked, but somebody had once left a lot of rusty old metal pipes stacked in an angle of the wall; Emmeline, who weighed very little more than old Scrawny, clambered carefully up them, and so over.

Inside, the churchyard was completely overgrown. Blackthorn, plane and sycamore trees were entangled with great clumps of bramble. Groves of mares'-tails, chin-high to Emmeline, covered every foot of the ground. It made a perfect place to come and hide by day, but was too dark at night and too full of pitfalls; pillars and stone slabs leaned every which way, hidden in the vegetation.

Emmeline flung herself down on the flat tomb of Admiral Sir Horace Tullesley Campbell and read her book; for three hours she never moved; then she closed it with a sigh, so as to leave some for the evening in case Mrs Vaughan went out.

A woodpecker burst yammering from the tallest tree as Emmeline shut the book. Could that be the Druids' oak, she wondered, and started to push her way through to it. Brambles scratched her face and tore her clothes; Mrs Vaughan would punish her but that couldn't be helped. And at last she was there. The tree stood in a little clear space of bare leaf-mould. It was an oak, a big one, with a gnarled, massive trunk and roots like knuckles thrusting out of the ground. This made an even better secret place for reading than the Admiral's tomb, and Emmeline wished once again that it wasn't too dark to read in the churchyard at night.

St Chad's big clock said a quarter to six, so she left *The Ancient History of Kimball's Green* in its plastic bag hidden in a hollow of the tree and went draggingly home; then realized, too late, that her book would be exceedingly hard to find once dark had fallen.

Mrs Vaughan, who had not yet spent all her week's money, went out to bingo again that evening, so Emmeline returned to the telephone box and rang up King Cunobel.

"Is that the King? I have to tell you that your enemies are five miles nearer. Queen Belavaun is driving a chariot with scythes on its wheels, and her wicked son Coluon leads a band of savage followers; he carries a sling and a gold-handled javelin and is more cruel than any of the band. Has the Chief Druid prepared the magic drink yet?"

She listened and old Scrawny, who as usual was sitting at her feet, said "Prtnrow?"

"The Chief Druid says they have made the drink, Scrawny, and put it in a flagon of beaten bronze, which has been set beneath the sacred oak until it is needed. Meanwhile the warriors are feasting on wheat-cakes, boars' flesh and mead."

Next she rang up Queen Belavaun and hissed, "Oh wicked queen, your enemies are massing against you! You think that you will triumph, but you are wrong! Your son will be taken prisoner, and you will be turned out of your kingdom; you will be forced to take refuge with the Iceni or the Brigantes."

It was still only half-past nine, and Mr Iachimo probably would not come this evening, for two nights out of three he went to play his flute outside a theatre in the West End of London.

"Long ago I was a famous player and people came from all over Europe to hear me," he had told Emmeline sadly, one wet evening when they were sheltering together in the church porch.

"What happened? Why aren't you famous now?"

"I took to drink," he said mournfully. "Drink gives you hiccups. You can't play the flute with hiccups."

"You don't seem to have hiccups now."

"Now I can't afford to drink any longer."

"So you can play the flute again," Emmeline said triumphantly.

"True," he agreed; he pulled out his instrument and blew a sudden dazzling shower of notes into the rainy dark. "But now it is too late. Nobody listens; nobody remembers the name of Iachimo. And I have grown too old and tired to make them remember."

"Poor Mr Yakkymo," Emmeline thought, recalling this conversation. *"He* could do with a drop of King Cunobel's magic drink; then he'd be able to make people listen to him."

She craned out of the telephone box to look at St Chad's clock: quarter to ten. The streets were quiet tonight: Colin's gang had got money from somewhere and were down at the Wansea Palais.

"I'm going to get my book," Emmeline suddenly decided. "At least I'm going to try. There's a moon, it shouldn't be too dark to see. Coming, Scrawny?"

Scrawny intimated, stretching, that he didn't mind.

The churchyard was even stranger under the moon than by daylight; the mares'-tails threw their zebra-striped shadows everywhere and an owl flew hooting across the path; old Scrawny yakkered after it indignantly to come back and fight fair, but the owl didn't take up his challenge.

"I don't suppose it's really an owl," Emmeline whispered. "Probably one of Queen Belavaun's spies. We must make haste."

Finding the oak tree was not so hard as she had feared, but finding the book was a good deal harder, because under the tree's thick leaves and massive branches no light could penetrate; Emmeline groped and fumbled among the roots until she was quite sure she must have been right round the tree at least three times. At last her right hand slipped into a deep crack; she rummaged about hopefully, her fingers closed on something, but what she pulled out was a small object, tapered at one end. She stuck it in her coat pocket and went on searching. "The book must be here somewhere, Scrawny; unless Queen Belavaun's spy has stolen it."

At last she found it; tucked away where she could have sworn she had searched a dozen times already.

"Thank goodness! Now we'd better hurry, or there won't be any time for reading after all."

Emmeline was not sorry to leave the churchyard behind; it felt *crowded,* as if King Cunobel's warriors were hiding there, shoulder to shoulder among the bushes, keeping vigilant watch; Sylvan Street outside was empty and lonely in comparison. She scurried into the phone box, clutching Scrawny against her chest.

"Now listen while I read to you about the Druids, Scrawny: they wore long white robes and they liked mistletoe—there's some mistletoe growing on that oak tree, I'm positive!—and they used rings of sacred stones, too. Maybe some of the stones in the churchyard are left over from the Druids."

Scrawny purred agreeingly, and Emmeline looked up the hill, trying to move St Chad's church out of the way and replace it by a grove of sacred trees with aged, white-robed men among them.

Soon it was eleven o'clock: time to hide the book behind the stone and wait for Mrs Vaughan on the doorstep. Along with his mother came Colin, slouching and bad-tempered.

"Your face is all scratched," he told Emmeline. "You look a sight."

"What have you been up to?" Mrs Vaughan said sharply.

Emmeline was silent but Colin said, "Reckon it's that mangy old cat she's always lugging about."

"Don't let me see you with a cat around *this* house," Mrs Vaughan snapped. "Dirty, sneaking things, never know where they've been. If any cat comes in here, I tell you, I'll get Colin to wring its neck!"

Colin smiled; Emmeline's heart turned right over with horror. But she said nothing and crept off upstairs to bed; only, when Scrawny arrived later, rather wet because it had begun to rain, she clutched him convulsively tight; a few tears wouldn't make much difference to the dampness of his fur.

*   *   *

"Humph!" said Mrs Vaughan, arriving early and unexpectedly in Emmeline's attic. "I thought as much!"

She leaned to slam the window but Scrawny, though startled out of sleep, could still move ten times faster than any human; he was out and over the roof in a flash.

"Look at that!" said Mrs Vaughan. "Filthy, muddy cat's footprints all over my blankets! Well that's one job you'll do this morning, my young madam—you'll wash those blankets. And you'll have to sleep without blankets till they've dried— I'm not giving you any other. Daresay they're all full of fleas' eggs too."

Emmeline, breakfastless, crouched over the tub in the back wash-house; she did not much mind the job, but her brain was giddy with worry about Scrawny; how could she protect him? Suppose he were to wait for her, as he sometimes did, outside the house. Mrs Vaughan had declared that she would go after him with the chopper if she set eyes on him; Colin had sworn to hunt him down.

"All right, hop it now," Mrs Vaughan said, when the blankets satisfied her. "Clear out, don't let me see you again before six. No dinner? Well, I can't help that, can I? You should have finished the washing by dinner-time. Oh, all right, here's a bit of bread and marge, now make yourself scarce. I can't abide kids about the house all day."

Emmeline spent most of the afternoon in a vain hunt for Scrawny. Perhaps he had retired to some hidey-hole for a nap, as he often did at that time of day; but perhaps Colin had caught him already?

"Scrawny, Scrawny," she called softly and despairingly at the mouths of alleys, outside gates, under trees and walls; there was no reply. She went up to the churchyard, but a needle in a hundred haystacks would be easier to find than Scrawny in that wilderness if he did not choose to wake and show himself.

Giving up for the moment Emmeline went in search of Mr Iachimo, but he was not to be found either; he had never told Emmeline where he lived and was seldom seen by daylight; she thought he probably inhabited one of the condemned houses and was ashamed of it.

It was very cold; a grey, windy afternoon turning gloomily to dusk. Emmeline pushed cold hands deep in her pockets; her fingers met and explored a round, unusual object. Then she remembered the thing she had picked up in the dark under the oak tree. She pulled it out, and found she was holding a tiny flask, made of some dark lustreless metal tarnished with age and crusted with earth. It was not quite empty; when Emmeline shook it she could hear liquid splashing about inside, but very little, not more than a few drops.

"Why," she breathed, just for a moment forgetting her fear in the excitement of this discovery, "it is—it *must* be the Druids' magic drink! But why, why didn't the warriors drink it?"

She tried to get out the stopper; it was made of some hard blackish substance, wood, or leather that had become hard as wood in the course of years.

"Can I help you, my child?" said a gentle voice above her head.

Emmeline nearly jumped out of her skin—but it was only Mr Iachimo, who had hobbled silently up the street.

"Look—look, Mr Yakkymo! Look what I found under the big oak in the churchyard! It must be the Druids' magic drink—mustn't it? Made of mallow and vetch and succory, steeped in mead, to give warriors courage. It must be!"

He smiled at her; his face was very kind. "Yes, indeed it must!" he said.

But somehow, although he was agreeing with her, for a moment Emmeline had a twinge of queer dread, as if there were nothing—nothing at all—left in the world to hold on to; as if even Mr Iachimo were not what he seemed but, perhaps, a spy sent by Queen Belavaun to steal the magic flagon.

Then she pushed down her fear, taking a deep breath, and said, "Can you get the stopper out, Mr Yakkymo?"

"I can try," he said, and brought out a tiny foreign-looking penknife shaped like a fish with which he began prising at the fossil-hard black substance in the neck of the bottle. At last it began to crumble.

"Take care—do take care," Emmeline said. "There's only a very little left. Perhaps the defenders did drink most of it. But anyway there's enough left for you, Mr Yakkymo."

"For me, my child? Why for me?"

"Because you need to be made brave so that you can make people listen to you play your flute."

"Very true," he said thoughtfully. "But do not you need bravery too?"

Emmeline's face clouded. "What good would bravery do me?" she said. "*I'm* all right—it's old Scrawny I'm worried about. Oh, Mr Yakkymo, Colin and Mrs Vaughn say they are going to *kill* Scrawny. What can I do?"

"You must tell them they have no right to."

"*That* wouldn't do any good," Emmeline said miserably. "Oh!— You've got it out!"

The stopper had come out, but it had also crumbled away entirely.

"Never mind," Emmeline said. "You can put in a bit of the cotton-wool that you use to clean your flute. What does it smell of, Mr Yakkymo?"

His face had changed as he sniffed; he looked at her oddly. "Honey and flowers," he said.

Emmeline sniffed too. There was a faint—very faint— aromatic, sweet fragrance.

"Wet your finger, Mr Yakkymo, and lick it! Please do! It'll help you, I know it will!"

"Shall I?"

"Yes, do, do!"

He placed his finger across the opening, and quickly turned the bottle upside down and back, then looked at his fingertip. There was the faintest drop of moisture on it.

"Quick—don't waste it," Emmeline said, breathless with anxiety.

He licked his finger.

"Well? does it taste?"

"No taste." But he smiled, and bringing out a wad of cotton tissue, stuffed a piece of it into the mouth of the flask, which he handed to Emmeline.

"This is yours, my child. Guard it well! Now, as to your friend Scrawny—I will go and see Mrs Vaughan tomorrow, if you can protect him until then."

"Thank you!" she said. "The drink *must* be making you brave!"

Above their heads the clock of St Chad had tolled six.

"I must be off to the West End," Mr Iachimo said. "And you had better run home to supper. Till tomorrow, then— and a thousand, thousand thanks for your help."

He gave her a deep, foreign bow and limped, much faster than usual, away down the hill.

"Oh, do let it work," Emmeline thought, looking after him.

Then she ran home to Mrs Vaughan's.

Supper was over; Colin, thank goodness, did not come in, and Mrs Vaughan wanted to get through and be off; Emmeline bolted down her food, washed the plates, and was dismissed to the streets again.

As she ran up to the churchyard wall, with her fingers tight clenched round the precious little flask, a worrying thought suddenly struck her.

The magic drink had mead in it. Suppose the mead were to give Mr Iachimo hiccups? But there must be very little mead in such a tiny drop, she consoled herself; the risk could not be great.

When she pulled her book from the hole in the wall a sound met her ears that made her smile with relief: old Scrawny's mew of greeting, rather creaking and scratchy, as he dragged himself yawning, one leg at a time, from a clump of ivy on top of the wall.

"*There* you are, Scrawny! If you knew how I'd been worrying about you!"

She tucked him under one arm, put the book under the other, and made her way to the telephone box. Scrawny settled on her feet for another nap, and she opened *The Ancient History of Kimball's Green.* Only one chapter remained to be read; she turned to it and became absorbed. St Chad's clock ticked solemnly round overhead.

When Emmeline finally closed the book, tears were running down her face.

"Oh, Scrawny—they didn't win! They *lost!* King Cunobel's men were all killed—and the Druids too, defending the stronghold. Every one of them. Oh, how can I bear it? Why did it have to happen, Scrawny?"

Scrawny made no answer, but he laid his chin over her ankle. At that moment the telephone bell rang.

Emmeline stared at the instrument in utter consternation. Scrawny sprang up; the fur along his back slowly raised, and his ears flattened. The bell went on ringing.

"But," whispered Emmeline, staring at the broken black receiver, "it's out of order. It *can't* ring! It's never rung! What shall I do, Scrawny?"

By now, Scrawny had recovered. He sat himself down again and began to wash. Emmeline looked up and down the empty street. Nobody came. The bell went on ringing.

* * *

At that same time, down below the hill and some distance off, in Wansea High Street, ambulance attendants were carefully lifting an old man off the pavement and laying him on a stretcher.

"Young brutes," said a bystander to a policeman who was taking notes. "It was one of those gangs of young hooligans from up Kimball's Green way; I'd know several of them again if I saw them. They set on him—it's the old street musician who comes from up there too. Seems he was coming home early tonight, and the boys jumped on him—you wouldn't think they'd bother with a poor fellow like him, he can't have much worth stealing."

But the ambulance men were gathering up handfuls of half-crowns and two-shilling pieces which had rolled from Mr Iachimo's pockets; there were notes as well, ten shillings, a pound, even five- and ten-pound notes. And a broken flute.

"It was certainly worth their while tonight," the policeman said. "He must have done a lot better than usual."

"He was a game old boy—fought back like a lion; marked some of them, I shouldn't wonder. They had to leave him and run for it. Will he be all right?"

"We'll see," said the ambulance man, closing the doors.

* * *

"I'd better answer it," Emmeline said at last. She picked up the receiver, trembling as if it might give her a shock.

"Hullo?" she whispered.

And a voice—a faint, hoarse, distant voice—said,

"This is King Cunobel. I cannot speak for long. I am calling to warn you. There is danger on the way—great danger coming towards you and your friend. Take care! Watch well!"

Emmeline's lips parted. She could not speak.

"There is danger—danger!" the voice repeated. Then the line went silent.

Emmeline stared from the silent telephone to the cat at her feet.

"Did you hear it too, Scrawny?"

Scrawny gazed at her impassively, and washed behind his ear.

Then Emmeline heard the sound of running feet. The warning had been real. She pushed the book into her pocket and was about to pick up Scrawny, but hesitated, with her fingers on the little flask.

"Maybe I ought to drink it, Scrawny? Better that than have it fall into the enemy's hands. Should I? Yes, I will! Here, you must have a drop too."

She laid a wet finger on Scrawny's nose; out came his pink tongue at once. Then she drained the bottle, picked up Scrawny, opened the door, and ran.

Turning back once more to look, she could see a group of dark figures coming after her down the street. She heard someone shout,

"That's her, and she's got the cat too! Come on!"

But beyond, behind and *through* her pursuers, Emmeline caught a glimpse of something else: a high, snow-covered hill, higher than the hill she knew, crowned with great bare trees. And on either side of her, among and in front of the dark houses, as if she were seeing two pictures, one printed on top of the other, were still more trees, and little thatched stone houses. Thin animals with red eyes slunk silently among the huts. Just a glimpse she had, of the two worlds, one behind the other, and then she had reached Mrs Vaughan's doorstep and turned to face the attackers.

Colin Vaughan was in the lead; his face, bruised, cut, and furious, showed its ugly intention as plainly as a raised club.

"Give me that damn cat. I've had enough from you and your friends. I'm going to wring its neck."

But Emmeline stood at bay; her eyes blazed defiance and so did Scrawny's; he bared his fangs at Colin like a sabre-toothed tiger.

Emmeline said clearly, "Don't you dare lay a finger on me, Colin Vaughan. Just don't you dare touch me!"

He actually flinched, and stepped back half a pace; his gang shuffled back behind him.

At this moment Mrs Vaughan came up the hill; not at her usual smart pace but slowly, plodding, as if she had no heart in her.

"Clear out, the lot of you," she said angrily. "Poor old Mr Iachimo's in the Wansea Hospital, thanks to you. Beating up old men! That's all you're good for. Go along, scram, before I set the back of my hand to some of you. Beat it!"

"But we were going to wring the cat's neck. You wanted me to do that," Colin protested.

"Oh, what do I care about the blame cat?" she snapped, turning to climb the steps, and came face to face with Emmeline.

"Well, don't *you* stand there like a lump," Mrs Vaughan said angrily. "Put the blasted animal down and get to bed!"

"I'm not going to bed," Emmeline said. "I'm not going to live with you any more."

"Oh, indeed? And where are you going, then?" said Mrs Vaughan, completely astonished.

"I'm going to see poor Mr Yakkymo. And then I'm going to find someone who'll take me and Scrawny, some place where I shall be happy. I'm never coming back to your miserable house again."

"Oh, well, suit yourself," Mrs Vaughan grunted. "You're not the only one. I've just heard: fifty years in this place and then fourteen days' notice to quit; in two weeks the bulldozers are coming."

She went indoors.

But Emmeline had not listened; clutching Scrawny, brushing past the gang as if they did not exist, she ran for the last time down the dark streets of Kimball's Green.

The Boy Who Read Aloud

Once there was a boy called Seb who was unfortunate. His dear mother had died, his father had married again, and the new wife brought in three daughters of her own. Their names were Minna, Hanna, and Morwenna, and they were all larger and older than Seb—big, fat, red-haired hateful girls. Minna pinched, Hanna tweaked hair and kicked shins, while Morwenna could pull such terrible faces that she put even the birds in a fright and her mother had forbidden her to do it indoors in case she cracked the cups and plates on the kitchen dresser. The mother was just as bad as her daughters, greedy, unkind, and such a terrible cook that nine months after they were married Seb's father wasted away and died from the food she fed him on. As for Seb, he had to manage on crusts, for that was all he got.

Now Seb had three treasures which his true mother had left him when she died. These were a little silver mug, a little silver spoon, and a book of stories. The book of stories was what he prized most, for when she was alive his true mother had read them aloud to him every day and as soon as he grew old enough to learn his letters he read them back to her while she did the ironing or peeled the potatoes or rolled out the pastry. So, now, when he opened the book, it was as if his true mother were back with him, telling him a story, and for a little he could forget how things had changed with him.

You can guess how hard Seb tried to keep these treasures

hidden from his step-sisters. But they were prying, peering, poking girls, and presently Minna came across the silver cup hidden under Seb's mattress.

"You mean little sniveller, keeping this pretty cup hidden away!" she cried. "I am the eldest, it should be mine, and I'll pinch and pinch you till you give it to me!"

"For shame, Seb!" said his step-mother when she heard him crying out at the pinches. "Give the cup to your sister at once!"

So poor little Seb had to give it up.

Then Hanna found the silver spoon hidden under Seb's pillow.

"Let me have it, let me have it, you little spalpeen!" she screeched, when he tried to keep it from her. "Or I'll drag out every hair in your head."

And her mother made Seb give her the little spoon.

Now Seb took particular pains to keep his precious book out of view, hiding it first in one place and then in another, between the bins of corn, under a sitting hen, inside a hollow tree, beneath a loose floorboard. But one evening Morwenna found it tucked up on a rafter, as they were going to bed. Quickly Seb snatched the book from her and darted off to his attic room, where he shut himself in, pushing the bed against the door. Morwenna was after him in a flash— though, mind you, it was only pure spite that made her want the book for, big as she was, she could read no more than a gatepost can.

"You'd better give it to me, you little mizzler!" she bawled through the door. "Or I shall make such a fearsome face at you that you'll very likely die of fright."

Seb trembled in his shoes at this threat, but he knew that Morwenna could do nothing till morning, since she was not allowed to pull faces indoors.

Huddling in bed, clutching the book to him, he decided

that the only thing for him to do was to run away. He would get up very early, climb out of the window, and slide down the roof.

But where should he go and how should he live?

For a long time, no plan came to him. But at last, remembering the book in his hands, he thought, "Well, there is one thing I can do. I can read. Perhaps somebody in the world would like me to read stories to them."

"In the village," he thought, "by the inn door, there is a board with cards stuck up on it, showing what work is to be had. I will go that way in the morning and see if anybody wants a reader."

So at last he went to sleep, holding the little book tight against his chest.

In the morning he woke and tiptoed out of the house long before anyone else was stirring. (Minna, Morwenna and Hanna were all lazy, heavy sleepers who never clambered from their beds till the sun was half across the sky.)

Seb went quietly through the garden and quietly down the village until he came to the notice-board. On it there were cards telling of jobs for gardeners, jobs for cooks, jobs for postmen, ploughmen and painters. Looking at them all he had begun to think there was nothing for him when up in the top corner he noticed a very old, dog-eared card with a bit torn off. It said:

> ELDERLY BLIND RETIRED SEA
> WOULD LIKE BOY TO READ
> ALOUD DAILY

What a strange thing, thought Seb. Fancy reading aloud to the sea! Fancy the sea going blind at all!

But still, he supposed, thinking it over, the sea could get old like anybody else, old and blind and bored. Didn't the emperor Caligula have chats with the sea, and who takes

the trouble nowadays even to pass the time of day with his
neighbour, let alone have a conversation with the ocean?

There would be no harm, anyway, in going to find out
whether the job had been taken already. Seb knew the way to
the sea because when his true mother had been alive they
had sometimes spent days at the shore. It was about twenty
miles but he thought he could walk it in a couple of days. So
he started at once.

Now, had Seb but known it, the truth of the matter was
this: that card had been up on the board such a long time
that it had been torn, and some of the words were missing. It
should have read:

> ELDERLY BLIND RETIRED SEA CAPTAIN
> WOULD LIKE BOY TO READ NEWSPAPER
> ALOUD DAILY. APPLY WITHIN.

Nobody ever had applied for the job, and in the end the
sea captain had grown tired of waiting and had gone off to
another town.

But Seb knew nothing of all this, so he started off to walk
to the sea, with his treasured book of stories in his pocket.

It was still very early and few folk were about.

As he walked along Seb began to worry in case he had
forgotten how to read aloud, because it was now a long time
since his true mother had died. "I had better practise a bit,"
he thought.

When he had gone about five miles and felt in need of a
rest he came to a gate leading into a deserted barn-yard.

"I'll go in here," he thought, "and practise my reading.
Because there's no doubt about it at all, it's going to seem
very queer reading to the sea till I've grown accustomed to
it."

There was an old rusty Rolls-Royce car in the yard, which
looked as if it had not been driven since the days when ladies

wore long trailing skirts and you could get four ounces of bull's-eyes for a halfpenny. Seb felt rather sorry for the poor thing, so broken-down, forlorn and battered did it seem, and he decided to read to it.

He sat down cross-legged in front of the radiator, took out his book and read a story about the sun-god's flaming chariot, and how once it was borrowed by a boy who had not passed his driving-test, and how he drove the chariot, horses and all, into the side of a hill.

All the time Seb was reading there came no sound or movement from the car. But when he had finished and stood up to go, he was astonished to hear a toot from behind him. He turned himself about fast, wondering if somebody had been hiding in the car all the time. But it was empty, sure enough.

Then he heard a voice, which said,

"Was that a true tale, boy?"

"As to that," said Seb, "I can't tell you."

"Well, true or not," said the voice (it came from the radiator and had a sort of purring rumble to it, like the sound of a very large cat), "true or not, it was the most interesting tale I have ever heard. In fact it was the *only* tale I have heard, and I am greatly obliged to you, boy, for reading it to me. No one else ever thought of doing such a thing. In return I will tell you something. In a well in the corner of the yard hangs a barrel of stolen money; five days ago I saw two thieves come here and lower it down. Wind the handle and you will be able to draw it up."

"Did you ever!" said Seb, and he went to the well in the corner and turned the handle which pulled the rope. Up came a barrel filled to the top with silver coins.

"There's too much here for me," Seb said. "I could never carry it all." So he took enough to fill one pocket (the book was in the other), wound the barrel down into the well again, and went on his way, waving goodbye to the Rolls-Royce car as long as he could see it.

He bought some bread with his money at the next village, and a bottle of milk.

After another five miles' walking he began to feel tired again, so he stepped aside from the road into the garden of an old empty house.

This would be a good place to read another of my stories, he thought.

So he read aloud a tale of two friends who arranged to meet one night near a hole in a wall. But they were frightened away by a lion and so they missed seeing one another.

When Seb had finished he heard a harsh voice behind him (he was sitting with his back to the house) which said,

"Was that a true tale, boy?"

"As to that," said Seb, "I can't tell you."

"True or not," said the voice, "it has given me something to think about in the long, empty days and nights. I never heard a tale before. So in return I will tell you something useful. Growing in my garden you will find a red flower which, if you pick and eat it, will cure any illness."

"But I haven't got any illness," Seb said. "I am quite well."

"If you eat this flower you will never fall ill, in the whole of your life. But take care not to pick the yellow flower which grows next it, for that is poisonous and would kill you at once."

Seb wandered through the garden until he found the red and yellow flowers growing side by side.

" 'Twould be a pity to pick the red one," he thought, "so pretty it looks growing there. Anyway I daresay somebody will come along who needs it more than I do."

So he thanked the house kindly and went on his way, waving until he was out of sight.

Presently it grew dark, so he ate some more of his bread, drank the milk, and went to sleep under an old thorn tree. Next morning, to thank the tree for watching over him all night, he read aloud a story about a girl who ran away from a suitor and turned herself into a laurel bush.

"Boy," said a rough, prickly voice when he had finished, "is that a true tale?"

"As to that," said Seb, "I don't know."

"True or not," said the voice, "I enjoyed it and it sounds true, so I will tell you something in return. Lodged in my topmost fork is the blue stone of eternal life, which a swallow dropped there a hundred years ago. If you care to climb up you may have it. Carry it in your pocket and you will live for ever."

Seb thanked the tree and climbed up. The stone was very beautiful, dark blue, with gold marks on it and white lines. But, he said to himself, do I really want to live for ever? Why should *I* do so out of all the people in the world?

So he put the stone back in the crotch of the tree. But, unknown to him, as he turned to climb down, he dislodged the stone again and it fell into his pocket.

He went on, waving goodbye to the tree as long as it was in sight, and now he came to the sea itself, with its green waves rolling up on to the sand, each one breaking with a roar.

"Will the sea be able to hear me if I read aloud?" Seb wondered.

Feeling rather foolish, because the sea was so very large and made so much noise, he sat down on the sand. Taking out his book he read first one story and then another. At first it seemed as if nobody heard him, but then he began to hear voices, many voices, saying,

"Hush! Hush!"

And looking up he noticed that all the waves had started to smooth out as if a giant palm had flattened them, so that hardly a ripple stirred as far as he could see. The water creamed and lapped at his feet, like a dog that wants to be patted, and as he waited, not knowing whether to go on or not, a long, thin white hand came out of the green water and turned over the page.

So Seb read another story and then another.

*   *   *

Meanwhile what had happened at home?

When they found Seb had run away the three sisters were very angry, but specially Morwenna.

"Just let him wait till I catch him!" she said. "I'll make such a face at him that his hair turns to knitting needles."

"Oh, let him go," said the mother. "What use was he at all, but only a mouth to feed?"

None the less Morwenna and her sisters went off looking for Seb. They asked of this one and that one in the village, who had seen him, and learned that he had taken the road to the sea. So they followed after until they came to the barn-yard, and there they heard a plaintive voice wailing and sighing.

"Oh, won't some kind soul tell me a story?" it sighed. "Alack and mercy and curse it. I have such a terrible craving to hear another tale! Oh, won't somebody take pity on me?"

"Who's been telling you tales?" said Morwenna, seeing it was the old Rolls-Royce car that spoke. "Was it a little runt of a boy with a book he'd no right to sticking out of his breeches pocket? Speak the truth now, and I'll tell you another story."

"Yes 'twas a boy," the old car said. "He read me from a wondrous book and in return I told him about the silver in the well."

"Silver in the well? Where?" screeched Minna and Hanna. Colliding together in their greed they made a rush for the well-head and wound up the handle. But Minna was so eager to get at the silver and keep her sisters from it that she jumped right on to the barrel when it came up, the rope broke, and down she went. So that was the end of Minna.

"Oh, well, never mind her," said Morwenna. "Come on,

let you, for it's plain 'twas this way he went." And she hurried on, taking no notice at all of the poor old car crying out, "My story, my story!"

"Bother your story, you miserable old heap of tin!" she shouted back.

So they came to the empty house, and here again they heard a voice moaning and lamenting.

"Ochone, ochone, why did I ever listen to that boy's tale? Now I've nothing in me but an insatiable thirst to hear another."

"Was it a bit of a young boy with a little black book?" Morwenna said. "Answer me that and I'll tell you a story."

"Ah, it was, and in return for the tale he told me I showed him where to find the red flower that cures you of any sickness."

"Where is it? Where?" And the sisters went ramping through the garden till they found it. But in her haste to snatch it before her sister, Hanna grabbed the yellow flower as well, ate it, and dropped down dead on the very spot.

"Oh, well, she's done for," said Morwenna, and she hurried on, taking no notice of the old house which wailed, "My story, my story!" behind her.

"Plague take your story, you mouldy old heap of brick," she called back.

So she came to the thorn tree.

"Have you seen a boy?" she asked it. "Did he tell you a story?"

"Indeed he did, and in return I was telling him about the stone of eternal life in my topmost fork."

"Let me lay my hands on that same stone!" said Morwenna, and she made haste to scramble up the tree. But because she was such an awkward, clumsy girl she fell from the top fork in her greedy hurry, and hung head down among the thorns.

"If you'd waited a moment longer," said the tree, "I could have told you that the boy took the stone with him."

"Oh, you villainous old tree!" cried Morwenna, kicking and twisting, and making such faces as turned the birds pale in their tracks. But she was stuck fast, and hangs there to this day.

Meanwhile Seb's step-mother had married again, a man as mean-natured as she was herself. By and by they began to hear tales of a marvellous boy, who sat on the shore and read tales to the sea.

"And the sea's given him great gifts!" said one. "They say he's been shown where the lost treasure of the Spanish galleon lies, with cups of gold and plates of pearl and wine-glasses all carved out of great rubies, and a hundred chests of silver ingots!"

"They say he's been told where every storm is, all over the world, and which way it's heading!" said another.

"They say he can listen to the voice of the sea as if it were an old friend talking to him!" said a third. "And devil a bit of a tide has there been since he began reading aloud, and a great inconvenience it is to the navigation in all realms of the world!"

"Can that boy be Seb?" wondered the step-mother and her husband. They resolved to go and see for themselves. So they harnessed up the pony-cart and made their way to the sea.

Sure enough, there on the sand was Seb, reading away from his little book. So many times he'd been through it now, he and the sea just about knew it by heart, between them.

"Why, Seb!" says his step-mother, sugar-sweet. "We've been in such an anxiety about you, child, wondering where you'd got to. Sure you'll be catching your mortal end of cold, sitting out on this great wet beach. Come home, come home, dear, for there's a grand cup of cocoa waiting for you, and a loaf with honey."

"That's very kind of you, ma'am," Seb says back, all polite.

"But if my sisters are there I'd just as lief not, if it's all the same to you."

"Oh, they've left," she says quickly. "So come along, dear, because the pony's beginning to fidget."

And without waiting for yea or nay she and her husband hustled Seb into the pony-cart and drove quickly home. Didn't they give him a time, then, as soon as they got in, pinching, poking and slapping one minute, buttering him up with sweet talk the next, as they tried to find out his secrets.

"Where's the sunken Spanish galleon? Where's the plates of pearl and glasses of ruby and the hundred chests of silver ingots?"

"I'm not remembering," says Seb.

"Didn't the sea tell you?"

"Sure, the sea told me one thing and another, but I was paying no heed to tales of ruby glasses and silver ingots. What do I care about silver ingots?"

"You little wretch!" she screamed. "You'd better remember, before I shake the eyes out of your head!"

"But I do remember one thing the sea told me," he says.

"What was that?"

He'd got his head turned, listening, towards the window, and he said, "The sea promised to come and help me if ever I was in trouble. And it's coming now."

Sure enough, the very next minute, every single wall of the house burst in, and the roof collapsed like an eggshell when you hit it with a spoon. There was enough sea in the garden to fill the whole Atlantic and have enough left over for the Pacific too. A great green wave lifted Seb on its shoulder and carried him out, through the garden and away, away, over the fields and hills, back to his new home among the conches and coral of the ocean bed.

As for the step-mother and her husband, they were never seen again.

But Seb is seen, it's said; sometimes at one great library,

sometimes at another, you'll catch a glimpse of him, taking out longer and longer books to read aloud to his friend the sea. And so long as he keeps the blue stone in his pocket, so long he'll go on reading, and hearing wonderful secrets in return, and so long the tides will go on standing still while they listen.

Is this a true tale, you ask?

As to that, I can't tell . . .

The Cost of Night

There was once a king called Merrion the Carefree who was inclined to be foolish. Perhaps this was because his wife had died when her baby daughter was born some years before, and so there was no one to keep an eye on the king. His worst failing was that he could never resist a game of chance; but of course all his subjects knew about this, and none of them would have dreamed of suggesting a game.

However it happened once that the king was returning home after a visit to a distant province of his kingdom. Towards twilight he came to a great river that was swift-flowing and wide. As he hesitated on the brink, for he was but an indifferent swimmer, he saw, moving through the reeds, an enormously large crocodile, with teeth as big as tenpins, cold expressionless yellow eyes, and a skin that looked as old and wrinkled and horny as the world itself.

"Ho, crocodile!" said King Merrion. "I am your lord and ruler, Merrion the Carefree, so it is plainly your duty to turn crossways over the river and make a bridge, in order that I may walk dry-shod from bank to bank."

At this the crocodile gave a great guttural choking bark, which might have been either a sardonic laugh or a respectful cough.

"Ahem, Your Majesty! I am no subject of yours, being indeed a traveller like yourself, but out of courtesy and good fellowship I don't mind making a bridge across the river for you, on one condition: that you play a game of heads or tails with me."

Now at this point, of course, the king should have had the sense to draw back. Better if he had slept all night on the bank, or travelled upstream till he came to the next bridge, however far off it lay. But he was tired, and eager to be home; besides, at the notion of a game, all sense and caution fled out of his head.

"I'll be glad to play with you, crocodile," he said. "But only one quick game, mind, for I am already late and should have been home hours ago."

So the crocodile, smiling all the way along his hundred teeth, turned sideways-on, and King Merrion walked on his horny back dry-shod from one river-bank to the other. Although the crocodile's back was covered in mud it was not slippery because of all the wrinkles.

When the king had stepped right over the hundred-tooth smile, and off the crocodile's long muddy snout, he looked about him and picked up a flat stone which was white on one side and brown on the other.

"This will do for our game, if you agree," he said.

"Certainly I agree," said the crocodile, smiling more than ever.

"What shall we play for?"

"The loser must grant the winner any gift he asks. You may throw first," the crocodile said politely.

So the king threw, and the crocodile snapped, "White!" Sure enough, the stone landed white side up.

Then the crocodile threw, and the king called, "Brown!" But again the stone landed white side up.

Then the king threw, and again the crocodile said "White!" and the stone landed white side up. For the fact of the matter was that the crocodile was not a genuine crocodile at all, but a powerful enchanter who chose to appear in that shape.

So the crocodile guessed right every time, and the king

guessed wrong, until he was obliged to acknowledge that he had lost the game.

"What do you want for your gift?" said he.

The crocodile smiled hugely, until he looked like a tunnel through the Rocky Mountains.

"Give me," he said, "all the dark in your kingdom."

At this the king was most upset. "I am not sure that the dark is mine to give away," he said. "I would rather that you had asked me for all the gold in my treasury."

"What use is gold to me?" said the crocodile. "Remember your kingly word. The dark I want, and the dark I must have."

"Oh, very well," said the king, biting his lip. "If you must, you must."

So the crocodile opened his toothy mouth even wider, and sucked, with a suction stronger than the widest whirlpool, and all the dark in King Merrion's kingdom came rushing along and was sucked down his great cavernous throat. Indeed he sucked so hard that he swallowed up, not only the dark that covered King Merrion's country, but the dark that lay over the entire half of the world facing away from the sun, just as you might suck the pulp off a ripe plum. And he smacked his lips over it, for dark was his favourite food.

"That was delicious!" he said. "Many thanks, Majesty! May your shadow never grow less!"

And with another loud harsh muddy laugh he disappeared.

King Merrion went home to his palace, where he found everyone in the greatest dismay and astonishment. For instead of there being night, as would have been proper at that time, the whole country was bathed in a strange unearthly light, clear as day, but a day in which nothing cast any shadow. Flowers which had shut their petals opened them again, birds peevishly brought their heads out from under their wings, owls and bats, much puzzled, returned to their thickets, and the little princess Gudrun refused to go to bed.

Indeed, after a few days, the unhappy king realized that he had brought a dreadful trouble to his kingdom—and to the whole world—by his rash promise. Without a regular spell of dark every twelve hours, nothing went right—plants grew tall and weak and spindly, cattle and poultry became confused and stopped producing milk and eggs, winds gave up blowing, and the weather went all to pieces. As for people, they were soon in a worse muddle than the cows and hens. At first everybody tried to work all night, so as to make the most of this extra daylight, but they soon became cross and exhausted and longed for rest. However it was almost impossible to sleep, for no matter what they did, covering their windows with thick curtains, shutting their doors, hiding under the bedclothes and bandaging their eyes, not a scrap of dark could anybody find. The crocodile had swallowed it all.

As for the children, they ran wild. Bed-time had ceased to exist.

The little princess Gudrun was the first to become tired of such a state of affairs. She was very fond of listening to stories, and what she enjoyed almost more than anything else was to lie in bed with her eyes tight shut in the warm dark, and remember the fairy-tales that her nurse used to tell her. But in the hateful daylight that went on and on it was not possible to do this. So she went to confide in her greatest friend and ask his service.

Gudrun's greatest friend was a great black horse called Houniman, a battle-charger who had been sent as a gift to King Merrion several years before; battles were not very frequent at that time, so Houniman mostly roamed, grazing the palace meadows. Now Gudrun sought him out, and gave him a handful of golden corn, and tried to pretend, by burying her face in his long, thick black mane, that the dark had come again.

"What shall we do about it, Houniman?" she said.

"It is obviously no use expecting your silly father to put matters right," Houniman replied.

"No, I am afraid you are right," Gudrun said, sighing.

"So, as he has given away all the dark in the entire world, we shall have to find out where dark comes from and how we can get some more of it."

"But who," she said, "would know such a thing?"

Houniman considered, "If we travel towards Winter," he said at length, "perhaps we might learn something, for in winter the dark grows until it almost swallows up the light."

"Good," said the princess, "let us travel towards Winter." So she fetched a woolly cloak, and filled her pockets with bread-and-cheese, and brought a bag of corn for Houniman, and they started out. Nobody noticed them go, since all the people in the kingdom were in such a state of muddle and upset, and King Merrion worst of all.

The princess rode on Houniman and he galloped steadily northwards for seven days and what ought to have been seven nights, over a sea of ice, until they came to the Land of Everlasting Winter, where the words freeze as you speak them, and even thoughts rattle in your head like icicles.

There they found the Lord of Winter, in the form of a great eagle, brooding on a rock.

"Sir," called Gudrun from a good way off—for it was so cold in his neighbourhood that the very birds froze in the air and hung motionless—"can you tell us where we can find a bit of dark?"

He lifted his head with its great hooked beak and gave them an angry look.

"Why should I help you? I have only one little piece of dark, and I am keeping it for myself, under my wing, so that it may grow."

"Does dark grow?" said Gudrun.

"Of course it grows, stupid girl! Cark! Be off with you!" And the eagle spread one wing (keeping the other tight folded) so that a great white flurry of snow and wind drove towards Gudrun and Houniman, and they turned and galloped away.

At the edge of the Land of Winter they saw an old woman leading a reindeer loaded with wood.

"Mother," called Gudrun, "can you tell us where we might find a bit of dark?"

"Give me a piece of bread-and-cheese for myself and some corn for my beast and I will consider."

So they gave her the bread and corn and she considered. Presently she said,

"There will be plenty of dark in the past. You should go to No Man's Land, the frontier where the present slips into the past, and perhaps you might be able to pick up a bit of dark there."

"Good," said the princess, "that sounds hopeful. But in which direction does the past lie?"

"Towards the setting sun, of course!" snapped the old woman, and she gave her reindeer a thump to make it jog along faster.

So Gudrun and Houniman turned towards the setting sun and galloped on for seven days and what should have been seven nights, until they reached No Man's Land. This was a strange and misty region, with low hills and marshes; in the middle of it they came to a great lake, on the shore of which sat an old poet in a little garden of cranberry shrubs. Instead of water the lake was filled with blue-grey mist, and the old poet was drawing out the mist in long threads, and twisting them and turning them into poems. It was very silent all around there, with not a living creature, and the old poet was so absorbed in what he did that he never lifted his head until they stood beside him.

"Can you tell us, uncle poet," said Gudrun, "where we might pick up a bit of dark?"

"Dark?" he said absently. "Eh, what's that? You want a bit of dark? There's plenty at the bottom of the lake."

So Gudrun dismounted and walked to the edge of the lake, and looked down through the mist. Thicker and thicker it grew, darker and darker, down in the depths of the lake, and as she looked down she could see all manner of strange shapes, and some that seemed familiar too—faces that she had once known, places that she had once visited, all sunk down in the dark depths of the past. As she leaned over, the mist seemed to rise up around her, so that she began to become sleepy, to forget who she was and what she had come for . . .

"Gudrun! Come back!" cried Houniman loudly, and he stretched out his long neck and caught hold of her by the hair and pulled her back, just as she was about to topple into the lake.

"Climb on my back and let's get out of here!" he said. "Dark or no dark, this place is too dangerous!"

But Gudrun cried to the poet, "Uncle poet, isn't there any other place where we might pick up a bit of dark?"

"Dark?" he said. "You want a bit of dark? Well, I suppose you might try the Gates of Death; dark grows around there."

"Where are the Gates of Death?"

"You must go to the middle of the earth, where the sky hangs so low that it is resting on the ground, and the rivers run uphill. There you will find the Gates of Death."

And he went back to his poem-spinning.

So they galloped on for seven days and what should have been seven nights, until the mountains grew higher and higher, and the sky hung lower and lower, and at last they came to the Gates of Death.

This place was so frightening that Gudrun's heart went small inside her, because everything seemed to be turning into something else. The sky was dropping into the mountains, and the mountains piercing into the sky. A great river ran uphill, boiling, and in front of the Gates of Death themselves a huge serpent lay coiled, with one yellow eye half open, watching as they drew near.

"Cousin serpent," called Gudrun, trying not to let her teeth chatter, "can you tell us where we might pick up a little piece of dark?"

"Ssss! Look about you, stupid girl!" hissed the serpent.

When Gudrun looked about her she saw that the ground was heaving and shuddering as if some great live creature were buried underneath, and there were cracks and holes in the rock, through which little tendrils of dark came leaking out.

But as fast as they appeared, the serpent snapped them off and gobbled them up.

Gudrun stretched out her hand to pick an uncurling frond of dark.

"Sssstop!" hissed the serpent, darting out his head till she drew back her hand in a fright. "All this dark is mine! And since my brother the crocodile ate all the dark in the world I will not part with one sprig of it, unless you give me something in return."

"But what can I give you?" said Gudrun, trembling.

"You can give me your black horse. He is the colour of night, he will do very well for a tasty bite. Give him to me and you may pick one sprig of dark."

"No, no, I cannot give you Houniman," cried Gudrun weeping. "He belongs to my father, not to me, and besides, he is my friend! I could not let him suffer such a dreadful fate. Take me instead, and let Houniman carry the dark back to my father's kingdom."

"*You* wouldn't do at all," hissed the serpent. "You have golden hair and blue eyes, you would give me indigestion. No, it must be the horse, or I will not part with any dark. But you must take off his golden shoes, or they will give me hiccups."

And Houniman whispered to the princess, "Do as the serpent says, for I have a notion that all will come right. But take care to keep my golden shoes."

So Gudrun wiped the tears from her eyes and Houniman lifted each foot in turn while she pulled off his golden shoes. And she put them in her pockets while the serpent sucked with a great whistling noise and sucked in Houniman, mane, tail and all.

Then Gudrun picked one little sprig of dark and ran weeping away from the Gates of Death. She ran on until she was tired, and then she turned and looked back. What was her horror to see that the serpent had uncoiled himself and was coming swiftly after her. "For," he had thought to himself, "I merely told her that she could *pick* one sprig in exchange for the horse, I did not say that she could carry it away. It would be a pity to waste a good sprig." So he was coming over the rocky ground, faster than a horse could gallop.

Quick as thought, Gudrun took one of the gold horseshoes out of her pocket and flung it so that it fell over the serpent, pinning him to the rock. Twist and writhe as he might, he could not get free, and she was able to run on until he was left far behind.

She passed through No Man's Land, but she was careful not to go too near the lake of mist. And she passed through the Land of Everlasting Winter, where the eagle sat guarding his little bit of dark. Then she came to the sea of ice, but now spring was coming, and the ice was beginning to melt.

"How shall I get over the sea?" Gudrun wondered. "Oh, how I wish my dear Houniman were here to advise me."

But then she remembered the gold horseshoes and thought they might help. So she pulled another from her pocket, and directly she did so it spread and stretched and turned into a boat. So Gudrun stepped into it, all the time hugging the little sprig of dark carefully against her heart, and the boat carried her safe across the sea.

Then she came to the borders of her father's kingdom, but it was still a long and weary way to his palace. For the journey that on Houniman's back had lasted only three times seven days and what should have been nights, took much longer on foot, and it was almost a year since she had left the Gates of Death. But the little sprig of dark had been growing and growing all the time.

Now Gudrun came to a wide, swift river.

In the reeds by the edge lay a crocodile, and he watched her approach with his yellow expressionless eyes.

"Ho there, little princess," he said. "I will play a game of heads or tails with you. If you win, I will turn my length across the river to make a bridge for you. And if I win, you shall give me the sprig of dark that you carry."

But Gudrun did not share her father's fondness for games of chance.

"Thank you," she said to the crocodile, "but I have a bridge of my own."

And she took out her third horseshoe, which immediately grew into a golden bridge, over which she crossed, leaving the crocodile to gnash his teeth with rage.

Gudrun ran on, slower and slower, for by now she was very tired, and the sprig of dark she carried had grown to the size of a young tree. But at last she reached her father's palace, and all the people ran out, with King Merrion in front, clapping their hands for joy.

"She has brought back the dark! Our darling princess has brought back the dark!"

"You must plant it in a safe, warm place and cherish it," said Gudrun faintly. "For I am afraid that the serpent and the crocodile may still come after it."

So it was planted in the palace garden, and it slowly grew bigger and bigger—first as big as a nut tree, then big as a young birch, then big as a spreading oak. And King Merrion's subjects took turns to guard it, and Gudrun stayed beside it always.

But one day the envious crocodile came creeping along, in the shadow thrown by the tree of dark. The man set to guard the tree was almost asleep, for the shadow made him drowsy after so many months of daylight, but Gudrun saw the crocodile.

Quick as a flash she pulled out her fourth horseshoe and threw it, pinning the crocodile to the ground.

But then she grew very anxious, "For," she said, "what shall we do if the serpent comes? Now I have no more horseshoes! Oh, my dear, good, faithful friend Houniman, how I do miss you!"

And she laid her head against the trunk of the tree and wept bitter tears.

Now this watering was just what the tree needed, and that very minute it grew and flourished until its branches spread right across the sky and true night had come at last. Directly this happened, all the creatures of night who had stayed sulking in their hiding-places for so long, the owls and moths and night-herons, the bats, bitterns, nightjars and nightingales, and all the beasts of darkness, came out rejoicing and calling down blessings on the little princess Gudrun. But she still knelt weeping beside the tree.

Then the king of the night creatures, who was an enormous owl, looked down with his great eyes and saw the serpent creeping through the dark. (In the end, after many days, he had managed to wriggle out from under the horseshoe.)

"Thief, thief!" cried the owl. "Kill him! Kill him!" And all the creatures of dark flew down, pecking and tearing, until they had pecked the serpent into a thousand pieces. And out of the pieces sprang Houniman, alive and well!

Then Gudrun flung her arms round Houniman's neck and wept for joy, and King Merrion offered him any reward he cared to name for helping to bring back dark to the world.

"All I ask," said Houniman, "is that you set me free, for in my own land, far to the east, where night begins, I was king and lord over all the wild horses."

"Willingly will I grant what you ask," said King Merrion.

So Houniman was given his freedom and he bade a loving farewell to the princess Gudrun and galloped away and away, home to his own country. But he sent back his son, the black colt Gandufer, to be the princess's lifelong companion and friend.

The creatures of night offered to peck the crocodile to pieces too, but King Merrion said no to that.

"I shall keep him a prisoner always, and the sight of him will be a reminder to me never again to get mixed up in a game of chance!" he said.

And so this was done.

A Leg Full of Rubies

Night, now. And a young man, Theseus O'Brien, coming down the main street of Killinch with an owl seated upon his shoulder—perhaps the strangest sight that small town ever witnessed. The high moors brooded around the town, all up the wide street came the sighing of the river, and the August night was as gentle and full as a bucket of new milk.

Theseus turned into Tom Mahone's snug, where the men of the town were gathered peaceably together, breathing smoke and drinking mountain dew. Wild, he seemed, coming into the lamplit circle, with a look of the night on him, and a smell of loneliness about him, and his eyes had an inward glimmer from looking into the dark. The owl on his shoulder sat quiet as a coffee-pot.

"Well, now, God be good to ye," said Tom Mahone. "What can we do for ye at all?"

And he poured a strong drop, to warm the four bones of him.

"Is there a veterinary surgeon in this town?" Theseus inquired.

Then they saw that the owl had a hurt wing, the ruffled feathers all at odds with one another. "Is there a man in this town can mend him?" he said.

"Ah, sure Dr Kilvaney's the man for ye," said they all. "No less than a magician with the sick beasts, he is." "And can throw a boulder farther than any man in the land." "'Tis the same one has a wooden leg stuffed full of rubies." "And keeps a phoenix in a cage." "And has all the minutes of his life numbered to the final grain of sand—ah, he's the man to aid ye."

And all the while the owl staring at them from great round eyes.

No more than a step it was to the doctor's surgery, with half Tom Mahone's customers pointing the way. The doctor, sitting late to his supper by a small black fire, heard the knock and opened the door, candle in hand.

"Hoo?" said the owl at sight of him, "who, whoo?" And, *who* indeed may this strange man be, thought Theseus, following him down the stone passageway, with his long white hair and his burning eyes of grief?

Not a word was said between them till the owl's wing was set, and then the doctor, seeing O'Brien was weary, made him sit and drink a glass of wine.

"Sit," said he, "there's words to be spoken between us. How long has the owl belonged to you?"

"To me?" said Theseus. "He's no owl of mine. I found him up on the high moor. Can you mend him?"

"He'll be well in three days," said Kilvaney. "I see you are a man after my heart, with a love of wild creatures. Are you not a doctor, too?"

"I am," answered Theseus. "Or I was," he added sadly, "until the troubles of my patients became too great a grief for me to bear, and I took to walking the roads to rid me of it."

"Come into my surgery," said the doctor, "for I've things to show you. You're the man I've been looking for."

They passed through the kitchen, where a girl was washing the dishes. Lake-blue eyes, she had, and black hair; she was small, and fierce, and beautiful, like a falcon.

"My daughter," the doctor said absently. "Go to bed, Maggie."

"When the birds are fed, not before," she snapped.

Cage after cage of birds, Theseus saw, all down one wall of the room, finches and thrushes, starlings and blackbirds, with a sleepy stirring and twittering coming from them.

In the surgery there was only one cage, but that one big enough to house a man. And inside it was such a bird as Theseus had never seen before—every feather on it pure gold, and eyes like candle-flames.

"My phoenix," the doctor said, "but don't go too near him, for he's vicious."

The phoenix sidled near the end of the cage, with his eyes full of malice and his wicked beak sideways, ready to strike. Theseus stepped away from the cage and saw, at the other end of the room, a mighty hour-glass that held in its twin globes enough sand to boil all the eggs in Leghorn. But most of the sand had run through, and only a thin stream remained, silting down so swiftly on the pyramid below that every minute Theseus expected to see the last grain whirl through and vanish.

"You are only just in time," Dr Kilvaney said. "My hour has come. I hereby appoint you my heir and successor. To you I bequeath my birds. Feed them well, treat them kindly, and they will sing to you. But never, never let the phoenix out of his cage, for his nature is evil."

"No, no! Dr Kilvaney!" Theseus cried. "You are in the wrong of it! You are putting a terrible thing on me! I don't want your birds, not a feather of them. I can't abide creatures in cages!"

"You must have them," said the doctor coldly. "Who else can I trust? And to you I leave also my wooden leg full of rubies—look, I will show you how it unscrews."

"No!" cried Theseus. "I don't want to see!"

He shut his eyes, but he heard a creaking, like a wooden pump-handle.

"And I will give you, too," said the doctor presently, "this hour-glass. See, my last grain of sand has run through. Now it will be *your* turn." Calmly he reversed the hour-glass, and started the sand once more on its silent, hurrying journey. Then he said,

"Surgery hours are on the board outside. The medicines are in the cupboard yonder. Bridget Hanlon is the midwife. My daughter feeds the birds and attends to the cooking. You can sleep tonight on the bed in there. Never let the phoenix out of its cage. You must promise that."

"I promise," said Theseus, like a dazed man.

"Now I will say goodbye to you." The doctor took out his false teeth, put them on the table, glanced round the room to see that nothing was overlooked, and then went up the stairs as if he were late for an appointment.

All night Theseus, uneasy on the surgery couch, could hear the whisper of the sand running, and the phoenix rustling, and the whet of its beak on the bars; with the first light he could see its mad eye glaring at him.

In the morning Dr Kilvaney was dead.

It was a grand funeral. All the town gathered to pay him respect, for he had dosed and drenched and bandaged them all, and brought most of them into the world, too.

" 'Tis a sad loss," said Tom Mahone, "and he with the grandest collection of cage-birds this side of Dublin city. 'Twas in a happy hour for us the young doctor turned up to take his place."

But there was no happiness in the heart of Theseus O'Brien. Like a wild thing caged himself he felt, among the rustling birds, and with the hating eye of the phoenix fixing him from its corner, and, worst of all, the steady fall of sand from the hour-glass to drive him half mad with its whispering threat.

And, to add to his troubles, no sooner were they home from the funeral than Maggie packed up her clothes in a carpet-bag and moved to the other end of the town to live with her aunt Rose, who owned the hay and feed store.

"It wouldn't be decent," said she, "to keep house for you,

and you a single man." And the more Theseus pleaded, the firmer and fiercer she grew. "Besides," she said, "I wouldn't live another day among all those poor birds behind bars. I can't stand the sight nor sound of them."

"I'll let them go, Maggie! I'll let every one of them go."

But then he remembered, with a falling heart, the doctor's last command. "That is, all except the phoenix."

Maggie turned away. All down the village street he watched her small, proud back, until she crossed the bridge and was out of sight. And it seemed as if his heart went with her.

The very next day he let loose all the doctor's birds—the finches and thrushes, the starlings and blackbirds, the woodpecker and the wild heron. He thought Maggie looked at him with a kinder eye when he walked up to the hay and feed store to tell her what he had done.

The people of the town grew fond of their new doctor, but they lamented his sad and downcast look. "What ails him at all?" they asked one another, and Tom Mahone said, "He's as mournful as old Dr Kilvaney was before him. Sure there's something insalubrious about carrying on the profession of medicine in this town."

But indeed, it was not his calling that troubled the poor young man, for here his patients were as carefree a set of citizens as he could wish. It was the ceaseless running of the sand.

Although there was a whole roomful of sand to run through the glass, he couldn't stop thinking of the day when that roomful would be dwindled to a mere basketful, and then to nothing but a bowlful. And the thought dwelt on his mind like a blight, since it is not wholesome for a man to be advised when his latter end will come, no matter what the burial service may say.

Not only the sand haunted him, but also the phoenix, with its unrelenting stare of hate. No matter what delicacies he brought it, in the way of bird-seed and kibbled corn, dry mash and the very best granite grit (for his visits to the hay and feed store were the high spots of his days) the phoenix was always waiting with its razor-sharp beak ready to lay him open to the bone should he venture too near. None of the food would it more than nibble at. And a thing he began to notice, as the days went past, was that its savage brooding eye was always focused on one part of his anatomy—on his left leg. It sometimes seemed to him as if the bird had a particular stake or claim to that leg, and meant to keep watch and see that its property was maintained in good condition.

One night Theseus had need of a splint for a patient. He reached up to a high shelf, where he kept the mastoid mallets, and the crutches, and surgical chisels. He was standing on a chair to do it, and suddenly his foot slipped and he fell, bringing down with him a mighty bone-saw that came to the ground beside him with a clang and a twang, missing his left knee-cap by something less than a feather's breadth. Pale and shaken, he got up, and turning, saw the phoenix watching him as usual, but with such an intent and disappointed look, like the housewife who sees the butcher's boy approaching with the wrong joint!

A cold fit of shivering came over Theseus, and he went hurriedly out of the room.

Next day when he was returning home over the bridge, carrying a bag full of bird-mash, with dried milk and antibiotics added, and his mind full of the blue eyes and black hair of Maggie, a runaway tractor hurtled past him and crashed into the parapet, only one centimetre beyond his left foot.

And again Theseus shuddered, and walked home white and silent, with the cold thought on him. He found the phoenix hunched on its perch, feathers up and head sunk.

"Ah, Phoenix, Phoenix," he cried to it, "why will you be persecuting me so? Do you want to destroy me entirely?" The phoenix made no reply, but stared balefully at his left leg. Then he remembered the old doctor's wooden leg full of rubies. "But I'll not wear it!" he cried to the bird, "not if it was stuffed with rubies and diamonds too!"

Just the same, in his heart he believed that the phoenix would not rest satisfied while he had the use of both his legs. He took to walking softly, like a cat, looking this way and that for all possible hazards, watching for falling tiles, and boiling saucepans, and galloping cattle; and the people of the town began to shake their heads over him.

His only happy hours were with Maggie, when he could persuade her to leave the store and come out walking with him. Far out of the town they'd go, forgetting the troubles that lay at home. For Maggie had found her aunt was a small, mean-minded woman who put sand in with the hens' meal and shingle among the maize, and Maggie couldn't abide such dealings.

"As soon as I've a little saved," said she, "I'll be away from this town, and off into the world."

"Maggie!" cried Theseus, and it was the first time he'd plucked up courage to do so. "Marry me, and I'll make you happier than any girl in the length and breadth of this land."

"I can't marry you," she said. "I could never marry a man who kept a phoenix in a cage."

"We'll give it away," he said, "give it away and forget about it." But even as he spoke he knew they could not. They kissed despairingly, up on the moors in the twilight, and turned homewards.

"I always knew that phoenix was a trouble-bringer," said Maggie, "from the day when Father bought it off a travelling tinker to add to his collection. He said at the time it was a bargain, for the tinker threw in the wooden leg and the great hour-glass as well, but ever after that day Father was a changed man."

"What did he give for it?" Theseus asked.

"His peace of mind. That was all the tinker asked, but it

was a deal too much, I'm thinking, for that hateful bird with his wicked look and his revengeful ways."

When he had seen Maggie home, Theseus went to the Public Library, for he couldn't abide the thought of the doctor's house, dark and cold and silent with only the noise of the phoenix shifting on its perch. He took down the volume OWL to POL of the encyclopedia and sat studying it until closing time.

Next day he was along to see Maggie.

"Sweetheart," he said, and his eyes were alive with hope, "I believe I've found the answer. Let me have a half-hundred-weight sack of layers' pellets."

"Fourteen shillings," snapped Aunt Rose, who happened to be in the shop just then. Her hair was pinned up in a skinny bun and her little green eyes were like brad-awls.

"Discount for cash payment," snapped back Theseus, and he planked down thirteen shillings and ninepence, kissed Maggie, picked up the sack, and hurried away home. Just as he got there a flying slate from the church roof struck him; if he'd not been wearing heavy boots it would have sliced his foot off. He ran indoors and shook his fist at the phoenix.

"There!" he yelled at it, pouring a troughful of layers' pellets. "Now get that in your gizzard, you misbegotten fowl!"

The phoenix cocked its head. Then it pecked a pellet, neck feathers puffed in scorn, and one satiric eye fixed all the while on Theseus, who stood eagerly watching. Then it pecked another pellet, hanging by one claw from its perch. Then it came down on to the floor entirely and bowed its golden head over the trough. Theseus tiptoed out of the room. He went outside and chopped up a few sticks of kindling—not many, but just a handful of nice, dry, thin twigs. He came back indoors—the phoenix had its head down, gobbling—and laid the sticks alongside the cage, not too close, an artful width away.

Next evening, surgery done, he fairly ran up to the hay and

feed store. "Come with me," he said joyfully to Maggie, "come and see what it's doing."

Maggie came, her eyes blazing with curiosity. When they reached the surgery she could hear a crackling and a cracking: the phoenix was breaking up twigs into suitable lengths, and laying them side by side. Every now and then it would try them out in a heap; it had a great bundle in the bottom of its cage but it seemed dissatisfied, and every now and then pulled it all to pieces and began again. It had eaten the whole sackful of pellets and looked plump and sleek.

"Theseus," said Maggie, looking at it, "we must let it out. No bird can build inside of a cage. It's not dignified."

"But my promise?"

"*I* never promised," said Maggie, and she stepped up to the cage door.

Theseus lifted a hand, opened his mouth in warning. But then he stopped. For the phoenix, when it saw what Maggie was at, inclined its head to her in gracious acknowledgment, and then took no further notice of her, but, as soon as the door was opened, began shifting its heap of sticks out into the room. If ever a bird was busy and preoccupied and in a hurry, that phoenix was the one.

"But we can't let it build in the middle of the floor," said Theseus.

"Ah, sure, what harm?" said Maggie. "Look, the poor fowl is running short of sticks."

As soon as Theseus had gone for more, she stepped over to the hour-glass, for her quick eye had noticed what he, in his excitement, had failed to see—the sand was nearly all run through. Quietly, Maggie reversed the glass and started the sand on its journey again, a thing she had often done for her father, unbeknownst, until the day when it was plain he would rather die than stay alive.

When Theseus came back the phoenix was sitting proudly on the top of a breast-high heap of sticks.

"We mustn't watch it now," said Maggie, "it wouldn't be courteous." And she led Theseus outside. He, however, could not resist a slant-eyed glance through the window as they passed. It yielded him a flash of gold—the phoenix had laid an egg in a kidney-basin. Moreover, plumes of smoke were beginning to flow out through the window.

"Goodbye, Phoenix," Maggie called. But the phoenix, at the heart of a golden blaze, was much too busy to reply.

"Thank heaven!" exclaimed Theseus. "Now I shall never know when the last of my sand was due to run through." Maggie smiled, but made no comment, and he asked her, "Is it right, do you think, to let the house burn down?"

"What harm?" said Maggie again. "It belongs to us, doesn't it?"

"What will the people of the town do, if I'm not here to doctor them?"

"Go to Dr Conlan of Drumanough."

"And what about your father's leg full of rubies?" he said, looking at the phoenix's roaring pyre.

"We'd never get it out now," said she. "Let it go on holding up the kitchen table till they both burn. We've better things to think of."

And hand in hand the happy pair of them ran out of the town, up along the road to the high moors and the world, leaving behind a pocketful of rubies to glitter in the ashes, and a golden egg for anyone who was fool enough to pick it up.

Hope

It was on a clear, frosty November evening, not many years ago, that Dr Jane Smith, having occasion to visit a patient in the part of London known as Rumbury Town, was suddenly overtaken by the impulse to call on an old teacher of hers, a Miss Lestrange, who had a bedsitting-room on the edge of that district, where she earned a meagre living by giving lessons on the harp.

Rumbury Town is a curious region of London. Not far from the big stations, adjacent to Islington, beyond, or anyway defying the jurisdiction of smokeless-fuel legislation, it lies enfolded generally in an industrial dusk of its own. The factories of Rumbury Town are not large, and their products are eccentric—artificial grass for butchers' windows, metal bedwinches, false teeth for sheep, slimmers' biscuits made from wood-pulp, catnip mice, plastic Christmas-tree decorations —these are a random sample of its exports. But the small gaunt chimneys, leaning from the factories at various precarious angles, belch black smoke as vigorously as any modern electric power station, and so do those of the houses, like rows of organ-stops, along the ill-lit, dour little terraced streets that lead up in the direction of Rumbury Waste, the ragged strip of tree-grown land fringing Rumbury Town on its eastern edge.

Rumbury Waste is a savage place enough, on no account to be visited after dark, but many a police officer would agree that the centre of Rumbury Town itself is far more of a hostile wilderness, far more dangerous. Here lies an area of mixed factories, business premises, and wholesale markets, interspersed with a few lanes of private dwellings and some dingy little shopping precincts; seamed by narrow alleys and shortcuts; a real maze where, it is said, only those born in Rumbury Town or who have spent at least forty years within earshot of the bells of St Griswold's, Rumbury, can ever hope to find their way.

So cold and clear was this particular evening, however, that even the smoke from the Rumbury chimneys had dwindled to a slaty wisp against the sky's duck-egg green; so little wind was there that in the derelict corners of factory lots where goldenrod and willowherb cloaked piles of rubble, the withered leaves and feathery seeds drifted straight and unswerving to the ground.

Engines and presses in the factories had ceased their clanging and thudding; workers had gone home; in the centre of Rumbury Town the only sound to be heard was the distant, muted roar of London; and a nearer surge of pop music, sizzle of fish frying, and shouts of children from the few inhabited streets. Dr Smith parked her car in one of these, locked it carefully, and went in search of her friend, Miss January Lestrange.

Rumbury Town seemed a curious environment for a spinster who taught the harp. And Miss Lestrange was a real spinster of the old-fashioned kind; she walked very slowly, with small, precise steps; she wore tight, pointed button boots, very shiny, which ended halfway up her calf, and long serge skirts, trimmed with rows of braid, which hung down over the boots; it was pure chance that Miss Lestrange's style of dressing was now once more the height of fashion, and a circumstance that she would certainly not have noticed; had she done so she might have been mildly irritated. Her grey hair was smoothly drawn back into a bun, and she wore pince-nez; all the children of Rumbury Town wondered how she managed to make them balance on her nose. Miss Lestrange kept herself to herself and never troubled her neighbours; many of them, if they had thought about it, would not have been surprised to be told that she was a thin, grey old ghost, occasionally to be seen gliding out on her small shopping errands. And the children, though they were not exactly frightened of her, never chalked on her door, or threw ice-lolly sticks after her, or sang rude rhymes about her, as they did about most other adults in the neighbourhood. Miss Lestrange, however, was no ghost, and although she had lived within sound of St Griswold's bells for forty years, was not a born citizen of the district; she still did not venture into the twilit heart of Rumbury Town.

"Why *do* you live here?" Dr Smith asked, when she had knocked on the faded blue door with its postcard, J. LESTRANGE, HARP TUITION, and had been admitted, passing a small frantic-looking boy on his way out with a music-case under his arm.

"It amazes me the way some of them keep on coming," murmured Miss Lestrange, zipping its case over the harp, which was as tall, gaunt and worn-looking as she herself. "I've told them and told them that you don't get a first-rate harpist once in a generation, but they all think they have the seed of it in them."

"What about that boy? Is he any good?"

Miss Lestrange shrugged.

"He's the same as the rest. I don't hold out false hopes and sweet promises. I send him away at the end of the lessons utterly despondent, limp as rhubarb, but by next time he's always plucked up heart again and thinks he'll be a second David. Well, Jane, it is nice to see you. What brings you here?"

"Suppose I said that *I* wanted some more lessons?" Dr Smith asked with a small, grim smile.

"I should tell you what I told your parents. It would be a

waste of their money, my time, and yours, to teach you for another five minutes."

"And they at least believed you. So I went away and trained for a doctor."

"And have turned into a good one, from what I hear." Miss Lestrange nodded at her ex-pupil affectionately. "I hope you will stay and take your evening meal with me and tell me about your work."

But her glance strayed a little doubtfully to the screened corner of the room where she cooked over a methylated-spirit lamp; she had been about to brew herself a nourishing, or at least vitamin-rich soup, made from hot water, parsley, grown in her window-box, and salt.

"No, no, I came to invite you out. I have to pay one call on a patient not far from here, and then I thought we'd go to the Chinese Restaurant at the corner of Inkermann Street. Put on your coat and let's be off."

Miss Lestrange was always businesslike.

"Well, that would certainly be a more enjoyable meal than the one I could have offered you," she said, put on her coat, and a black hat which had the shape though not the festive air of a vol-au-vent, and ushered out her visitor, locking the door behind them.

The little grimy street was silent and watchful. Half a dozen children stared, to see Miss Lestrange setting out at such an unwonted time of day, in such an unwonted manner, in a car, with a friend.

Dr Smith reverted to her first, unanswered question.

"Why *do* you live here?"

"The rents are very low," Miss Lestrange said mildly. "Five pounds a year for my room."

"But in a better part you might get more pupils—brighter ones . . ."

"The world is not that full of gifted harpists," Miss Lestrange said drily. "And this neighbourhood suits me."

"You have friends here?"

"Once I did. One friend. We have not seen each other for some time. But as one grows older," Miss Lestrange said calmly, "one requires fewer friends."

Reflecting that it would be difficult to have fewer friends than *one,* Dr Smith brought her car to a halt by a large, grim tenement with a dozen arched entrances. The road that passed it was an old, wide, cobbled one, and on the opposite side began the cluttered, dusky jumble of piled-up factory, warehouse, shed, storehouse, office, factory and lumber-yard that like a great human badger-warren covered the heart of Rumbury Town.

"My patient lives just through here; I shan't be long."

"Who is your patient?" inquired Miss Lestrange, as the doctor turned to lift her black case from the rear seat of the car.

"Well, as a matter of fact he's quite well known—the writer Tom Rampisham. Why, like you, he chooses to live in this godforsaken spot I don't know, but here he's lived for goodness knows how many years. He has a ground-floor flat in that gloomy block."

"Tom Rampisham," Miss Lestrange said musingly. "It is some time since he did one of his broadcasts. What's his trouble?"

"Heart. Well, I probably shan't be more than a few minutes. But here's a spare car-key in case you want to stroll about."

It looked an unpromising area for a stroll. But when Dr Smith's few minutes lengthened to ten, and then to fifteen, Miss Lestrange, who seemed restless and disinclined to sit still, even after a long day's work, got out of the car, locked it, and stood irresolutely on the pavement.

For a moment she stared at the large forbidding block into which the doctor had vanished. Then, with decision, she turned her back on it and struck off briskly across the road. Almost immediately opposite the car was a little opening in the clifflike façade of warehouses, one of those narrow lanes which the denizens of Rumbury Town call *hackets,* which led inwards, with many angles and windings and sudden changes of direction, towards the heart of the maze.

Along this alley Miss Lestrange rapidly walked. It seemed as if she walked *from* rather than *to* anything in particular; her head was bent, her eyes fixed on the greasy cobbles, she ignored the entrances with their mysterious signs: Wishaw, Flock Sprayers; Saloop, Ear Piercing Specialists; Ample Tops; The Cake Candle Co.; Madame Simkins, Feathers; Sugg, Ganister Maker and Refractory Materials Manufacturer; Toppling Seashell Merchants; Shawl, String, and Sheepskin Co.; Willow Specialists and Wood Wool Packers. One and all, she passed them without a glance, even the Shawl, String, and Sheepskin office, which was in fact the source of her new harp-strings when the old ones had snapped under the inexpert fingers of the youth of Rumbury Town.

Miss Lestrange walked fast, talking to herself, as elderly people do who lead solitary lives.

"If he were ill he might ask for me," she muttered, going past Gay Injectors and Ejectors without sparing a thought to wonder what obscure goods or services their name denoted. "He once said he might; I remember his saying that if he were taken ill he might get in touch with me; it's queer that I can hardly remember what we quarrelled about, and yet I can remember that."

The alley took a turn, widened, and led her into a melancholy little area of street market: crockery stalls, cheap clothing stalls, vegetable stalls, second-hand book and junk stalls. The traders were just closing up for the night, piling their unsold wares—of which there seemed a great many—back into cartons; the way was impeded by boxes of rubbish, and slippery with squashed vegetables, but Miss Lestrange stepped briskly round and over these obstacles without appearing to notice them.

"What did we quarrel about, all that long time ago?" she mused, neatly by-passing a pram loaded with dusty tins of furniture polish and stepping over a crate labelled SUPER-SHINE WHOLESALE : WE PROMISE DAZZLING RESULTS. "It was something to do with his poetry, was it?"

The lane narrowed again and she went on between great overhanging cliffs of blackened brick, frowning a little, over her pince-nez, as she tried to summon up a young, lively, impatient face. What had he looked like, exactly? At one time she had known his face by heart—better than her own, for Miss Lestrange had never been one to spend much time gazing at herself in mirrors. Noticeable cheekbones; a lock of hair that always fell forward; that was all she could remember.

We Promise Dazzling Results.

"I don't *know* anything about poetry, Tom. How can I say if it's good or bad?"

"You've got an *opinion,* haven't you, girl? You can say what you *think?*"

"You don't really want me to say what I think. You just want me to praise them."

"Damn it, that's not true, January. January!" he said bitterly. "There never was a more appropriate bit of classification. If ever anybody was ice-cold, frozen hard, ungenerous, utterly unwilling to give an inch, it's you!"

"*That's* not true!" she had wanted to cry. "It's just that I can't praise what I don't understand, I won't make pretty speeches just to encourage. How can I tell about your poetry? How can I say if I don't know? It wouldn't be right."

But he had already stuffed the disputed poems into an old black satchel and gone striding off; that was the last time she had seen him.

She passed a café with an inscription in what looked like white grease on its window-glass: Sausages, potatoes, onions, peas; frying now, always frying. Why not try our fry?

A staggeringly strong, hot waft of sausage and onion came

from the open door; inside were boys with tiny heads, tiny eyes, and huge feet in huge boots; as she hurried by, Miss Lestrange felt their eyes investigating her and then deciding that she was not worth the trouble. The hot smell of food made her feel sick and reminded her that she was trembling with hunger; for her lunch at midday she had eaten half a hard-boiled egg, for her breakfast a cup of milkless tea.

"I suppose I shall have to put my fees up," she thought, frowning again.

A shrill whistle, with something familiar about it, disturbed her train of thought, and she glanced ahead. It was the tune, not the whistle, that was familiar: in a moment she identified it as a tune she had written herself, an easy tune for beginners on the harp; she had called it *Snowdrops*.

And, rollerskating heedlessly in her direction, whistling it shrilly, but in tune, came the boy to whom she had just finished giving a lesson earlier that evening when Dr Smith arrived.

Their surprise at meeting was equal. He had almost run into her; he skidded to a jerky stop, braking himself with a hand on the alley wall.

"Miss Lestrange! Coo, you're a long way from home, aren't you? You lost your way?"

"Good evening, David. No, I have not lost my way," Miss Lestrange replied briskly. "I am simply taking a walk." What is there surprising in that? her tone expressed.

David looked startled; then he gave her a teasing, disbelieving grin, which made his crooked eyebrows shoot off round the corners of his face. She had never noticed this trick before; but then of course in his lessons he never *did* grin; he was always sweatingly anxious and subdued.

"*I* don't believe you're just out for a walk; I think you're after that there buried treasure!"

"Buried treasure? What buried treasure, pray?"

"Why, the treasure they say's buried somewhere under the

middle o' Rumbury Town. That's what *you're* after. But you won't find it! They say the old Devil's keeping an eye on it for himself. If I were you, Miss Lestrange, I'd turn back before you *do* get lost!"

"I shall do no such thing," Miss Lestrange said firmly, and she went on her way, and David went skating zigzag on *his* way, whistling again the little tune, *Snowdrops*—"Mi, re, doh, Snowdrops in the snow . . ."

But Miss Lestrange did turn and look once after David, slightly puzzled. He was so different, so much livelier and more sure of himself than during her lessons; he had quite surprised her.

But as for getting lost—what nonsense.

Nevertheless, in a couple of minutes, without being aware of it, Miss Lestrange did lose herself. She came to a point where five alleys met at an open space shaped like a star, chose one at random, walked a fair way along it, came to another similar intersection, and chose again. Rumbury Town folded itself round her. The green sky overhead was turning to navy-blue.

And all around her was dark, too; like the crater of an extinct volcano. An occasional orange streetlight dimly illuminated the alleyway. Not a sound was to be heard. It was a dead world.

Suddenly Miss Lestrange felt uneasy. Her thoughts flew to the professional visit taking place behind her, from the vision of which she had so determinedly started away. Jane must have left him by now. Probably in the car, wondering where I've got to. I had better turn back.

She turned back. And came to the first of the star-shaped conjunctions of lanes.

"Which was mine?" She stood wondering. All four openings facing her looked blank, like shut drawers; she could find no recognizable feature in any of them. The names were just visible: Lambskin Alley, New Year Way, Peridot Lane, Hell

Passage; none of them did she consciously remember seeing before.

"I'd surely have noticed New Year Way," she thought, and so chose Hell Passage—not that it looked any more familiar than the rest. What may have caught her unwitting ear was the faint thrum and throb of music, somewhere far away in that direction; as she proceeded along the narrow passage the sound became steadily more identifiable as music, though Miss Lestrange could not put a name to the actual *tune;* but then the world of pop music was unfamiliar territory to her. At least, though, music meant people, and inhabited regions; just for a minute or two, back there, although she would not have admitted it to anybody, Miss Lestrange had felt a stirring of panic at the vacuum of silence all round her.

On she went; crossed another star-shaped conjunction of alleys and, by the light of one high-up orange sodium tube, hung where the youth of Rumbury Town were unlikely to be able to break it by throwing bottles, saw that Hell Passage still continued, bisecting the angle between Sky Peals Lane and Whalebone Way.

"Curious names they have hereabouts; it must be a very old quarter. I shall look up the names on the map if—when I get home. *Did* I come this way?" Miss Lestrange asked herself; another surge of anxiety and alarm swept over her as she passed the closed premises of the Prong, Thong, and Trident Company—surely she would have noticed *that* on the way along?

But the music was much louder now; at least, soon, she must encounter somebody whom she could ask.

Then, without any question, she knew that she was lost. For Hell Passage came to a stop—or rather, it opened into a little cul-de-sac yard out of which there was no other exit. Miss Lestrange could see quite plainly that there was no other exit because the yard was illuminated by a fierce, flickering, variable light which came from bundles of tarry rags stuffed into roadmenders' tripods and burning vigorously. These were set against the walls. There were about a dozen people in the yard, and Miss Lestrange's first reaction was one of relief.

"It's one of those pop groups," she thought. "I've heard it's hard for them, when they're starting, to find places to practise; I suppose if you can't afford to hire a studio, somewhere like this, far off and out of earshot, would be a godsend."

Somehow the phrase *out of earshot,* though she had used it herself, made her feel uncomfortable; the beat and howl of the music, failing to fight its way out of the narrow court, was so tremendous, that it gave her a slight chill to think what a long way she must be from any residential streets, for people not to have complained about it.

She glanced again at the group; decided not to ask them her way, and turned to go quickly and quietly back. But she was too late; she found somebody standing behind her: an enormously large, tall man, dressed in red velvet trousers and jacket, with a frilled shirt.

"Hey, now, you're not thinking of *leaving,* are you—when you just got here?" His voice was a genial roar, easily heard even above the boom of the music, but there was a jeering note under its geniality. "Surely not going to run off without hearing us, were you? Look, boys and girls," he went on, his voice becoming, without the slightest difficulty, even louder, "Look who's here! It's Miss Lestrange, Miss January Lestrange, come to give us her critical opinion!"

A wild shout of derisive laughter went up from the group in the court.

"Three cheers for Miss January Lestrange—the hippest harpist in the whole of toe-tapping Rumbury Town!"

They cheered her, on and on, and the tall man led her with grinning mock civility to a seat on an upturned Snowcem tin. The players began tuning their instruments, some of which, trumpets and basses, seemed conventional enough, but others were contrivances that Miss Lestrange had never laid eyes on before—zinc washtubs with strings stretched across, large twisted shells, stringed instruments that looked more like weapons—crossbows, perhaps—than zithers, strange prehistoric-looking wooden pipes at least six or seven feet long—and surely that was an actual *fire* burning under the kettle-drum?

"January!" the large man boomed, standing just behind the shoulder of Miss Lestrange. "Now, *there's* a chilly sort of name to give a spirited lady like yourself—a downright cold, miserable kind of a dreary name, isn't it, boys and girls? The worst month of the year!"

"It is not!" snapped Miss Lestrange—but she did wish he would not stand so close, for his presence just out of sight gave her the cold grue—for some odd reason the phrase *Get thee behind me, Satan,* slipped into her mind—"January means hope, it means looking forward, because the whole year lies ahead."

But her retort was drowned in the shout from the group of players— *"We'll* soon warm her up!"

"Happy lot, ain't they?" confided the voice at her back. "Nick's Nightflowers, we call ourselves—from the location, see?" He pointed up and, by the light of the flaring rags, Miss Lestrange could just read the sign on the wall: OLD NICK'S COURT, E.I. "And I'm Old Nick, naturally—happy to have you with us tonight, Miss Lestrange."

She flicked a glance sideways, to see if it would be possible to slip away once they began playing, but to her dismay most of the group were now between her and the entrance, blocking the way; from their grins, it was plain that they knew what she had in mind. And she had never seen such an unattractive crew— "Really," she thought, "if they had *tails* they could hardly look less human."

Old Nick, with his red velvet and ruffles, was about the most normal in appearance and dress, but she cared for him least of all, and unobtrusively edged her Snowcem tin cornerways until at least she had the wall at her back.

"Ready, all? Cool it now—real cool," called Nick, at which there was a howl of laughter. "One, two, three—*stomp!*"

The music broke out again. If music it could be called. The sound seemed to push Miss Lestrange's blood backward along her arteries, to flog on her eardrums, to slam in her lungs, to seize hold of her heart and dash it from side to side.

"I shan't be able to endure it for more than a minute or two," she thought quite calmly. "It's devilish, that's what it is —really devilish."

Just at the point when she had decided she could stand it no longer, half a dozen more figures lounged forward from a shadow at the side of the court, and began to dance. Boys or girls? It was hard to say. They seemed bald, and extraordinarily *thin*—they had white, hollow faces, deepset eyes under bulging foreheads, meaningless grins. "White satin!" thought Miss Lestrange scornfully. "And ruffles! What an extraordinarily dated kind of costume—like the pierrot troupes when I was young."

But at closer view the satin seemed transparent gauze, or chiffon. "I've never *seen* anyone so thin—they are like something out of Belsen," thought Miss Lestrange. "That one must have had rickets when young—his legs are no more than bones. They must all have had rickets," she decided.

"D'you like it?" boomed the leader in her ear. It seemed amazing that he could still make his voice heard above the row, but he could.

"Frankly, no," said Miss Lestrange. "I never laid eyes on such a spiritless ensemble. They all dance as if they wanted dosing with Parrish's Food and codliver oil."

"Hear that, gang?" he bawled to the troupe. "Hear that? The lady doesn't care for your dancing; she thinks you're a lily-livered lot."

The dancers paused; they turned their bloodless faces towards Miss Lestrange. For a moment she quailed, as tiny lights seemed to burn in the deep eye-sockets, all fixed on her. But then the leader shouted,

"And what's more, I think so too! Do it again—and this time, put some guts into it, or it'll be prong, thong, and trident, all right!"

The players redoubled their pace and volume, the dancers broke into a faster shuffle. And the leader, still making himself heard above the maniac noise, shouted,

"Hope! Where are you? Come along out, you mangy old tom-cat, you!" And, to the group, *"He'll* soon tickle you up!"

A dismal and terrified wailing issued from the dancers at these words.

"Hope's a little pet of mine," confided the leader to Miss Lestrange. "Makes all the difference when they're a bit sluggish; *you* ought to like him too."

She distrusted his tone, which seemed to promise some highly unpleasant surprise, and looked round sharply.

A kind of ripple parted the musicians and dancers; at first Miss Lestrange could not see what had caused this, but, even through the music, she thought she could hear cries of pain or terror; then a wave of dancers eddied away from her and a gold-brown animal bounded through, snatching with sabre-teeth at a bony thigh as it passed.

"That's Hope," said the leader with satisfaction. *"That's* my little tiger-kitten. Isn't he a beauty? Isn't he a ducky-did-dums? I powder his fur with pepper and ginger before we start, to put him in a lively mood—and *then* doesn't he chase them about if they're a bit mopish!"

Hope certainly had a galvanizing effect upon the dancers; as he slunk and bounded among them, their leaps and gyrations had the frenzy of a tarantella; sometimes he turned and made a sudden snarling foray among the musicians, which produced a wild flurry of extra discords and double drum-beats.

"Here, puss, puss! Nice pussy, then! There's a lady here who'd like to stroke you."

Hope turned, and silently sprang in their direction. Miss Lestrange had her first good look at him. He was bigger than a leopard, a brownish-ginger colour all over, with a long, angrily switching tail; his fangs glistened white-gold in the fiery light, his eyes blazed like carbuncles; he came towards Miss Lestrange slowly, stalking, with head lowered.

And she put out her right hand, confidently running it over his shoulder-blades and along the curving, knobbed spine; its bristles undulated under the light pressure. "There, then!" she said absently. Hope turned, and rubbed his harsh ruff against her hand; elevated his chin to be scratched; finally sat down beside her and swung the long tail neatly into place over formidable talons.

Miss Lestrange thoughtfully pulled his ears; she had always liked cats.

She turned to the leader again.

"I still don't think much of your dancers. And, to be honest, your music seems to me nothing but a diabolical row!"

Silence followed her words. She felt the dark cavities in their faces trained on her, and forced herself not to shrink.

"However, thank you for playing to me. And now I must be going," she ended politely.

"Dear me." The leader's tone was thoughtful. "That fairly puts us in our place, don't it, boys and girls? You certainly are a free-spoken one, Miss January Lestrange. Come now— I'm sure a nice lady, a dyed-in-the-wool lady like you, wouldn't want to be too hard on the lads, and *really* upset them. Just before you go—if— you *do* go—tell me, don't you think that, in time, if they practise hard enough, they might amount to something?"

"I am absolutely not prepared to make such a statement," Miss Lestrange said firmly. "Your kind of music is quite outside my province. And I have never believed in flattery." A kind of rustle ran through the group; they moved closer.

"Our kind of music ain't her province," the leader said. "That's true. Tell you what, Miss Lestrange. *You* shall give *us* a tune. Let's have some of *your* kind of music—eh? That'd be a treat for us, wouldn't it, gang?"

They guffawed, crowding closer and closer; she bit her lip.

"Fetch over the harp!" bawled Nick. "No one in our ensemble actually plays it," he explained to Miss Lestrange. "But we like to have one along always—you never know when someone may turn up who's a harp fancier. Like you. No strings, I'm afraid, but we can fix that, easy."

A warped, battered, peeling old harp was dumped down before her; it had no strings, but one of the dancers dragged up a coil of what looked like telephone cable and began rapidly stringing it to and fro across the frame.

"Now," said Nick, "you shall delight us, Miss Lestrange! And if you *do,* then maybe we'll see about allowing you to leave. Really, you know, we'd hate to part from you."

An expectant silence had fallen: an unpleasant, mocking, triumphant silence.

"I haven't the least intention of playing that ridiculous instrument," Miss Lestrange said coldly. "And now, I'm afraid you'll have to excuse me; my friend will be wondering where I've got to. Come, Hope."

She turned and walked briskly to the entrance of the court; there was no need to push her way, they parted before her. Hope trotted at her side.

Far off, down Hell Passage, could be heard a faint, clear whistle, coming her way.

But, once out in the alley, Miss Lestrange tottered, and nearly fell; she was obliged to put a hand against the wall to support herself. Seized with a deep chill and trembling, she was afraid to trust her unsteady legs, and had to wait until the boy David reached her, whistling and zig-zagging along on his rollerskates.

"Coo, Miss Lestrange, I *knew* you'd get lost; and you did, didn't you? Thought I'd better come back and see where you'd got to. You all right?" he said, sharply scrutinizing her face.

"Yes, thank you, David. I'm quite all right now. I just went a bit farther than I intended. I'm a little tired, that's all."

She glanced back into Old Nick's Court. It was empty: empty and silent. The flares had gone out.

"Well, come on then, Miss Lestrange, just you follow me and I'll take you back to the other lady's car. You can hold on to my anorak if you like," he suggested.

"That's all right, thank you, David, I can manage now."

So he skated slowly ahead and she walked after him, and a little way in the rear Hope followed, trotting silently in the shadows.

When they came within view of the car—it took a very short time, really—David said, "I'll say goodnight then, Miss Lestrange. See you Thursday."

"Good night, David, and thank you." Then she called after him: "Practise hard, now!"

"Okay, Miss Lestrange."

There was an ambulance drawn up behind the car.

"Wait there!" she said to Hope. He sat down in the shadows of the alley-mouth.

As Miss Lestrange crossed the road, the ambulance rolled off. Dr Smith stood looking after it.

"Sorry to be such a time," she said. "That poor man—I'm afraid he's not going to make it."

"You mean—Tom Rampisham?"

"I shouldn't be surprised if he dies on the way in. Oh—excuse me a moment—I'll have to lock up his flat and give the key to the porter."

Without thinking about it, Miss Lestrange followed her ex-pupil. She walked into the untidy room that she had last entered—how long? thirty years ago?—and looked at the table, covered with scrawled sheets of paper.

"I don't know who ought to take charge of this," Dr Smith said, frowning. "I suppose he has a next-of-kin somewhere. Well—I'll worry about that tomorrow. Come along—*you* must be starving and exhausted—let's go."

Miss Lestrange was looking at the top sheet, at the heading HOPE, which was printed in large capitals. Halfway down the page a sentence began.

"It was on a clear, frosty November evening, not many years ago . . ."

The words tailed off into a blob of ink.

Dr Smith led the way out. "It's terribly late. We can still get a meal at the Chinese place, though," she was saying. "And afterwards I'll phone up Rumbury Central and find out how—and find out. I really am sorry to have kept you so long. I hope you weren't frozen and bored."

"No . . . No. I—I went for a walk."

Miss Lestrange followed the doctor along the echoing concrete passage. And as she went—"I do hope," she was thinking, "oh, I do *hope* that Hope will still be there."

More Than You Bargained For

Once there was a little girl called Ermine Miggs, who lived with her mother in a flat in Southampton Row. Her real name was Erminetrude, but that was too long for anyone to pronounce. Her mother went out to work every day except Sundays, but Ermine was not strong, so she did not go to school. In the winter she sat in the big front room by the warm, popping gas fire and read and read and read. In the summer she used to wander along Theobalds Road, Lambs Conduit Street, Great Ormond Street and the Grays Inn Road, or sit in Russell Square or Lincoln's Inn Fields.

They were very poor—the furniture in the flat consisted of a tin box, a home-made table, a stool and a bed, and they had painted the floor green to do for a carpet, but they were happy; they had enough to eat, the gas fire to sit by, hot water for baths, and the sun shone into their window; moreover there was a fig tree across the street in a bit of garden behind a wall, and in the summer Ermine used to drag the bed up to the window and lie there looking at it. Their greatest treasure was an old gramophone and half a dozen records which they played again and again; Mrs. Miggs when she was ironing or mending and Ermine when she was by herself in the flat and feeling lonely. The only thing she did long for was a cat to keep her company, but Mrs. Miggs said that it was unkind to keep a cat where there was no grass for it, so Ermine had to do without. She always stopped to stroke the black cat in the ABC, the tortoise-shell in the grocery, the kitten in the laundry and the putty-coloured cat in the bicycle shop.

It was a hot, dusty May. Everything seemed very grimy. Layers of soot settled more quickly on the window ledges because of the lack of wind, and the pavements looked dirty because it had not rained for weeks. People went about saying how they longed to get away from London into the country. Ermine and her mother did not wish it. They liked London in the summer, and Ermine, in any case, had never been in the country and did not know what it was like at all.

They kept the flat cool and clean with the floor scrubbed and the curtains drawn, and a bunch of radishes soaking in a blue bowl of water, ready for anyone who came in to take a cool peppery bite. Ermine used to take an apple and some cheese, and twopence to buy ice-cream, and go out for the whole day into one or another of the squares or the cool galleries of the British Museum.

One evening as she was coming home under the dusty blue dome of sky she found a dirty-looking shilling lying on a path in Bloomsbury Square. She took it home and left it to soak in the radish-bowl (when they had eaten all the radishes).

"You'd better keep it," said her mother. "It's your birthday in a few days and I'm afraid you won't be getting any present except a new shirt, and that you need anyway."

Ermine polished the shilling with the dishcloth, wondering what she should do with it—there were so many different possibilities. A shilling would buy quite a few books off a twopenny or threepenny stall in the Charing Cross Road—but in a way it was wasteful to buy books when she could get them at the Public Library for nothing. Or she could go on a river trip or a long bus ride, or wander round Woolworth's and find half a dozen pretty trifles.

On her birthday she put on the new blue shirt, polished her sandals, took her apple and the special birthday cream cheese which her mother had left for her and went out into the hot May day. She ate her lunch in Russell Square and then strolled down to the little streets south of the British Museum where there are all sorts of odd small shops selling secondhand books and antiques. She spent an hour or so browsing through dirty old books and looking at twisted Persian slippers, little brass figures from Burma, Italian powder horns, Egyptian wall hangings and many other things, without finding anything that she wanted.

She was delving in a box of articles marked "Ninepence" outside a shop in Museum Street when she felt a pain in her finger as if something had jabbed it. She withdrew her hand hurriedly—it must have been pricked by an old brooch or pin —and stood sucking it. Then she noticed something covered with bright beads underneath the heap of bric-à-brac. She pulled it out. It was a little snake, about a foot long, worked all over with tiny glass beads—red, blue and black. On its stomach the black beads were formed into letters which read: "Turkish Prisoners, 1917."

"What a queer creature," thought Ermine, dangling it between her hands. She did not quite like it, but somehow it interested her.

"Do you want the snake, dear?" said a brisk little sandy-haired woman, coming to the door of the shop.

"I don't think so, thank you," Ermine answered.

"It's a real bargain—you won't often find a thing like that for ninepence."

"No, I think I won't, just the same, thank you."

"Well put it back in the box then," the woman snapped angrily, and went inside. Ermine could see her looking through the window, and hurriedly moved on to the next shop which sold secondhand gramophone records.

"Of course," she thought, "I'll get a record—something we've never heard before. Then it will be a surprise for Mother as well."

She stooped over the box marked 1/- and started looking slowly through the records, twisting her head about to read the titles which always seemed to be upside down. Most of the records looked rather battered, and some were bent or cracked, but one seemed to be brand-new—it was clean and glossy and its paper case was uncrumpled. Ermine studied the title. It was a concerto grosso for oboe and orchestra by Mr. Handel. The name was unfamiliar to her, but she preferred that—it would be more of a surprise, and it would take them longer to learn it. She was standing half-decided, holding her shilling, when a man came out from inside the shop with a huge stack of records in his arms. All of a sudden they began to slip different ways, and the whole pile would have crashed on to the pavement had not Ermine jumped forward and steadied them with both hands.

"Thank you duck," said the man. "That wouldn't have done, would it? They're a lot of junk but still, no one wants broken records all over the street. Just help me tip them into the two-and-sixpenny box would you? That's the stuff."

"May I have this one, please?" Ermine said, going back to the shilling box and pulling out her concerto grosso.

"Ah, you've found yourself something nice there," said the man cheerfully. "I guess that one slipped in out of the five bob box by mistake—however, that's my lookout. But you can reckon you've got quite a bargain."

"I'm glad of that," said Ermine, following him in to the shop. "It's my birthday present."

"Is it then? Well, you treat it carefully and it'll last you for plenty of birthdays. I'll tell you what—seeing you've saved me the trouble of sweeping fifty records off the pavement, I'll give you some fibre needles. And a sharpener, as it's your birthday."

"Oh, thank you *very* much," said Ermine, overwhelmed, as he handed her the two parcels.

"Now don't run home with it—walk."

"I shouldn't dream of playing it until Mother gets home anyway," she replied with dignity. He laughed. "Goodbye, and thank you—it *was* kind of you to give me these."

Towards tea-time she walked slowly and happily home, hugging her presents. The sun was still very hot, and it was pleasant to go into the cool, curtained flat and wash her dusty hands and feet. She cut some bread and butter, made lemonade in a jug, and then carefully undid the record and put it on the turntable, wound the gramophone and put in one of the new needles, all ready for her mother's arrival.

Soon she heard a quick footstep on the stairs, and Mrs. Miggs came in saying: "Ouf, isn't it hot. Had a nice birthday, lovey? What did you get yourself?"

"A new record—and the man gave me some needles and a sharpener because it's my birthday; wasn't it nice of him? And it was really a five-shilling one anyway, got into the shilling box. It's all ready to play while we're having tea."

"Shan't be a second then—I must wash and I'll be with you. Oh, lovely, you've made cress sandwiches."

She was back in a moment with a tiny birthday cake decorated with pink candles and silver balls.

"There you are dearie—I made it last night when you were asleep."

"Oh *Mother*—"

"Come on, goose—let's hear this record."

As soon as Ermine put the needle down and the disk began to revolve, a strange thing happened.

Ermine found herself walking down a steep, narrow lane, in between two high walls. At the bottom of the lane she crossed a cobbled road and came to another wall in which there was a door. She opened the door, and passing through found herself in a garden. There were tall trees close at hand, interspersed with holly bushes. A little path led among them, and following it she came to a wide lawn, with a stone terrace at one end and a pool at the other. Beyond the pool was a hedge and an arched gateway with a glimpse of bright flowers through it. Ermine went this way and found a little formal garden with brick paths and all sorts of sweet-smelling flowers whose names she did not know, besides roses and wallflowers and others which she remembered seeing in flower shops. Another archway led from the paved garden to a smaller lawn, in the centre of which grew a huge tree, all covered with blossom. Ermine thought it was an apple tree, but she had never seen one so large. She started to cross the grass to it, but at that moment the music slowed down and came to an end.

Ermine rubbed her eyes in bewilderment, and looked at the record, lying quietly on its turntable.

"Goodness," said her mother. "That music made me think of all sorts of things I haven't remembered for years. I was in such a dream I never even noticed you turn over."

"I didn't turn over." But when Ermine looked at the record the uppermost side was numbered "2." "It must have turned itself—we certainly started it on the right side."

"What a curious record," said her mother. "And only a shilling—there's a bargain for you. Come on now—cut your cake."

Ermine wondered if her mother had seen the garden too, but did not quite like to ask her.

Later on in the evening when Mrs. Miggs was having a bath Ermine played the record again, and exactly the same thing happened. She walked down the alley between the walls, went across the road and through the door, under the trees, and then wandered about in the garden. She went a different way this time, past a lily pond and a little brick-paved stream with forget-me-nots trailing on its banks, but as before, finally came to the lawn with the great apple tree on it, and as before, was just starting to cross the grass when the music ceased. She looked at the record. It was on its second side.

Next day she went back to the shop and told the man how much they had enjoyed it.

"Glad you liked it," he said. "Come in and have a look round any time you like, and a chat. Always pleased to see friends in the shop."

As Ermine left, her eye was caught again by the little bead-covered snake in the box next door. She glanced down at it, and then looked up to see the woman staring at her in an unfriendly manner through the window. She went hastily on.

That evening she told her mother about the woman and the snake.

"Funny to be so cross just because you didn't buy it," commented Mrs. Miggs. "Ninepence wouldn't make much difference to her, you'd think. But I expect the people who keep those curio shops do get rather odd—it's only natural when you think that they spend their lives among stuffed crocodiles and the like. Let's play your record again—I've taken a great fancy to it."

Goodness knows how many times Ermine played her record over during the next month or two. She never tired of it, and every time she played it, it performed its trick of turning over in the middle without any help—only Ermine never saw this happen because by that time she was in the garden, finding some new path to walk down, or some new flower to examine. On the hottest days she had only to wind the gramophone, place the needle on the disk, and at once be transported to the shade of those trees and the spreading green of the great lawn. The apple tree gradually shed its blossom in a pale carpet on the grass and small green apples formed. More roses came out, and the narcissi withered.

In London it grew hotter. Ermine became disinclined to go out, and spent more and more time indoors listening to the record. One afternoon she had only been as far as the bottom of Southampton Row to buy a lettuce, but when she came home her head ached and she could hardly drag herself up the stairs.

"You look feverish, dearie," said her mother. "Better go to bed. Goodness, your head is as hot as fire."

Ermine gratefully climbed in between the cold sheets, but she could not get comfortable. She seemed to ache all over, and the bed soon became hot and tangled. She moved about miserably, listening to the lorries rattling past outside; it seemed to become dark all of a sudden, though of course the street lamps were shining on the ceiling.

"Try to keep still," her mother's voice said. "Would you like some music? Do you think that would help you to sleep?"

"Oh yes," Ermine answered eagerly. Now she was going down the walled lane. It was dark, and a single lamp threw leaf-shadows across the road at the bottom.

When she reached the garden she saw bright moonlight falling across the lawns. She wandered for some time in and out of the shadows and at length came to the apple tree. She could dimly distinguish green apples the size of plums hanging among the leaves. Below them something glittered. She crossed the grass (which she had never been able to do before) and then stood drenched with icy fear. A great serpent was twined round the trunk of the tree, gazing at her with ruby-coloured eyes. The moonlight struck on it here and there, and she could see that it was striped and barred, red, black and blue. She opened her mouth to shriek but no sound came out; it was like a nightmare. And then, thank heaven, the music stopped and she was back in her hot bed, tossing and turning.

"The snake, the snake!" she said desperately, but her mouth seemed to be clogged with fur, and her tongue was as large as a football.

"What snake, lovey?" she heard her mother say, and then she was swept off into red-hot darkness. People came and went, her mother and a doctor; drinks and medicine were trickled between her lips, darkness alternated with light. Sometimes she was tormented by a glimpse of apples, hanging in cool clusters among leaves, sometimes she saw a huge snake spiralling round and round like a catherine wheel on the gramophone and playing a jangling tinny tune. Sometimes everything vanished altogether and she was only conscious of her aching self.

One day she began to get better and sat propped up on pillows sipping chicken broth.

"Well, you gave us a fright," said her mother, who looked pale and thin, but cheerful.

"I had a fright too," Ermine answered slowly, thinking of the snake. Speech was tiring, and she lay silent, staring about the room at the dusty golden sunlight. Presently her eyes dropped to the little home-made table by her bed and she gave a faint cry.

"What is it, ducky?" said Mrs. Miggs coming anxiously.

"That snake. How did it get here?"

"Well, when you were feverish—you know you've been ill for three weeks darling—you kept calling out the snake, the snake! and I thought perhaps you were thinking of the one in the shop that you'd told me about. So I went along and bought it in case you were fretting for it."

Fretting for it! Ermine eyed the snake with revulsion. She wanted to cry Take it away! but that would have seemed rude and heartless.

Suddenly a thought struck her.

"Mother!"

"Yes, ducky?"

"You've been here all day?"

"Yes, what about it?"

"But what about your job?"

"Oh, I had to give that up," said Mrs. Miggs lightly. "Never mind, I'll soon get another one when you're better. Don't you fret your head about that."

"But how have you been managing?" Ermine asked mistily,

and then another thing about the room struck her. "The gramophone?"

"Yes, I had to sell it. I'd much rather have you than a gramophone, after all. We'll get another one by and by. Now come along—drink up the last of that soup and off to sleep with you."

It took Ermine a long time to recover. She sat about the flat, thin and weak, looking wearily at her books. Sometimes she took the record out of its paper case and rubbed her finger round it curiously, wondering if she could hear a faint sound of the wind in those trees. She could not help longing to hear it again, though at the same time she dreaded it. Was the snake still twined in the apple tree? Had it been there all the time?

She always put the record back hurriedly if she heard her mother coming.

One day she announced that she was perfectly able to look after herself and was going out to sit in the square.

Mrs. Miggs looked at her searchingly, gave her a quick pat, and said:

"Take care of yourself then. I'll go off and do a bit of job-hunting if you're sure you're all right."

"Quite sure."

The leaves were beginning to hang heavily on the trees, and the grass was yellow and parched. Ermine walked very slowly to a seat in Bloomsbury Square and sank on to it. Her legs felt like skeins of wool.

Everything round her was dead and quiet. People were away on holiday, she supposed, and London was empty. It smelt of tar and dust. She thought of early morning in her garden, the dew thick on uncut grass and apples hanging among the leaves.

Suddenly behind her she heard a faint mew, a tiny note of distress. Turning her head she saw a strange little animal with a head like a cat, but a long thin body and a rusty-coloured coat. When she put out her hand he ran up eagerly and rubbed against it, purring.

"Well, you funny puss," she said, stroking it. "Where do you come from?"

Her finger found a collar, and running it round she came to a little engraved nameplate which said "Adamson" and gave a number in Museum Street.

"I'd better take you home," she said, and picked it up. It seemed quite willing to be carried and sat with its forepaws dangling over her arm, looking alertly round as she walked along Great Russell Street and turned into Museum Street.

When she came to the number on the collar she found to her surprise that it was the record shop.

"Mr. Adamson?" she said.

"Hullo, it's the birthday girl. What's happened to you, though? You've grown, or got thinner or something. And you've brought back Ticky for me—I was beginning to worry about him. You're a fine one, you are," he scolded the cat. "Giving me heart failure like that. I suppose you want some milk. Now *you* sit down *there*—" he moved an armful of sheet music off a backless chair and pushed Ermine gently on to it—"while I give Ticky his milk. Where did you find him?"

"Only in Bloomsbury Square, but he seemed very miserable."

"He's partly mongoose, you see—his granny was one. He's not used to city life and he goes out and gets scared. He's taken a fancy to you, though, I can see. Now, what shall I give you for bringing him back? Like another record? You're fond of Handel, I seem to remember."

"It wouldn't be much use to me now, I'm afraid," she said, laughing a little. "I got ill, and Mother lost her job and had to sell our gramophone."

"A lady selling a gramophone, eh? Rather thin, youngish, dark hair? An old model in a walnut box with a detachable handle?"

He went to the back of the shop and pulled it out from under a typing desk.

"Haven't got rid of it yet, you see. To tell the truth, never thought I would. People won't go for this sort of thing now, all for these automatic pickups with short- and long-playing, though mark you, this has a beautiful tone, one of the best I've heard for a long time. But I could see she wanted to sell it pretty badly, so I thought, Well, why not let it lodge here for a bit. So you've been ill eh? And your ma's out of a job? That won't do. Well now, I'll tell you what. I'll put on my jacket and shut up, because it's closing time anyway, and we'll take this gramophone, which is your reward for bringing back Ticky, and we'll go and call on your ma and have a chat with her."

He began putting up the shutters, slamming them into their grooves.

"Oh, you are kind," said Ermine, her eyes full of tears.

"Nonsense, nonsense. One good turn deserves another. Are we ready now?

"Yes, you take Ticky, he won't be left behind. Southampton Row? Blimey, did your ma come all that way with this?"

It only took them five minutes, though. It was dusk by now, and Ermine saw a crack of light under the flat door which showed that her mother was back. Her footsteps sounded discouraged, though she put on a cheerful smile for Ermine as she said:

"No luck yet, ducky—" Then she saw Mr. Adamson behind, and her expression became inquiring.

"I expect you remember me, Ma'am," he said. "Your daughter did me a good turn this afternoon—brought back my cat that had been missing for two days. So I'm just carrying home her reward, a gramophone I happened to have by me."

Mrs. Miggs's jaw dropped.

"I—I don't know what to say," she began. "You must let me—"

"No, I certainly will not let you."

Ermine noticed that Ticky, whom she still held in her arms, was beginning to get very restless and anxious. She let him jump down, and he raced across to the little bedside table and pounced upon something that lay on it.

"What's he got there?" asked Mr. Adamson anxiously, turning from Mrs. Miggs. "You don't keep pet mice, do you?"

"No, it's the snake," said Ermine, fascinated. "He's tearing it to bits." Tiny beads and bits of stuffing were flying about as Ticky, growling tremendously, worried and gnawed at it.

"Oh, I say, what a shame. I *am* sorry. Here, Ticky, you bad—"

"No, no, don't stop him. It doesn't matter."

The elders fell into talk again. Ermine heard Mr. Adamson say:

"I'm opening another branch in St. Martin's Lane—think you could look after this one for me?" And her mother answered:

"Well it's very kind of you and I'd jump at the chance—"

"Kind? Nonsense. Then that's settled. Here, you, bright-eyes, put that Handel record on the gramophone and let's make sure it's still working."

Ermine was half afraid as she put on the record and wound the handle, but she could not have disobeyed. With the first notes she forgot her fear, for she was walking down the alley and a few red leaves were drifting ahead of her. Smoke from a bonfire hung cloudily among the trees in front. She went through the door in the wall, down the path among the hollies, along beside the lawn and through the paved garden. Then she came to the apple-tree lawn. The tree was weighed down by its heavy golden fruit, but today there was no serpent—not so much as a blue or red glass bead in the grass.

She ran to the tree, and reaching up, felt one of the apples come away, heavy and round, into her hand. Then the music stopped and she came back to herself, blinking, in the familiar room.

"That child's been asleep, I do believe," remarked her mother. "Look how pink her cheeks are."

"If I was asleep," said Ermine, "where did I find this?"

She held out her hand. In it, heavy and round, lay a golden apple.

The People in the Castle

The castle stood on a steep hill above the town. Round the bottom of the hill ran the outer castle wall with a massive gateway, and inside this gate was the doctor's house. People could only approach the castle by going in through his surgery door, out through his garden door, and up a hundred steps; but nobody bothered to do this, because the castle was supposed to be haunted, and in any case who wants to go and see an empty old place falling into ruins? Let the doctor prowl round it himself if he wanted to.

The doctor was thought to be rather odd by the townspeople. He was very young to be so well established, he was always at work writing something, and he was often quite rude to his patients if they took too long about describing their symptoms, and would abruptly tell them to get on and not beat about the bush.

He had arranged his surgery hour in a very businesslike way. The patients sat in rows in the large waiting-room amusing themselves with the illustrated papers or with the view of the castle, which filled up the whole of one window in a quite oppressive manner. Each patient picked up a little numbered card from a box as he arrived and then waited until the doctor rang the bell and flashed his number on the indicator. Then the patient hurried to the surgery, breathlessly recited his symptoms before the doctor grew impatient, received his medicine, dropped his card into another little box, paid for his treatment (or not, after the National Health Service arrived), and hurried out by another door which led straight back to the main castle gateway.

By this means the incoming and outgoing patients were not allowed to become entangled in halls and passageways creating confusion and holding up proceedings. The doctor was not very fond of people, and the sooner he could clear them all out of his house and get back to his writing, the better he was pleased.

One evening there were fewer patients than usual. It was late in October. The wind had been blowing in from the sea all day, but it dropped before sunset, and what leaves remained on the trees were hanging motionless in the clear dusk.

"Is there anyone after you?" the doctor asked old Mrs. Daggs, as he gave her some sardine ointment.

"Just one young lady, a stranger I reckon. Never seen her in the town."

"All right—good night," said the doctor quickly, and opened the door for the old woman, at the same time pressing the buzzer for the next number. Then he thought of a phrase for the paper he was writing on speech impediments and twiddled round in his revolving chair to put it down in the notebook on his desk. He was automatically listening for the sound of the waiting-room door, but as he heard nothing he impatiently pressed the buzzer again, and turning round shouted:

"Come along there."

Then he stopped short, for his last patient had already arrived and was sitting in the upright chair with her hands composedly folded in her lap.

"Oh—sorry," he said. "You must have come in very quietly. I didn't know you were in here."

She inclined her head a little, as if acknowledging his apology. She was very white-faced, with the palest gold hair he had ever seen, hanging in a mass to her shoulders. Even in that dusky room it seemed to shine. Her dress was white, and over it she wore a grey plaid-like cloak, flung round her and fastening on her shoulder.

"What's your trouble?" asked the doctor, reaching for his prescription block.

She was silent.

"Come along for goodness' sake—speak up," he said testily. "We haven't got all night." Then he saw, with surprise and some embarrassment, that she was holding out a slate to him. On it was written:

"I am dumb."

He gazed at her, momentarily as speechless as she, and she gently took the slate back again and wrote on it:

"Please cure me."

It seemed impolite to answer her in speech, almost like taking an unfair advantage. He felt inclined to write his message on the slate too, but he cleared his throat and said:

"I don't know if I can cure you, but come over to the light and I'll examine you." He switched on a cluster of bright lights by his desk, and she obediently opened her mouth and stood trustfully while he peered and probed with his instruments.

He gave an exclamation of astonishment, for at the back of her mouth he could see something white sticking up. He cautiously pulled it further forward with his forceps and discovered that it was the end of a long piece of cotton wool. He pulled again, and about a foot of it came out of her mouth, but that seemed to be nowhere near the end. He glanced at the girl in astonishment, but as she appeared quite calm he went on pulling, and the stuff kept reeling out of her throat until there was a tangle of it all over the floor.

At last the end came out.

"Can you speak now?" he asked, rather anxiously.

She seemed to be clearing her throat, and presently said with some difficulty:

"A little. My throat is sore."

"Here's something to suck. I'll give you a prescription for that condition—it's a result of pulling out the wool, I'm afraid. This will soon put it right. Get it made up as soon as you can."

He scribbled on a form and handed it to her. She looked at it in a puzzled manner.

"I do not understand."

"It's a prescription," he said impatiently.

"What is that?"

"Good heavens—where *do* you come from?"

She turned and pointed through the window to the castle, outlined on its hill against the green sky.

"From *there?* Who are you?"

"My name is Helen," she said, still speaking in the same husky, hesitant manner. "My father is King up there on the hill." For the first time the doctor noticed that round her pale, shining hair she wore a circlet of gold, hardly brighter than the hair beneath. She was then a princess?

"I had a curse laid on me at birth—I expect you know the sort of thing?" He nodded.

"A good fairy who was there said that I would be cured of my dumbness on my eighteenth birthday by a human doctor."

"Is it your birthday today?"

"Yes. Of course we all knew about you, so I thought I would come to you first." She coughed, and he jumped up and gave her a drink of a soothing syrup, which she took gratefully.

"Don't try to talk too much at first. There's plenty of time. Most people talk too much anyway. I'll have the prescription made up"—"and bring it round," he was going to say, but hesitated. Could one go and call at the castle with a bottle of medicine as if it was Mrs. Daggs?

"Will you bring it?" she said, solving his problem. "My father will be glad to see you."

"Of course. I'll bring it tomorrow evening."

Again she gravely inclined her head, and turning, was gone, though whether by the door or window he could not be sure.

He crossed to the window and stood for some time staring up at the black bulk of the castle on the thorn-covered hill, before returning to his desk and the unfinished sentence. He left the curtains open.

Next morning, if it had not been for the prescription lying on his desk, he would have thought that the incident had been a dream. Even as he took the slip along to Boots to have the medicine made up he wondered if the white-coated woman there would suddenly tell him that he was mad.

That evening dusk was falling as the last of his surgery patients departed. He went down and locked the large gates and then, with a beating heart, started the long climb up the steps to the castle. It was lighter up on the side of the knoll. The thorns and brambles grew so high that he could see nothing but the narrow stairway in front of him. When he reached the top he looked down and saw his own house below, and the town with its crooked roofs running to the foot of the hill, and the river wriggling away to the sea. Then he turned and walked under the arch into the great hall of the castle.

The first thing he noticed was the scent of lime. There was a big lime tree which, in the daytime, grew in the middle of the grass carpeting the great hall. He could not see the tree, but why was a lime tree blossoming in October?

It was dark inside, and he stood hesitating, afraid to step forward into the gloom, when he felt a hand slipped into his. It was a thin hand, very cool; it gave him a gentle tug and he moved forward, straining his eyes to try and make out who was leading him. Then, as if the pattern in a kaleidoscope had cleared, his eyes flickered and he began to see.

There were lights grouped round the walls in pale clusters,

and below them, down the length of the hall, sat a large and shadowy assembly; he could see the glint of light here and there on armour, or on a gold buckle or the jewel in a head-dress as somebody moved.

At the top of the hall, on a dais, sat a royal figure, cloaked and stately, but the shadows lay so thick in between that he could see no more. But his guide plucked him forward; he now saw that it was Helen, in her white dress with a gold belt and bracelets. She smiled at him gravely and indicated that he was to go up and salute the King.

With some vague recollection of taking his degree he made his way to the dais and bowed.

"I have brought the Princess's linctus, Sire," he said, stammering a little.

"We are pleased to receive you and to welcome you to our court. Henceforth come and go freely in this castle whenever you wish."

The doctor reflected that he always *had* come and gone very freely in the castle; however, it hardly seemed the same place tonight, for the drifting smoke from the candles made the hall look far larger.

He lifted up his eyes and took a good look at the King, who had a long white beard and a pair of piercing eyes. Helen had seated herself on a stool at his feet.

"I see you are a seeker after knowledge," said the King suddenly. "You will find a rich treasure-house to explore here— only beware that your knowledge does not bring you grief."

The doctor jumped slightly. He had indeed been thinking that the King looked like some Eastern sage and might have information which the doctor could use in his study on occult medicine.

"I suppose all doctors are seekers after knowledge," he said cautiously, and handed Helen her bottle of medicine. "Take a teaspoonful after meals—or—or three times a day." He was not sure if the people in the castle had meals in the ordinary way, though some kind of feast seemed to be in progress at the moment.

From that time on the doctor often made his way up to the castle after evening had fallen, and sat talking to the King, or to some of the wise and reverend knights who formed his court, or to Helen. During the daytime the castle brooded, solitary and crumbling as always, save for some archaeologist taking pictures for a learned monthly.

On Christmas Eve the doctor climbed up with a box of throat tablets for Helen, who still had to be careful of her voice, and a jar of ointment for the King who had unfortunately developed chilblains as a result of sitting in the chill and draughty hall.

"You really should get him away from here, though I'd miss him," he told Helen. "I don't know how old he is—"

"A thousand—" she interjected.

"—Oh," he said, momentarily taken aback. "Well in any case it really is too damp and cold for him here. And you should take care of your throat too; it's important not to strain it these first months. This castle really is no place for either of you."

She obediently flung a fold of her grey cloak round her neck.

"But we are going away tomorrow," she said. "Didn't you know? From Christmas to Midsummer Day my father holds his court at Avignon."

The doctor felt as if the ground had been cut from under his feet.

"You're going away? You mean you'll none of you be here?"

"No," she answered, looking at him gravely.

"Helen! Marry me and stay with me here. My house is very warm—I'll take care of you, I swear it—" He caught hold of her thin, cold hand.

"Of course I'll marry you," she said at once. "You earned

the right to my hand and heart when you cured me—didn't you know that either?"

She led him to her father and he formally asked for her hand in marriage.

"She's yours," said the King. "I can't prevent it, though I don't say I approve of these mixed marriages. But mind you cherish her—the first unkind word, and she'll vanish like a puff of smoke. That's one thing we *don't* have to put up with from mortal man."

As soon as Helen married the doctor and settled in his house she became a changed creature. The people in the town were surprised and charmed to find what a cheerful, pretty wife their hermit-like doctor had found himself. She left off her magic robes and put on check aprons; she learned to cook and flitted around dusting and tidying; moreover as her newly won voice gathered strength she chattered like a bird and hummed the whole day long over her work.

She abolished the buzzer in the surgery because she said it frightened people. She used to look through the door herself and say:

"The doctor will see you now, Mrs. Jones, and will you try not to keep him waiting please—though I know it's hard for you with your leg. Is it any better, do you think? And how's your husband's chest?"

"She's like a ray of sunshine, bless her," people said.

The doctor was not sure about all this. What he had chiefly loved in her was the sense of magic and mystery; she had been so silent and moved with such stately grace. Still, it was very pleasant to have this happy creature in his house attending to his comfort—only she did talk so. In the daytime it was not so bad, but in the evenings when he wanted to get on with his writing it *was* trying.

By and by he suggested that she might like to go to the cinema, and took her to a Disney. She was enchanted, and after that he was ensured peace and quiet on at least two evenings a week, for she was quite happy to go off by herself and leave him, only begging him not to work too hard.

One night he had nearly finished the chapter on Magic and its Relation to Homeopathic Medicine, and was wishing that he could go up and discuss it with the King. He heard her come in and go to the kitchen to heat the soup for their late supper.

Soon she appeared with a tray.

"It was a Western," she said, her eyes sparkling. "The hero comes riding into this little town, you see, and he pretends he's a horse-dealer but really he's the D.A. in disguise. So he finds that the rustling is being run by the saloon keeper—"

"Oh, for goodness' sake, *must* you talk all the time," snapped the doctor. Then he stopped short and looked at her aghast.

A dreadful change had come over her. The gay print apron and hair ribbon dropped off her and instead he saw her clad in her white and grey robes and wreathed about with all her magic. Even as she held out her hands to him despairingly she seemed to be drawn away and vanished through the thick curtains.

"Helen!" he cried. There was no answer. He flung open the door and ran frantically up the steps to the castle. It was vacant and dark. The grass in the great hall was stiff with frost and the night sky showed pale above him in the roofless tower.

"Helen, Helen," he called, until the empty walls re-echoed, but no one replied. He made his way slowly down the steps again and back to his warm study where the steam was still rising from the two bowls of soup.

From that day the townspeople noticed a change in their doctor. He had been hermit-like before; now he was morose. He kept the castle gates locked except for the surgery hour and disconnected his telephone. No longer was there a pretty wife to tell them that the doctor would see them now; instead they were confronted by a closed door with a little grille, through which they were expected to recite their symptoms. When they had done so, they were told to go round by an outside path to another door, and by the time they reached it they found the necessary pill or powder and written instructions lying outside on the step. So clever was the doctor that even with this unsatisfactory system he still cured all his patients, and indeed it seemed as if he could tell more about a sick person through a closed door than other doctors could face to face; so that although people thought his treatment strange, they went on coming to him.

There were many queer tales about him, and everyone agreed that night after night he was heard wandering in the ruined castle calling "Helen! Helen!" but that no one ever answered him.

Twenty years went by. The doctor became famous for his books, which had earned him honorary degrees in all the universities of the world. But he steadfastly refused to leave his house, and spoke to no one, communicating with the tradespeople by means of notes.

One day as he sat writing he heard a knock on the outer gate, and something prompted him to go down and open it. Outside stood a curious looking little woman in black academic robes and hood, who nodded to him.

"I am Dr. Margaret Spruchsprecher, Rector of the University of Freiherrburg," she said, walking composedly up the path before him and in at his front door. "I have come to give you the degree of Master of Philosophy at our University, as you would not come to us or answer our letters."

He bowed awkwardly and took the illuminated parchment she offered him.

"Would you like a cup of coffee?" he said, finding his voice with difficulty. "I am most honoured that you should come all this way to call on me."

"Perhaps now that I have come so far I can help you," she

said. "You are seeking something, are you not? Something besides knowledge? Something that you think is in the castle, up there on the hill?"

He nodded, without removing his gaze from her. The keen, piercing look in her old eyes reminded him vividly of the King.

"Well! Supposing that all this time, what you seek is not *inside,* but has gone *outside;* supposing that you have been sitting at the mouth of an empty mouse-hole; what then?" There was something brisk, but not unkindly in her laugh as she turned and made off down the path again, clutching the voluminous black robes round herself as the wind blew them about. The gate slammed behind her.

"Wait—" the doctor called and ran after her, but it was too late. She was lost in the crowded High Street.

He went out into the town and wandered distractedly about the streets staring into face after face, in search of he hardly knew what.

"Why, it's the doctor, isn't it," a woman said. "My Teddy's been a different boy since that medicine you gave him, Doctor."

Someone else came up and told him how thankful they were for his advice on boils.

"My husband's never forgotten how you cured his earache when he thought he'd have to throw himself out of the window, the pain was so bad."

"I've always wanted to thank you, Doctor, for what you did when I was so ill with the jaundice—"

"You saved my Jennifer that time when she swallowed the poison—"

The doctor felt quite ashamed and bewildered at the chorus of thanks and greeting which seemed to rise on every side. He finally dived into a large doorway which seemed to beckon him, and sank relieved into a dark and sound-proof interior—the cinema.

For a long time he took no notice of the film which was in progress on the screen, but when he finally looked up his attention was attracted by the sight of galloping horses; it was a Western. All of a sudden the memory of Helen came so suddenly and bitterly into his mind that he nearly cried aloud.

"Excuse me, sir, that's the one and nine's you're sitting in. You should be in the two and three's."

He had no recollection of having bought any ticket, but obediently rose and followed his guide with her darting torch. His eyes were full of tears and he stumbled; she waited until he had caught her up and then gave him a hand.

It was a thin hand, very cool; it gave him a gentle tug. He stood still, put his other hand over it and muttered:

"Helen."

"Hush, you'll disturb people."

"Is it you?"

"Yes. Come up to the back and we can talk."

The cinema was pitch dark and full of people. As he followed her up to the rampart at the back he could feel them all about him.

"Have you been here all these years?"

"All these years?" she whispered, mocking him. "It was only yesterday."

"But I'm an old man, Helen. What are you? I can't see you. Your hand feels as young as ever."

"Don't worry," she said soothingly. "We must wait till this film ends—this is the last reel—and then we'll go up to the castle. My father will be glad to see you again. He likes your books very much."

He was too ashamed to ask her to come back to him, but she went on:

"And you had better come up and live with us in the castle now."

A feeling of inexpressible happiness came over him as he

stood patiently watching the galloping horses and feeling her small, cool hand in his.

Next day the castle gates were found standing ajar, and the wind blew through the open doors and windows of the doctor's house. He was never seen again.

Don't Pay the Postman

Young Miss Wind lived with her father in his cottage on an island north of the Hebrides. It was a lonely life for her, as her mother was dead, and her father, Wind, was out all day, and often all night too, on his work, blowing.

Miss Wind kept the cottage tidy, dusted (which she did very well), knitted warm woolly socks for her father and generally looked after him as far as she was able, cooked the supper and dug in their little patch of garden where nothing would ever grow. Her only possessions were a comb and a gold ring, which had been her mother's. She spent long hours sitting gazing out to sea, wondering what life was like in the south, where she had never been.

The cottage was built of breeze-blocks, with huge windows made from slices of wind, and dark curtains of night-wind for use in the summer when the sun is still shining at midnight in those northern regions. No one ever called there except the postman who visited all the islands in his motor boat. Old Wind did not encourage callers. He could not prevent the postman, who had to bring his licence to blow, certificates of proficiency and other government documents, but he told his daughter never to let the man into the cottage, and that she was not to gossip with him.

Wind was not fond of society. By the time he came home from his work all he wanted to do was fall on his great bed and pass into a sleep so heavy that it took three alarm clocks and Miss Wind with a cup of boiling tea to wake him.

On Sundays he went to be cleaned, for by the end of the week he had collected up so much dust, paper, straws, leaves, bits of wool and general odds and ends, not to mention chimneypots, masts of ships, trees and waterspouts that he was quite choked up and unable to function. The cleaning took all day, and was done backwards and forwards, many times over.

Miss Wind used to find Sunday her loneliest day until she learned about the Sunday paper, and then it was her happiest. She was very fond of reading, but there were no books or magazines in the cottage, as Wind did not hold with them. He said that paper was flimsy, useless stuff and it stood to reason that anything written on it would be useless too. So Miss Wind had to hide her Sunday paper, and when she had read it right the way through she burned it, though very regretfully.

The postman brought the Sunday paper when he made his weekly visit on Saturday afternoon. Miss Wind did not obey her father's rule. She always asked the postman in and gave him a cup of tea. Moreover, she paid him twopence for the paper and another penny for delivery; he had told her that this was the regular fee. This was not the case, but Miss Wind, who lived very much out of the world, believed him. He also told her that the reason for the arrival of the Sunday paper on a Saturday was that, as they were so far north and the sun rose at midnight, their day began before everybody else's. Miss Wind did not quite understand this, but she believed it too.

She always turned first to the Great Fashion Competition and filled in her entry for it while the postman drank his tea. Then she would give him some money for stamps to stick on the completed form and he would take it away when he went. She had never won anything, and this was not surprising for she knew very little about fashion. When the postman had gone she used to read her horoscope. This was the treat of the week. She took it most seriously, and would often become very excited if it said something like:

"A promising social opening this week will mean a widening of your horizon and many new friendships," or

"After a gay and lively week you will need to relax at the weekend," or

"A new business contact will lead to heavy and important responsibilities."

Miss Wind faithfully followed their directions as well as she was able.

One Saturday she was feeling low. Her father had been bad-tempered all week because it was the Equinox and he had extra work to do with the gales and spring tides. Moreover, Miss Wind was beginning to think about the spring-cleaning. She wished that she could get a woman in to help her, but unfortunately there was no one available within fifty miles. She was afraid that her father might decide to help, and find one or two cherished horoscopes which she had not been able to resist cutting out and keeping.

When she heard the chug of the postman's motor boat she put the kettle on for tea and decided that she would cheer herself up by turning to her horoscope first instead of doing the fashion competition.

She saw the postman into his chair, with the sugar bowl beside him, and eagerly turned to page three, looking for the square block in the two middle columns. When she had read through it she looked up with an exclamation of dismay.

"What's up?" asked the postman, drinking his tea.

"It says 'Don't pay the postman who brings you this paper. He is paid by the Government and requires nothing further from you. You will receive a newspaper bill in due course.'"

"Eh? What's that?" said the postman, grabbing the paper from her. When he read it an ugly expression came over his face.

"And I suppose you'll believe a wretched, twopenny paper

rather than me, who's been bringing it regularly all these months."

"I must believe it," replied Miss Wind with dignity, though she was rather frightened. "I always believe my horoscope."

"Anyway it's last week's so it doesn't apply," snapped the postman.

She looked at the date (which she had never thought to do before) and turned pale.

"So you've been deceiving me when you said it was tomorrow's paper," she said slowly. "In that case I certainly shall not continue paying you."

The postman swore in a nasty way, took hold of her wrist before she realized what he was going to do, and snatched off her gold ring. Then he made off with it, shouting:

"That'll pay you out, you miserly little skinflint."

She heard the chug-chug of his boat as she reached the door, and knew she could never hope to catch him.

Wind arrived home early that day, and in a bad temper. He had become quite clogged up with blowing on a fire in a sock factory in Glasgow. He wanted his tea and he wanted to go to bed. When he entered the cottage he found his daughter in tears seated before a fire which was nearly out, surrounded by the pages of the *Sunday Illustrated*. There was no kettle on, no hot scones, no girdle cakes, no kippers.

"What's the meaning of this?" asked Wind furiously.

Poor Miss Wind sobbingly let out the whole story—the postman, the papers, the tea, the horoscopes, the payments, the fashion competitions, and worst of all, the loss of the ring.

As Wind listened his face grew darker and darker, and finally at the end of the recital he gave her a stinging slap on the cheek—the sort that you feel when you go out in a northeast gale.

"This is a pretty kettle of fish!" he said. "I knew how it would be if you let anyone into the house. Here's this fellow been cheating you out of threepence every week—I don't suppose the newsagents saw a penny of it—not to mention the entry money for the competitions—and now he's got away with your mother's ring. Perhaps you'll obey my orders another time. Now leave the house, and don't come back unless you have the ring with you—and take that disgusting trash out of my sight."

Poor Miss Wind picked up her Sunday paper and wrapped her comb and some oatcakes in it. Then she went down to the anchorage where she kept her little boat, for she guessed that the postman would never come back to the island, and if she wanted the ring she would have to go after him.

Wind raged furiously round the house trying to light the fire. He blew so hard that a great clot of half-burned socks, which had been stopping him up, suddenly flew out and finished off the fire completely. That made him angrier than ever, and he determined to go in search of the postman himself. He set off across the islands, and by pure chance met the postman's motor boat just rounding a promontory. Wind pounced on him, intending to grab the ring, but the man had it in his pocket. The motor boat capsized, the wicked postman was drowned, and the ring was lost.

Then Wind was sorry, and went looking for his daughter to tell her to come home again and cook his supper, but she was nowhere to be seen.

Miss Wind had gone in quite the other direction, and was rowing her boat slowly south. She felt very sad. Her father was angry, she had lost her ring, and she had been following the wrong horoscope every week. She felt that she had nothing left but the fashion competition, so in order to cheer herself a little she turned over the scattered pages of her paper until she found it, and set seriously to work, trying to judge the merits of twelve different hair styles.

Miss Wind had quite a lot of hair herself, of a strange, silvery colour. She never wore it in any particular *style,* merely keeping it combed and wishing that she could cut it short—

but she had no scissors. So she gazed with interest at the different pictures of curled hair, waved hair, upswept hair, downswept hair, and sideswept hair. The last picture was one which particularly took her fancy; it was short and comfortable-looking, not too tidy (she had such difficulty in keeping her own hair tidy) and the caption underneath was "Windswept." That decided her; she unhesitatingly put a cross under it and wished that she had some stamps, or some money to buy them.

These reflections had taken time, and when she looked over her shoulder she found that she was approaching the mainland. A row of mountains stood up out of the sea, and at the foot of them was a little fishing village.

"Hey there, are you a mermaid?" somebody called, and she saw a young fisherman bobbing in a boat nearby.

"No I am not," she replied with dignity. "My name is Miss Wind and I am looking for the postman. Can you assist me?"

"I'm afraid you're unlucky, Miss," he said. "The postman was drowned in a gale this afternoon off Point Ness."

"Oh dear," exclaimed Miss Wind.

"I shouldn't worry," the fisherman consoled her. "He was a bad lot. Been taking money out of the registered envelopes for years. He's no loss."

"No, but he had my ring in his pocket," said Miss Wind sadly. "Now I shall never get it back."

"Oh I don't know. Rings often turn up inside fish. You stay around in Port Lomas for a while, and it's odds someone finds your ring in a herring."

"Is this Port Lomas?"

"Yes it is. My dad keeps the fish shop."

A fat man in a white apron appeared in a door and stuck up a notice which said "Frying Tonight." When he saw them he shouted:

"Jock! The fan's gone wrong again."

"That's bad," said Jock gloomily. "I've no more repair

parts left. It's the fan we use for cooling the fish," he explained to Miss Wind.

"Perhaps I could do it instead," she suggested. "I'm very good at blowing."

They agreed to take her on temporarily until the fan was mended, and Mrs. Andrews, the fishmonger's wife, let Miss Wind have a room. Her pay was five shillings a week.

Miss Wind liked her work, and the Andrews family took a great fancy to her. Mr. Andrews started teaching her to play the bagpipes, and Mrs. Andrews helped her fill in and post her fashion competition entry.

Unfortunately the time came when the fan was mended, and then Miss Wind was out of a job. There were only two other shops in Port Lomas, a butcher and a baker. The butcher kept his meat in a huge refrigerator, and the baker heated his oven by means of an electric bellows, so neither of them needed Miss Wind's services; moreover, the baker said that Miss Wind's presence in the bakehouse was enough to make the dough sink.

Luckily the Provost, who had seen her at work in the fishmonger's, offered her a job as a street cleaner. It was not very well paid, but she did not mind; she tied up her hair in a blue and white cloth to keep out the dust and toffee papers, and much enjoyed seeing all the people go by and saying good morning to them.

One day she was working hard clearing away a lot of confetti left over from a wedding when the sky became black, and looking up she saw her father standing with arms folded and regarding her in a very awful manner.

"So this is where you have got to! What is the meaning of employing yourself in the public streets in this manner?" he said.

"Well," replied Miss Wind with spirit, for she was no longer the timid little thing she had been when she lived at home, "you turned me out, so I had to earn my own living."

"It is quite out of the question for you to do it in *this* way," said Wind. "You have no training, no diploma, no certificate, no licence to blow, and you are not a union member. You had better come home right away before the union gets to hear about this."

"I don't want to come home—it's too dull—besides I haven't found the ring yet. And I like street cleaning, and I do it just as well as anybody else."

"That is not the point," pronounced Wind. "Are you coming home or not?"

"Not."

Wind flung his plaid round him and stalked off to the post office without another word. His daughter placidly continued removing the bits of confetti and sweet papers from the pavement.

Wind sent telegrams, saying that a non-union cleaner was operating in Port Lomas, to the Amalgamated Union of Trade Winds, the International Transport, Propulsion and Motivation Workers' Union (a somewhat sluggish union generally known as the Doldrums), the Federated Roaring Forties (a progressive splinter group), the Sirocco, Simoon and Mistral Co-operative Union, and the North-East Trades Council.

As a result of these telegrams the various wind unions met and decided to work to rule. This meant that there was just enough wind to encourage housewives to hang out their washing, but not enough to dry it; enough wind to get yachtsmen out on the water but not enough to move them; enough wind to persuade farmers to cut their grass, but not enough to make hay.

Still Miss Wind went on with her job. She did not see why she should stop for a lot of unions, though she was visited by dozens of shop stewards who tried to persuade her to stop, and picketed by breezes, light airs, gusts, eddies and capfuls of wind who got in her way and tried to hinder her work.

Then a general strike of wind was decided on, and this was more serious.

Poor Miss Wind began to get beseeching letters: from drought-parched farmers in California who saw rain-clouds in the next valley which never moved; from ship-owners; from millers; from the Lord Mayor of London to say that the city was enveloped in a dark cloud of smog and people would soon be dying of it; from gliding clubs; from children who could not fly their kites; from directors of airlines; all imploring her to leave her job and allow the winds of the world to get started again.

In the end she gave in. With tears in her eyes she pounced on her last bit of newspaper and then started slowly back to her digs at the Andrews's. As she came within sight of the door she saw them all there, jumping up and down and waving.

"You've won it, lass!" shrieked Mrs. Andrews. "You've won the hair-style competition."

A fat agreeable man came forward, said he was from the *Sunday Illustrated,* and presented her with a cheque for £500.

"May I ask how you will use it?" he asked, whipping out his notebook.

"I shall start a hairdressing establishment in Port Lomas," replied Miss Wind at once. "I already have a comb and an interest in hair (not to mention waves) and I can do the drying myself; there is no hairdresser's for two hundred miles so I shall have plenty of custom."

This plan proved most popular and in no time Miss Wind was doing a roaring trade, creating newer and more elegant windswept styles, larger and more permanent waves.

A week after she was installed young Jock Andrews came into the shop with something in his hand.

"Guess what I found inside a herring?" he said.

"My ring," answered Miss Wind at once. She took it from him and put it in a registered envelope, addressing it to Wind,

Esq. "I hope the new postman is more reliable than the last one."

"Aren't you going to go back and live at home?"

"When I'm so happy here? Not likely. I'll visit Father on my half days and do a bit of cleaning for him."

"How about marrying me?" suggested Jock Andrews, pulling another ring out of his pocket.

So she married him and they lived happily ever after. If custom was ever slack, she went out with her husband in his smack and blew him along, and every August they went for their holiday to stay with Wind in the little house built of breeze-blocks.

The Third Wish

Once there was a man who was driving in his car at dusk on a spring evening through part of the forest of Savernake. His name was Mr. Peters. The primroses were just beginning but the trees were still bare, and it was cold; the birds had stopped singing an hour ago.

As Mr. Peters entered a straight, empty stretch of road he seemed to hear a faint crying, and a struggling and thrashing, as if somebody was in trouble far away in the trees. He left his car and climbed the mossy bank beside the road. Beyond the bank was an open slope of beech trees leading down to thorn bushes through which he saw the gleam of water. He stood a moment waiting to try and discover where the noise was coming from, and presently heard a rustling and some strange cries in a voice which was almost human—and yet there was something too hoarse about it at one time and too clear and sweet at another. Mr. Peters ran down the hill and as he neared the bushes he saw something white among them which was trying to extricate itself; coming closer he found that it was a swan that had become entangled in the thorns growing on the bank of the canal.

The bird struggled all the more frantically as he approached, looking at him with hate in its yellow eyes, and when he took hold of it to free it, hissed at him, pecked him, and thrashed dangerously with its wings which were powerful enough to break his arm. Nevertheless he managed to release

it from the thorns, and carrying it tightly with one arm, holding the snaky head well away with the other hand (for he did
not wish his eyes pecked out), he took it to the verge of the
canal and dropped it in.

The swan instantly assumed great dignity and sailed out to
the middle of the water, where it put itself to rights with much
dabbling and preening, smoothing its feathers with little showers of drops. Mr. Peters waited, to make sure that it was all
right and had suffered no damage in its struggles. Presently
the swan, when it was satisfied with its appearance, floated in
to the bank once more, and in a moment, instead of the great
white bird, there was a little man all in green with a golden
crown and long beard, standing by the water. He had fierce
glittering eyes and looked by no means friendly.

"Well, Sir," he said threateningly, "I see you are presump-
tuous enough to know some of the laws of magic. You think
that because you have rescued—by pure good fortune—the
King of the Forest from a difficulty, you should have some
fabulous reward."

"I expect three wishes, no more and no less," answered Mr.
Peters, looking at him steadily and with composure.

"Three wishes, he wants, the clever man! Well, I have yet
to hear of the human being who made any good use of his
three wishes—they mostly end up worse off than they started.
Take your three wishes then—" he flung three dead leaves in
the air "—don't blame me if you spend the last wish in un-
doing the work of the other two."

Mr. Peters caught the leaves and put two of them carefully
in his notecase. When he looked up the swan was sailing about
in the middle of the water again, flicking the drops angrily
down its long neck.

Mr. Peters stood for some minutes reflecting on how he
should use his reward. He knew very well that the gift of three
magic wishes was one which brought trouble more often than
not, and he had no intention of being like the forester who

first wished by mistake for a sausage, and then in a rage wished it on the end of his wife's nose, and then had to use his last wish in getting it off again. Mr. Peters had most of the things which he wanted and was very content with his life. The only thing that troubled him was that he was a little lonely, and had no companion for his old age. He decided to use his first wish and to keep the other two in case of an emergency. Taking a thorn he pricked his tongue with it, to remind himself not to utter rash wishes aloud. Then holding the third leaf and gazing round him at the dusky undergrowth, the primroses, great beeches and the blue-green water of the canal, he said:

"I wish I had a wife as beautiful as the forest."

A tremendous quacking and splashing broke out on the surface of the water. He thought that it was the swan laughing at him. Taking no notice he made his way through the darkening woods to his car, wrapped himself up in the rug and went to sleep.

When he awoke it was morning and the birds were beginning to call. Coming along the track towards him was the most beautiful creature he had ever seen, with eyes as blue-green as the canal, hair as dusky as the bushes, and skin as white as the feathers of swans.

"Are you the wife that I wished for?" asked Mr. Peters.

"Yes I am," she replied. "My name is Leita."

She stepped into the car beside him and they drove off to the church on the outskirts of the forest, where they were married. Then he took her to his house in a remote and lovely valley and showed her all his treasures—the bees in their white hives, the Jersey cows, the hyacinths, the silver candlesticks, the blue cups and the lustre bowl for putting primroses in. She admired everything, but what pleased her most was the river which ran by the foot of his garden.

"Do swans come up here?" she asked.

"Yes, I have often seen swans there on the river," he told her, and she smiled.

Leita made him a good wife. She was gentle and friendly, busied herself about the house and garden, polished the bowls, milked the cows and mended his socks. But as time went by Mr. Peters began to feel that she was not happy. She seemed restless, wandered much in the garden, and sometimes when he came back from the fields he would find the house empty and she would only return after half an hour or so with no explanation of where she had been. On these occasions she was always especially tender and would put out his slippers to warm and cook his favourite dish—Welsh rarebit with wild strawberries—for supper.

One evening he was returning home along the river path when he saw Leita in front of him, down by the water. A swan had sailed up to the verge and she had her arms round its neck and the swan's head rested against her cheek. She was weeping, and as he came nearer he saw that tears were rolling, too, from the swan's eyes.

"Leita, what is it?" he asked, very troubled.

"This is my sister," she answered. "I can't bear being separated from her."

Now he understood that Leita was really a swan from the forest, and this made him very sad because when a human being marries a bird it always leads to sorrow.

"I could use my second wish to give your sister human shape, so that she could be a companion to you," he suggested.

"No, no," she cried, "I couldn't ask that of her."

"Is it so very hard to be a human being?" asked Mr. Peters sadly.

"Very, very hard," she answered.

"Don't you love me at all, Leita?"

"Yes, I do, I do love you," she said, and there were tears in her eyes again. "But I miss the old life in the forest, the cool grass and the mist rising off the river at sunrise and the feel of the water sliding over my feathers as my sister and I drifted along the stream."

"Then shall I use my second wish to turn you back into a swan again?" he asked, and his tongue pricked to remind him of the old King's words, and his heart swelled with grief inside him.

"Who would darn your socks and cook your meals and see to the hens?"

"I'd do it myself as I did before I married you," he said, trying to sound cheerful.

She shook her head. "No, I could not be as unkind to you as that. I am partly a swan, but I am also partly a human being now. I will stay with you."

Poor Mr. Peters was very distressed on his wife's account and did his best to make her life happier, taking her for drives in the car, finding beautiful music for her to listen to on the radio, buying clothes for her and even suggesting a trip round the world. But she said no to that; she would prefer to stay in their own house near the river.

He noticed that she spent more and more time baking wonderful cakes—jam puffs, petits fours, éclairs and meringues. One day he saw her take a basketful down to the river and he guessed that she was giving them to her sister.

He built a seat for her by the river, and the two sisters spent hours together there, communicating in some wordless manner. For a time he thought that all would be well, but then he saw how thin and pale she was growing.

One night when he had been late doing the accounts he came up to bed and found her weeping in her sleep and calling:

"Rhea! Rhea! I can't understand what you say! Oh, wait for me, take me with you!"

Then he knew that it was hopeless and she would never be happy as a human. He stooped down and kissed her goodbye, then took another leaf from his notecase, blew it out of the window, and used up his second wish.

Next moment instead of Leita there was a sleeping swan lying across the bed with its head under its wing. He carried it out of the house and down to the brink of the river, and then he said "Leita! Leita!" to waken her, and gently put her into the water. She gazed round her in astonishment for a moment, and then came up to him and rested her head lightly against his hand; next instant she was flying away over the trees towards the heart of the forest.

He heard a harsh laugh behind him, and turning round saw the old King looking at him with a malicious expression.

"Well, my friend! You don't seem to have managed so wonderfully with your first two wishes, do you? What will you do with the last? Turn yourself into a swan? Or turn Leita back into a girl?"

"I shall do neither," said Mr. Peters calmly. "Human beings and swans are better in their own shapes."

But for all that he looked sadly over towards the forest where Leita had flown, and walked slowly back to his empty house.

Next day he saw two swans swimming at the bottom of the garden, and one of them wore the gold chain he had given Leita after their marriage; she came up and rubbed her head against his hand.

Mr. Peters and his two swans came to be well known in that part of the country; people used to say that he talked to the swans and they understood him as well as his neighbours. Many people were a little frightened of him. There was a story that once when thieves tried to break into his house they were set upon by two huge white birds which carried them off bodily and dropped them in the river.

As Mr. Peters grew old everyone wondered at his contentment. Even when he was bent with rheumatism he would not think of moving to a drier spot, but went slowly about his work, milking the cows and collecting the honey and eggs, with the two swans always somewhere close at hand.

Sometimes people who knew his story would say to him:

"Mr. Peters, why don't you wish for another wife?"

"Not likely," he would answer serenely. "Two wishes were enough for me, I reckon. I've learned that even if your wishes are granted they don't always better you. I'll stay faithful to Leita."

One autumn night, passers-by along the road heard the mournful sound of two swans singing. All night the song went on, sweet and harsh, sharp and clear. In the morning Mr. Peters was found peacefully dead in his bed with a smile of great happiness on his face. In between his hands, which lay clasped on his breast, were a withered leaf and a white feather.

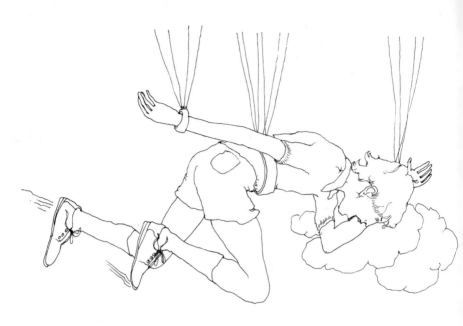

Pigeon Cake for Miss Samphire

A salesman was walking along a lonely coast road in the west of England. He carried a wicker suitcase, which he swung lightly in one hand, and a heavy bag hanging over his shoulder. In his pockets were a toothbrush, a razor, and some nylon webbing. He travelled in eggs, which sounds a risky proceeding, but was really very easy.

When he came to a house he knocked at the door and asked the housewife:

"Any delicious new-laid eggs today, Madam?"

If she said yes, or asked if the eggs really were fresh, he put down the suitcase on the step and opened it. It was empty. While the housewife laughed scornfully, or looked annoyed, he called:

"Pauline, Madeleine, Estelle, Annette, Louise, Sophie, Caroline, Odette, Marguerite, Josephine, Suzanne, Lily!"

At once twelve beautiful white pigeons would come wheeling down and each lay an egg in the suitcase. Then the salesman would hold it out to the astonished housewife and say:

"There you are, Madam. New laid, as you can see for yourself."

On another occasion it would be Jacqueline, Marianne, Lucille, Antoinette, Seraphine, Diane, Nicolette, Catherine, Charlotte, Adelaide, Stephanie and Claudette that he called. He had about fifty birds who took it in turns to lay eggs for him and followed him everywhere at a discreet distance. In the sack over his shoulder he carried grain for them, and at night, wherever he was staying, whether at an inn or under a hay-stack, he would clap his hands and the pigeons would come flocking round for their supper. Then, if it was a cold night, they would all sleep huddled together with the salesman underneath a sort of quilt of pigeons.

Housewives were always delighted to get such fresh eggs, even if they were only pigeon-size, and he was hardly ever turned away from a door, so that as his wants were few he made a comfortable living.

On this particular day the salesman had already sold three dozen eggs at a fishing village, and as the wind was rising and it was turning cloudy he decided to finish business and look for somewhere to pass the night. It was midsummer eve, but quite cold; the wind was whipping up the tops of the waves and blowing little eddies of sand or "travellers" off the beach, which stung the salesman's legs and got into his turnups.

The road ran right beside the beach across a bay between two headlands. Inland was a sandy marsh which stretched for miles. It was an isolated, empty part of the country, and the salesman began to wish that he had stayed in the village or struck inland instead of keeping along this deserted road. His pigeons trailed along dispiritedly after him, spread out across the bay in small groups. A casual eye would have taken them for gulls.

About two miles in front of him at the foot of the opposite headland he thought he could see a house. He wondered if the people in it would put him up for the night or tell him where he could get a lodging. As he walked on he came to a notice which said:

ONLY ANOTHER 1000 YARDS TO THE OYSTER CAFÉ
SHRIMP AND OYSTER TEAS

The salesman was encouraged by this. The notice looked quite new, so he hoped that he could get a meal at the Oyster Café, and possibly a bed too, if the proprietor was friendly.

At a nearer view of the place his hopes sank. It looked very quiet; there were no cars standing near, the garden was full of weeds and the house itself wanted a lick of white paint. He began to wonder if it was empty but as he came round the corner of the garden wall he heard children's voices and saw two boys playing on the grass. He went up a path made of oyster-shells to the front door and knocked. After a longish time it was opened and a pale, timid-looking woman peered at him.

"Did you want something?" she asked, looking nervously over his shoulder along the road.

"Can I get some supper here?" he asked.

"No we never serve suppers," she said flatly. "Only teas, and that's finished at six."

He looked at his watch. It was seven.

"Well, can you tell me where I can get a bite to eat and a bed for the night?"

"There's no other house round here, not till you get to Penbarrow and that's another seven miles. You might be able to stay at the Fisherman's, though they don't mostly take visitors."

His heart sank, as he thought of walking on through the chilly evening for another seven miles.

A couple of his pigeons, Jacqueline and Louise, fluttered near, hoping that it would soon be supper time, and he impatiently waved them off.

"Those are pretty," said the woman. "Are they yours?"

"Yes," he answered curtly. "Wouldn't like some eggs in return for a meal, I suppose?"

Her face lit up. "Oh yes, I *would!* It's my little boy's birthday tomorrow and I haven't an egg in the house to make him a birthday cake. The—the manager forgot to go in for the groceries. Could you spare me a dozen?"

The salesman called up some more pigeons and presented her with a dozen little white eggs.

"Come inside," she said quickly, glancing round once more.

"There isn't much in the larder but I'll see what I can do for you." She showed him into a chilly, dreary room full of flimsy little tables; its walls were decorated by lemonade and ginger beer advertisements.

He sat down at one of the tables and studied a menu which read:

Oyster Tea. Off.
Whelk Tea. Off.
Shrimp Tea. Off.
Prawns, Cockles, Mussels. Off.
Scones. Off.
Bread and Butter.
Cakes. Off.
Mustard and Cress. Off.
Salad. Off.
Devonshire Tea. Off.

In contrast to this discouraging list a savoury smell of frying bacon stole into the room. He looked idly out of the french window and saw the two boys playing close by. One of them, the larger, kept poking the other with a stick and teasing him until he was on the point of tears.

"You wouldn't do that if Miss Samphire was here," the smaller boy blubbered, trying ineffectually to grab the stick.

"Oh, go on. Who cares for you and your old Miss Samphire?" All the same, the salesman noticed that the bigger boy glanced behind him nervously. Then as if ashamed of himself, he leaned forward and viciously tugged at the other boy's nose, at the same time hitting him on the side of the head with the stick. The salesman opened the window and stepped through.

"Stop that, you bully," he said angrily to the bigger boy, who gaped at him in astonishment, and then ran off round the house.

The younger boy was almost as startled and gazed at the salesman as if he were a ghost.

"Who's Miss Samphire?" asked the salesman. "Your teacher?"

"Hush!" said the little boy hurriedly. "I'm not allowed to tell people about her."

Just at that moment the woman appeared at the french window to say that supper was ready.

"I must just feed my pigeons," said the salesman. He clapped his hands three times and the whole fifty dropped down round him like bullets for the grain he scattered. The woman and boy watched wide-eyed.

He found quite a good supper of fried ham, bread and butter and coffee waiting for him in the dining-room, and started eating ravenously. Presently he heard a car draw up outside and heavy footsteps clumped into the house. Then there was a silence, and looking up he saw a man staring at him through the dining-room door—a tall man with black hair and a pair of very cold eyes. The man turned on his heel and went on into the kitchen without saying a word. Then the salesman heard a deep growling voice in the next room:

"What's *he* doing here?"

There was a low, apologetic murmur from the woman.

"Eggs be blowed. You get him out, d'you understand? I've told you before that I won't have people here after six. I'm going to fetch Skid and Duke, and when I come back, he's got to be gone. Maybe this will help you to remember."

He heard a cry from the woman as if she had been hit.

"And put that snivelling brat of yours to bed."

Then there were running footsteps and the bigger boy went past the dining-room door. There was a confused mumble of complaint from him:

"—wasn't doing anything to Rob and he said he'd hit me—"

"Said he'd *what?*"

The black-haired man swung into the dining-room and leaned over the salesman's table.

"You leave my boy alone or I'll knock your block off."

"I didn't touch him. I told him not to hit his brother."

"Brother be hanged. That's the housekeeper's brat, and what Les does to him is none of your business. Now get out of here."

"I haven't paid my bill yet," the salesman said calmly. He got up and went into the kitchen to find the housekeeper, who was just putting a cake into the oven.

"That'll be two and six, please," she said. He noticed a red mark on her cheek. As he gave her the money he heard a car start, and looking out through the kitchen window saw the black-haired man and his boy drive off.

"A nasty type," he said. "What's his name?"

The woman looked so terrified. "Mr. Abel," she answered.

"What's going on here?" the salesman asked curiously. "Everyone seems to be frightened of something. What happens here in the evenings? And who's Miss Samphire?"

"Miss Samphire?" She looked bewildered. "Oh, that's just some nonsense of Robbie's—nothing to do with Mr. Abel."

"The other boy seemed to know about her."

"No, it's just children's games."

"What does Abel do, then?"

"I can't tell you about that—you must go. If he found you when he came back with Skid and Duke he'd probably kill you. This is a dreadful place—oh, why did I ever answer the advertisement for a housekeeper and come here?"

"Why don't you leave?"

"They'd murder me if I tried to—I know too much about what they do."

"Dear me," said the salesman. "This is all very shocking."

He was a good citizen, and did not at all approve of these sinister goings-on. Moreover, he was very curious to know what Abel and his associates *did* do in the evenings—could they be smugglers? Or wreckers?

Not wanting to get the woman into further trouble he said a polite goodbye, picked up his case and went out of the garden gate, but then he doubled back behind the wall and made his way round to some outbuildings at the back, wondering if they would hold any clue to Abel's activities. There was a farm-yard paved with loose oyster-shells. It was impossible to walk across it without making a noise, but the sea was beyond the further buildings and the sound of the waves drowned his footsteps.

The farm buildings seemed to be unused, and were in bad repair, but there was a tower behind them which attracted his attention. It was on the edge of the beach, solidly built of stone, standing in a shingle-bank. He went across to it and tried the door, which opened. Inside, a circular flight of stairs led upwards. It was dark and steep, and he had to feel his way carefully until he came to another door at the top which opened into a round room, lit by three small windows. It was nearly full of sacks, piled on top of each other. The salesman prodded them inquisitively. They might have contained grain or dried peas, but some of his pigeons who flew in after him displayed no interest in them.

The sound of the sea, which was now rolling in heavily, deadened all other noises, and the salesman did not hear the return of Abel's car. He pulled out his pocket-knife, and cutting the cord which tied one of the sacks, looked inside. It was full of large, pink pearls.

At this moment he heard a rasping voice from behind him which said:

"Hey, Abel. Abel! There's somebody in here. I can hear him feeling about."

The salesman turned round and saw a fat man with a bald, shiny head, who was standing still with his head in a listening attitude. He seemed to be blind. Next instant Abel's face appeared over his shoulder.

"It's you, is it? Poking about," Abel said savagely. "Well, I warned you to clear out before, but now you've gone too far and it's too late. Duke, bring that bit of rope up will you?"

A third man appeared, as tall as Abel, with a surly, brutish expression. He pulled out a rope without a word, and he and Abel closed in on the salesman. After a short struggle he was overpowered and they tied his hands.

"Now you can stay there for a bit," said Abel, "till we're ready for you. You're very clever to have found the pearls, and I dare say you've guessed that the oysters in this bay are pearl oysters, and that's the last guess you'll guess, because we're not fond of strangers poking into our affairs. When we've brought in tonight's haul we'll take you out and dump you in a sack to study the oysters close to, so you can be looking forward to that. I suppose that precious housekeeper of mine fetched you here—well, we'll dump her too, and her brat. I always said it was stupid to have them."

"How are we going to run the teashop then?" grumbled the blind man.

"Duke will have to—he can cut bread and butter. And you can count the change," Abel said sourly. "Come on now—tide's getting down."

They went off, slamming the door and bolting it on the outside, but reappeared in a few minutes shoving the housekeeper and Robbie in front of them. Their hands were tied as well.

"My cake's in the oven," the woman kept crying. "My cake!"

"Oh, bother your cake. You won't be there to eat it anyway."

Abel's boy accompanied them this time, and he came over and gave the salesman a kick.

"That'll teach you to butt in when I'm talking to Rob," he said vindictively. Then he gave a parting clump to Robbie and they went out, bolting the door again. Presently the three prisoners heard the chug of a motor boat starting up.

"How long do they take getting the pearls?" the salesman asked.

"A couple of hours," the woman told him. "Oh, why did you have to interfere?"

"Well, it's not hopeless yet," the salesman said, though he did not feel too cheerful. He went to the landward window and whistled to his pigeons, who came flocking in. He showed them by signs that he wanted them to peck through his ropes, and in a few minutes they got the idea and began hammering away with their beaks. They were constantly bumping each other as they fluttered over him, and his hands became very sore and started to bleed, from the pecks that missed the ropes. By and by, though, he felt the ropes begin to give as they became more ragged, and at last, with a terrific effort he was able to break them. Then he untied the other two captives.

"Thirty feet to the ground—and anyway that window's too small for me to climb through," he said thoughtfully. "It'll have to be you, sonny."

"He can't climb down the tower," the woman said, going pale.

"No, no, I don't mean him to. He's going to wear my pigeon harness."

He pulled a tangle of nylon webbing and cord out of his pocket and began fitting it round Robbie.

"I use this for crossing rivers, or if I get lost and want to take a sighting. The pigeons can't carry me very far, of course, too heavy, but they can manage a mile or so. They should be able to carry the boy a good long way. Where's your nearest police station?"

"Penbarrow," she said dully. "That's seven miles."

"I think they could do that."

"I'd sooner go and get Miss Samphire," the boy said, wriggling himself more comfortable in the straps.

"No fairy-tales now, son. This is serious. You go for the police and tell them we're shut up here and if they don't get here by," he glanced at his watch, "eleven o'clock it'll be all up with us. Can you do that?"

The boy nodded.

"Pull the left-hand bunch of cords to go left, right-hand to go right, one jerk with both hands to go up, two to come down. Now help me harness these pigeons—that's more tricky."

It was a long job, as each pigeon had to be securely buckled into her little harness, but at last it was done. The pigeons all flew out of the window at a signal from their master, and hovered outside, keeping the nylon cords just taut between them and the boy.

"Not frightened, are you?" asked the salesman.

He shook his head. He was rather pale, but he climbed up on to the window ledge. His mother hugged him goodbye with tears streaming down her face, and then he gave both bunches of rope a tug, and the birds rose a little and lifted him clean off the sill and up into the air. He swung in view for a moment and then was whisked away out of sight.

"Seven miles," said the salesman reflectively. "He ought to make it in an hour. Those birds can do thirty miles an hour easily without a load. I should think they could manage ten with the boy. I hope the police have a car."

But Robbie had gone for Miss Samphire.

It was a delightful sensation being swung along by the birds, once he had recovered from the first moment's sick fright, as he saw the ground wheeling such a long way below his feet. He took a deep breath and steered the pigeons down to the sea. Beyond the house the ground rose into a cliff, which formed one arm of the bay, and the beach came to an abrupt end. Only at the lowest tides was the foot of the cliff exposed, but an agile child could scramble across its face out to the point, and this Robbie had done. Now he made the birds take him the same way, out along by the black rocks and over the heaving water. The pigeons disliked it very much.

Dusk was falling, and he had to strain his eyes to see the place he was aiming for. Near the point of the headland there was a dark crack in the cliff face. Robbie tugged twice when they reached it, and the birds dropped until he was dangling just above the water outside it. He leaned forward, grabbed at a ledge and pulled himself up until he was kneeling on it.

"Miss Samphire!" he called urgently. "Miss Samphire!"

"Yes?" a voice answered him—a very long-drawn, echoing voice which seemed to come from somewhere deep, deep inside the cliff. "Yes, what is it?"

"Miss Samphire, Mr. Abel and those other two men have got Mother and a stranger shut up in the tower, and they are going to drop them into the sea in sacks. And me too. Please will you help us?"

"Well really," said the voice, which was half a snarl, half a yawn. "These men are unbearable. First they take my pearls, now they are going to start dropping people into my bay. I shall have to put a stop to it, once and for all."

She emerged suddenly from the mouth of her cleft, and the pigeons rose cawing and flapping, dragging Robbie off his rock most painfully. Many people would not have found Miss Samphire handsome, but Robbie was fond of her, as she had helped him on several occasions when he had been in difficulties.

She was eight feet high, or long, and her skin was bright blue-green. Her hair was not hair, but a series of flutes or folds something like a bat's wing, or an umbrella, which hung down from her head round her neck and waved in and out as she floated in the water. It was scarlet and white. Her arms were very, very long, and her fingers were curved, more like spines than real fingers. Her tail was covered, not with scales, but with thick, waterproof fur like that of a seal, grey-green in colour. She was rather phosphorescent.

"Where are those men now?" she asked Robbie, balancing herself with a downward thrust of her tail so that she bobbed in the swell underneath him.

"Across on the opposite rocks, getting the pearls. There would be time to go and rescue Mother and the man before they get back."

"You go back to the shore and wait there. I shan't be long."

The pigeons were only too glad to carry Robbie to the beach, and had started tugging him away before he gave the signal.

Miss Samphire disappeared in an arrowy flash of bubbles.

The three men and the boy had taken as many oysters as the boat would carry and were turning for home when they heard an echoing voice from the water which cried: "Stop!" and Miss Samphire, green and glittering, appeared ahead. With one sweep of her tail she overset the boat, and that was the end of them.

Then she turned and made for the shore. Robbie had unloosed his pigeons and tried to unlock the door at the foot of the tower. The key was in the lock, but it was too stiff for him. Miss Samphire's long green talons turned it in a second.

"There's another one at the top," said Robbie. "I can't reach the bolt."

She slithered up the stairs with the speed of someone used to crawling on slippery rocks, and bracing herself on her five-foot tail, undid the bolt at the top. The door opened inwards, and she practically fell into the round room.

Robbie's mother took one look at her and shrieked, but the salesman said:

"Ah! I thought there must be something of the kind about. Thank you, Miss."

He helped the housekeeper down the stairs (she was having hysterics) while Miss Samphire shot on ahead like an eel.

The salesman very politely invited her in to have a bite of something, and she rather doubtfully accepted. They had Robbie's birthday cake (which was just done) and a large omelette made from pigeon's eggs.

Robbie's mother kept on the house, which seemed to belong to nobody. Half the pearls went to the Crown, and the other half they were allowed to keep. The salesman always dropped in on them when he was round that way, and let them have a few dozen eggs for nothing, as compensation for having got them into such a tight corner. In return they gave him pearls, which he used to offer to the housewives on their doorsteps as an alternative to eggs.

If they saw a green shape at night, flashing across the bay, or heard a sad hoarse voice singing below the cliffs, they never mentioned it to anyone, knowing Miss Samphire's desire for privacy.

When Robbie was older he had a very beautiful pearl and silver necklace made, and left it in a little parcel beside the cleft in the rock.

Nutshells, Seashells

It was customary in the summer time for Miss Solliver's academy of dancing to remove itself to her farmhouse by the sea.

"Because," said Miss Solliver, "how can a lot of little cockneys express trees and grass and water in their dancing if they have never seen such things?" It was hardly true to say that her pupils were a lot of little cockneys—the members of her famous Ballets Doux had in their veins some of the bluest blood in Europe, but it was true that they were mostly city-bred and knew little about the country. Even the elegant Natasha Borodinova, whose father had once owned thousands upon thousands of acres, had never set foot in a real wood until she came to Miss Solliver's. The problem was soon solved, however, by hiring a large coach and taking them about on appropriate excursions—to a moonlit glade when they were doing *Sylphides*, a lake before a performance of *Swan Lake*, and so on.

This year there would be no need for the coach. The new ballet they were going to start rehearsing was called *Neptune*. It dealt with the sea, and there the sea was, ready to be studied, just at the foot of the cliffs. Several members of the corps de ballet looked at it carefully out of their bedroom windows as they unpacked; Natasha herself did so, and then glancing the other way into her mirror, performed some flowing, arching movements like those of a wave which at the last moment decides not to turn over.

Little Liz Miller, the youngest and smallest pupil, could not see the sea from her window. Her room, which she shared with two other girls, was downstairs and looked out into the garden, which was surrounded by a thick, high hazel hedge. Nothing could be seen of the sea from the garden; it was warm and sheltered even on the windiest days, and had a wide, flat lawn, admirable for practice.

After tea they all went out and limbered up. Presently Miss Solliver appeared and told them her plans, allotting the parts of Neptune, Alcestis, Tritons, Nereids, Dolphins and the rest. The part of Neptune was being taken by Boris Grigorieff and that of Alcestis by Natasha. Already they were in a far corner of the lawn practising a *pas de deux* which Miss Solliver was describing to them, and looking more like two swallows than two dancers as they curvetted about. The rest of the cast flitted and bounded in the wildest confusion enjoying themselves in the evening sun. Serious work would begin tomorrow.

Little Liz Miller escaped from it all and ran down the lane which she had been told led to the sea. In a moment she could hear nothing of the laughter and voices—the road was deep sunk between banks, and shared its course with a stream which poured out of a hole in the bank and then cataracted down among tall grasses towards the sea.

Liz was so happy that she thought she would burst. For one thing it was her birthday, and her mother had given her a box to open on the train which proved to contain a large cake iced with pink icing and covered with silver balls. And then it was so wonderful to have come here. Liz had never been away from home before; never imagined places like this, like the sprawling white-washed farmhouse all tangled round with fuchsia, or the strange bumpy up and down hills surrounding it, or the sudden swoop of cliff to the sea, or the sea itself, as blue as a street light and going in every direction at once.

Liz was the only real cockney in the school; she had been born within the sound of Bow Bells and her mother, Mrs. Miller, was the charwoman who polished the long long expanses of glassy floor in the London classrooms. Miss Solliver had taken in little Liz out of kindness to Mrs. Miller, who had difficulties with a sick father and no husband and very little money.

"Mrs. Miller is convinced that the child is an infant genius," said Miss Solliver, smiling indulgently, to the Assistant Principal, Madame Legume, "because she can skip and roller-skate. I am afraid it goes no further than that. But she will get good food with us and come to no harm, and be out of her mother's way. Poor little thing! She moves like a milkman's pony, all legs and joints. We shall never be able to make anything of her."

"It is very charitable of you to take her in, chérie," replied the ponderous Madame Legume.

Little Liz was not aware of this. She knew that her skipping and roller-skating were considered vulgar accomplishments, so she did not talk about them, but she had the purest and most loving admiration for all the other members of the school from Natasha downwards, and her only desire was to emulate them. She fully expected that in due time, if she worked hard, she would become a ballerina. She did not know that they were laughing at her and treating her like a mongrel puppy that had bounced in among a collection of aristocratic greyhounds.

She had to stop half way down the lane and sit on the bank for a moment, hugging herself with happiness. Her birthday; and the cake; and having the privilege of sharing it with all these godlike creatures; it was almost too much. Even Natasha had eaten a piece, after delicately removing the silver balls and dropping them back into the little girl's hand.

"You eat them for me, Baby. They will break my teeth."

The balls were in her pocket now, with some old hazel nuts found under the garden hedge as she came through.

But the last and almost unbearable happiness was that Miss Solliver had told her she could be a baby dolphin in the ballet. "If you are good and do as you are told and don't get in the way." To dance in a real ballet! She rolled round on to her stomach and lay kicking her legs. She did not know exactly what a dolphin was—some kind of a bird, perhaps.

There were harebells growing in the grass; she picked some and stuck them in her buttonhole, and then jumped up and ran on down the hill. Here was the sea, round this next corner, and a wonderful flat expanse of sand, just right for skipping on. Rather guiltily looking round to see that no one else from the school was about—but no, they were all up dancing in the garden—she pulled her skipping rope out of her pocket. When Liz was happy she had to skip. But first she must pick up those long pink shells and add them to the collection that was beginning to weigh down her pocket.

"Nutshells, seashells—" she sang, for she always made up her own skipping rhymes.

> "Nutshells, seashells,
> Silver balls, harebells,
> River lanes, waterfalls,
> Harebells, silver balls."

And she began to skip.

When Liz skipped it was something quite special. Perhaps Miss Solliver had never seen her do it? The rope that she held seemed to become alive and partner her in a whirling dance, thinking up things to do for itself. Other children, back in the alley where Liz had learned to skip, could twirl the rope under them twice while they were in the air. Liz could do it seven times; and while she was in the air she moved from side to side like a gull glancing about over the water. Other children could skip a hundred times running, or a thousand times, but Liz could probably have gone on for ever if she had wanted to. She could toss the rope from her, catch it in mid-air, cross it into a figure eight and skip forward through the top loop and back through the bottom one; she could dance a mazurka or a reel while the rope flashed round her like a sword, she could dance a waltz or a minuet while it wove a web round her as shining and insubstantial as the web of rib-bons round a maypole. She could swing the rope round underneath her by one handle until it made a spinning circular platform, while she spun round in the other direction above it; sometimes the rope was a planet and she was the sun, or the rope was Niagara and she was M. Blondin whirling down it in a barrel with her legs hooked over her ears; sometimes it was a tight-rope with its ends attached to nothing in particular and she was skipping along it; sometimes it was a cradle and she was rocking herself off to sleep in it.

As she skipped she sang her skipping rhyme, and at the end, when she had done all the different sorts of skipping that she could think of, she flipped out all the contents of her pockets and began to juggle with them. Pink shells, harebells, hazel nuts and silver balls tossed up and down over the rope, and Liz skipped underneath them, keeping them all in the air and herself as well. At last she flopped down on a rock, letting them scatter round her. To her surprise there was a loud burst of applause from the sea.

She looked round, rather pink and embarrassed, to see who had surprised her at her forbidden pastime. The whole sea appeared to be crammed with people.

In the midst of them all was a huge man, very like Mr. Sammons who kept the whelk stall in Vauxhall Bridge Road. He was sitting on something that might have been a whelk stall, trimmed up a bit; it rose up and down on the waves and was pulled by two great fish like the stone ones on either side of the Mercantile Insurance Building doorway, only these were very much alive, plunging and bouncing, and the man had to keep pulling on the reins. All around the stall, which was encrusted with lobsters and crabs, cockles and mussels, was swimming every sort of fish that Liz had ever seen on a barrow—cod, skate, halibut, herring, mackerel, sole, plaice and rock salmon—and many that she hadn't; not to mention sea lions and walruses which she had once seen at the zoo. But in among these were much odder creatures; girls with tails playing on combs wrapped in paper, men with faces of fish, playing on mouth-organs; fish with wings, blowing trumpets; young ladies coming out of large whelk shells; birds with fins riding on oysters; lobsters blowing out long paper snakes that rolled up again with a click; fish with the faces of men, carrying shrimping nets; and so forth.

"Coo," said Liz, shaken out of herself by this extraordinary scene. "It's like Hampstead Heath on Bank Holiday."

"Hello there, Liz," shouted Neptune, waving a three-pronged toasting fork with an ice-cream cone on each prong. "What can we do for you, dearie?"

"For *me?* Why?"

"You called us, didn't you? With your song about nutshells and seashells."

"But that was just a skipping song I made up."

"Any little song will do for an incantation," said Neptune, "if you're doing something important."

"But I wasn't doing anything important."

"Your skipping is important, my girl. It's Art, that's what it is."

"Miss Solliver says it's vulgar."

"Well, nuts to Miss Solliver, whoever she may be. But that isn't the point. The point is, you called for us, whether you meant to or not, and here we are, so what would you like? Anything you've a fancy for? Free cruise to Madeira? Streamlined modern kitchen installed in your home? Winning ticket for the pools? Pearl necklace? Strawberry or vanilla? Whelks in vinegar?"

"No, there's nothing at all, really, thank you," said Liz, beaming all over again at the thought of her happiness, "I've got all I want already."

A long sigh, of admiration, envy and amazement went up from the sea.

"Still," said Neptune rallying, "we could give her a good time, couldn't we, boys and girls? How about a bit of deep-sea rock, eh? Or a mug with a Present from Neptune on it? You come for a ride in my chariot and look at the sights before you go back."

So she skipped out over the heaving backs of dolphins into the chariot and they went careering off, everyone singing Cockles and Mussels and offering her ice-cream, potato crisps and prawns in jellyfish.

"There you are," said Neptune, when at last they put her down again after she had seen the sights. "Now don't forget, if there's ever anything you need, or if you're in any sort of trouble—I don't say it's likely, mind, but you never know your luck—don't forget your old pal. Ta, ta, now, don't lose the skipping rope."

Liz had thought she was happy when she went down the lane, but she was ten times happier when she ran up it. She was longing to confide in someone: perhaps she could tell one of the girls she slept with, but not tonight, it was far too late; the moon was up, and the lane was in deep shadow between its banks. It was strictly forbidden to be out after dark and Liz wondered if she could crawl through the hazel hedge and climb in her window without being caught. She resolved to try.

But as she stole along behind the hedge she was alarmed to hear the voices of Miss Solliver and Madame Legume who were, apparently, strolling in the moonlight on the other side.

"Yes, the casting is none of it bad except for the dolphins. It is a pity that we have to have the little Miller girl in the show—it will give people a wrong idea of our standards. But it would look so invidious if she were the only one left out, and her mother would be upset."

"Yes! That child!" sighed Madame. "No one could ever teach her to dance gracefully; too much vulgar bounce. I wonder if it would not be kinder to tell her and let her leave."

"No, we'll keep her a bit longer, till things are easier for her mother. Everyone in the school quite understands the position. It's a nuisance about *Neptune* though—we'll have to keep her well at the back of the stage—"

The voices moved away again.

Liz stood where she was, almost turned to stone. Her face, which had been flushed, became very white. After a little while she turned and walked slowly back into the lane. She was stiff, as if her arms and legs ached all over, there was no vulgar bounce about her now. Then she sat down and looked at the little stream which came pouring out of its hole in the bank, as if she could not understand what she had heard and needed time to take it in. The water tumbled down, making its gentle noise in the quiet night, and still she looked and looked, until presently tears began to run down her face and she stood up because she was too wretched to stay sitting still.

"I can't go back there," she thought, "they all laugh at me and know I'm no good. How silly I must have been not to see that before."

She did not blame them; in fact she felt sorry for them because it must have been so tiresome. It was not their laughter that ached in her bones; it was that dreadful sentence: "No one could ever teach her to dance gracefully."

Where was she to go? Then she saw a couple of harebells nodding in the moonlight and remembered her skipping rhyme:

> Nutshells, seashells,
> Silver balls, harebells—

It was easy to find a couple of nutshells in the hedge. She ran down to the beach and picked up a handful of shells.

But what about the silver balls? Then she remembered that her skipping rope had silver ball-bearings in the handles. She would have to break it to get them out. What did that matter when she was never going to skip or dance again—unless Neptune could help her? But suppose the song didn't work? She gave a little sob as she knelt down and cracked the handles on a rock.

Miss Solliver was very worried to hear next morning that Liz Miller was missing.

"It has occurred to me that we were rather near her window when we were talking last night," she said to Madame Legume. "Do you suppose she could have heard us? I don't know what I shall say to her mother if anything has happened to her."

Later on a pair of sandshoes and a broken skipping rope, identified as belonging to Liz, were found at the foot of the cliff. As nothing more was seen of her she was presumed to have been drowned; the whole school was much upset, the plans for the Neptune ballet were laid aside and they all went back to London earlier than usual. Miss Solliver wrote a polite note to Mrs. Miller regretting that her daughter had been drowned and suggesting that it would be best if she did not continue her employment as cleaner in the London school because the place would no doubt be painful to her; Miss Solliver enclosed a cheque in lieu of notice.

Seven years later a new ballerina took London by storm. Miss Solliver, full of curiosity, went to see her in the ballet *Atlantis,* produced by a Mr. Thalassoglu whom no one had ever heard of.

"She really is most strange," said Miss Solliver to Madame Legume, in between two scenes. "I suppose it's a trick of the lighting, but sometimes, it's hard to decide whether she's swimming or flying. Do you suppose she's really hanging on wires?"

She leaned forward and stared intently at the silvery figure darting about the streets of the drowned city.

"It's odd, she reminds me of someone a little—who can it be?"

After the performance a journalist friend of Miss Solliver's offered to introduce her to the ballerina. They went round to her dressing-room.

In the far corner was old Grandfather Miller in a bath-chair; knitting beside the fire was Mrs. Miller; on the dressing-table lay a skipping rope. The ball-bearings were made from pearls, and round the coral handles was inscribed: "A Present from Neptune."

Some Music for the Wicked Countess

Mr. Bond was a young man who had just arrived in a small village to take up the position of schoolmaster there. The village was called Castle Kerrig but the curious thing about it was that there was no castle and never had been one. There was a large wood round three-quarters of its circumference which came almost to the door of the schoolmaster's little house, and beyond that the wild hills and bog stretched for miles.

There were only ten children needing to be taught; it hardly seemed worth having a school there at all, but without it they would have had to travel forty miles by bus every day, and a schoolmaster was far cheaper than all that petrol, so Mr. Bond was given the job. It suited him very well, as he did not have to waste too much time in teaching and had plenty left for his collections of birds' eggs, moths, butterflies, fossils, stones, bones, lizards and flowers and his piano-playing.

There was a tinny old piano in the school, and when he and the children were bored by lessons he would play tunes and songs to them for hours at a time while they listened in a dream.

One day the eldest of the children, Norah, said to him:

"Faith, 'tis the way your Honour should be playing to the Countess up at the Castle for the wonder and beauty of your melodies does be out of this world entirely."

"The Castle?" said Mr. Bond curiously. "What castle is that? There's no castle near here, is there?"

"Ah, sure, 'tis the Castle in the forest I mean. The wicked Countess would weep the eyes out of her head to hear the tunes you do be playing."

"Castle in the forest?" The schoolmaster was more and more puzzled. "But there's no castle in the forest—at least it's not marked on the two and a half-inch ordnance survey."

"Begorrah, and doesn't your Honour know that the whole forest is stiff with enchantment, and a leprechaun peeking out of every bush in it, the way you'd be thinking it was nesting time and they after the eggs?"

"What nonsense, my dear Norah. You really must learn not to come to me with these tales."

But all the children gathered round him exclaiming and persuading.

"Faith, and isn't it the strange thing that your Worship should not be believing in these enchantments, and you playing such beautiful music that the very ravens from the Castle, and the maidens out of the forest are all climbing and fluttering over each other outside the windows to get an earful of it?"

Mr. Bond shooed them all off rather crossly, saying that school was over for the day and he had no patience with such silliness.

Next day was the last day of term, and Norah was leaving. Mr. Bond asked her what she was going to do.

"Going into service up at the Castle. They're in need of a girl in the kitchen, I'm told, and mother says 'twill be good experience for me."

"But there *isn't* any castle," said Mr. Bond furiously. Was the girl half-witted? She had always seemed bright enough in school.

"Ah, your Honour will have your bit of fun. And what else could I do, will you be telling me that?"

Mr. Bond was forced to agree that there were no other jobs

to be had. That afternoon he started out into the forest, determined to search for this mysterious castle and see if there really was some big house tucked away in the trees, but though he walked for miles and miles, and came home thirsty and exhausted long after dusk, not a thing did he see, neither castle, house, nor hut, let alone leprechauns peeking out of every bush.

He ate some bread and cheese in a bad temper and sat down to play it off at his own piano. He played some dances from Purcell's *Fairy Queen,* and had soon soothed himself into forgetfulness of the children's provoking behaviour. Little did he know that three white faces, framed in long golden hair, were gazing through the window behind his back. When he had finished playing for the night the maidens from the forest turned and went regretfully back to the Castle.

"Well," asked the Wicked Countess, "and does he play as well as the village talk has it?"

"He plays till the ears come down off your head and go waltzing off along the road. Sure there's none is his equal in the whole wide world at all."

"I expect you are exaggerating," said the Countess sadly, "still he would be a useful replacement for Bran the Harpist, ever since the fool went and had his head chopped off at the Debateable Ford."

She looked crossly over to a corner where a headless harpist was learning to knit, since being unable to read music he could no longer play.

"We must entice this schoolmaster up to the Castle," said the Wicked Countess. "'Twill cheer up our dull and lonely life to have a bit of music once again. Ah, that will be the grand day when they have the television broadcast throughout the length and breadth of the country for the entertainment and instruction of us poor warlocks. I've heard they do be having lessons in ballet and basket making and all sorts of wonderments."

"How will you entice him up?" asked one of the maidens.

"The usual way. I'll toss out me keys and let it be known that my hand and heart is in waiting for the lucky fellow is after finding them. Then we'll give him a draught of fairy wine to lull him to sleep for seven years, and after that he's ours for ever."

So the Countess arranged for the message about the keys to be relayed through the village and the keys were left lying in a conspicuous place in the middle of the schoolmaster's garden path, visible to him but invisible to everyone else. Quite a number of people became very excited at the thought of winning the Wicked Countess's heart and hand, and the forest was almost as crowded as Epping Forest at Bank Holiday, but the schoolmaster was very preoccupied just at that time with his search for the Scarlet Striped Orchis, which blooms only during the first week in May, and he hardly noticed the commotion.

He did observe the keys lying on his path, but he knew they did not belong to him, and they came into none of the categories of things that he collected, so he merely kicked them out of the way, and then forgot them in the excitement of noticing a rare orange fritillary by his garden gate.

"The man's possessed," exclaimed the Countess in vexation. It was mortifying to have her message so completely ignored, but she did not abandon her purpose.

"We'll try the snake trick—that'll be after fetching him in, and he interested in all manner of bugs and reptiles, the way it'd be a terrible life for his wife, poor woman."

The snake trick was a very old ruse for enticing mortals. One of the maidens of the forest changed herself into a beautiful many-coloured snake with ruby eyes and lay in the path of the intended victim, who would be unable to resist picking it up and taking it home. Once inside his house, it would change back into the forest maiden's form again, and the luckless man would be obliged to marry her. She would become more and more exacting, asking for a coat made from rose-petals, or cherries in midwinter, until her husband had to go up to the Castle and ask them to supply one of these difficult requirements. Then of course he was in their power.

"Indeed, why didn't we try the snake trick before," said the Countess. "'Twould have fetched him better than any old bit of a bunch of keys."

Accordingly, when next Mr. Bond went into the forest, looking for green-glass snails and the salmon-spotted hellebore, he found this beautiful coloured snake lying temptingly displayed in a wriggle of black, scarlet, white and lemon-yellow across his path.

"Bless my soul," said Mr. Bond. "That is something unusual. Can it be *T. vulgaris peristalsis?* I must certainly take it home."

He picked up the snake, which dangled unresistingly in his hands, and rushed home with it. All the forest maidens and the ravens leaned out of the high branches, and the leprechauns pried between the stems of the bushes to watch him go by. He ran up the garden path, shoved open the front door with his shoulder, and dropped the snake into a jar of brine which was standing ready for specimens on the kitchen table. He was unable to find a picture or description of the snake in any work of reference, and to his annoyance and disappointment the beautiful colours faded after a couple of hours. The Wicked Countess was also very annoyed. One of her forest maidens had been demolished, and she had been foiled again, which was galling to her pride.

"Maybe we could give him a potion?" suggested one of the maidens.

"He's teetotal, the creature," said the Wicked Countess in disgust. "Will you be after telling me how you can administer a potion to a man that will touch neither drop nor dram?"

"Well, but doesn't he take in each day the grandest bottle

of milk you ever laid eyes on that would make any cow in Kerry sigh with envy at the cream there is on it?"

"Very well, you can try putting the potion in the milk, but 'tis a poor way of instilling a magic draught into a man, I'm thinking, and little good will it do him."

Two enthusiastic maidens went to Mr. Bond's house at cockcrow the following morning and lay in wait for the milkman. As soon as he had left the bottle they removed the cardboard bottle-top, tipped in the potion (which was a powder in a little envelope, like a shampoo) put back the cap, and then hurried back to the Castle to report.

Unfortunately it was the schoolmaster's turn to be unwilling host to the village tits that morning. Shortly after the maiden had left, forty blue tits descended on to his doorstep, neatly removed the cap once more, and drank every drop of the milk. Mr. Bond was resigned to this happening every eleventh day, and swallowed his morning tea milkless, before setting off to open up the school, as the holiday was now over.

Up at the Castle the maidens had a difficult time explaining to the Wicked Countess the sudden appearance of forty blue tits who flew in through the window and absolutely refused to be turned out.

"How are we to get this miserable man up here, will you tell me that?" demanded the Countess. "I've lost patience with him entirely."

"You could write him a civil note of invitation, the way he'd be in no case to refuse without displaying terrible bad manners in it?"

"I never thought of that," admitted the Countess, and she sat down and penned a little note in her crabbed, runic handwriting, asking the schoolmaster for the pleasure of his company to a musical evening. She entrusted the note to Norah, who was now a kitchen-maid at the Castle, and asked her to give it into Mr. Bond's own hands. Norah skipped off, much pleased with the commission, and presented the note to Mr. Bond as he sat in morning school.

"Now isn't it herself has done you the great honour of requesting your worshipful presence at such a musical junketing and a singing and dancing you'd think it was King Solomon himself entertaining the Queen of Sheba."

Mr. Bond scrutinized the letter carefully.

"Now this is very interesting; the back of this document appears to be part of a version of the Cuchulainn legend written in a very early form of Gaelic. Dear me, I must write to the Royal Society about this."

He became absorbed in the legend on the back, and clean forgot to read what was on the other side.

The Countess was very affronted at this, and scolded Norah severely.

"I've no patience with the lot of you, at all. I can see I'll have to be after fetching him myself, the way otherwise we'll be having no music this side of winter."

It was now the middle of May, which is a very dangerous month for enchantment, the worst in the year apart from October.

The Wicked Countess sent out her spies to inform her when Mr. Bond next took an evening walk in the forest. A few days later it was reported that he had set out with a tin of golden syrup and a paintbrush and was busy painting the trunks of the trees. The Countess hastily arrayed herself with all her enchantments and made her way to where he was working. The whole forest hummed with interest and excitement and the leprechauns were jumping up and down in their bushes to such an extent that showers of hawthorn blossom kept falling down. Mr. Bond noticed nothing of all this, but he was just able to discern the Wicked Countess with her streaming hair and her beauty. He thought she must be the District Nurse.

"The top of the evening to you," she greeted him, "and isn't it a grand and strange thing you do be doing there, anointing the bark of the trees with treacle as if they were horses and they with the knees broken on them? But perhaps 'tis a compliment you do be after paying me, and it meaning to say that the very trees in my forest are so sweet they deserve to be iced like cakes."

"Good evening," said Mr. Bond, with reserve. "I'm out after moths."

"And isn't it a wonderful thing to be pursuing those pitiful brown things when you could be stepping up to the Castle like a civilized creature and passing a musical evening with me and my maidens, the way our hearts and voices would be singing together like a flock of starlings?"

"Are you the Countess by any chance? I seem to have heard some vague tales about you, but I never thought that you were a real person. I hope you will forgive me if I have been guilty of any impoliteness."

"Sure our hearts are warmer than that in this part of the world, and what's a trifle of an insult between friends? Do you be after strolling up with me this minute for a drop of something to drink and a few notes of music, for they say music be a great healer when there's hurt feelings in the case, and it smoothing away the sore hearts and wounded spirits."

Mr. Bond gathered that he *had* in some way offended this talkative lady, and his mind went back guiltily to the note Norah had given him, which he had sent off to the Royal Society and forgotten to read.

He turned and walked with her, and was surprised to notice a grey and vine-wreathed tower standing in a part of the forest where, he would have been ready to swear, there had been nothing before.

"Walk in this way," said the Countess holding open a little postern. "We won't stand on ceremony between friends."

They had to climb half a hundred steps of spiral staircase, but finally emerged in the Wicked Countess's bower, a dim, rush-strewn room full of maidens, leprechauns and wood-smoke.

"Pray be taking a seat," said the Countess, "the while you do be getting your breath. Fetch a drink for the poor gentleman, one of you," she commanded the maidens, "he has no more breath in him than a washed sheet, and it clinging together on the line."

"Nothing stronger than tea for me, please," said the schoolmaster faintly.

"Tea, is it? We must be after brewing you a terrible strong poteen of the stuff, for how can you make music worthy the name in a draught like that? Girls, put the kettle on."

"It's all right, thank you, I'm better now. Please don't trouble."

"Do be after playing us a tune then, for since you came here the village has hummed with your praise the way we've been after thinking 'twas a human nightingale had come to live among us."

"I will with pleasure," said Mr. Bond, "but I can't play without a piano, you know."

There was a disconcerted pause.

"Ah, sure, I'll send two of my leprechauns down to the little house for it," said the Countess rallying. "They'll be back in ten minutes, the creatures." Two of them scuttled off, in obedience to a ferocious look.

Mr. Bond gazed round him dreamily, lulled by the atmosphere of enchantment. The arrival of the tea roused him a little; he took one look at it and shuddered, for it was as black as the pit and looked as if it had been stewed for hours. The maidens were not very expert tea-makers. The Countess was delicately sipping at a tall flagon of mead.

Fortunately a diversion was created by the two leprechauns who came staggering back with the piano in an astonishingly short time. While they were getting it up the spiral staircase amid cries of encouragement from the maidens, Mr. Bond tipped his tea into the treacle tin.

"What shall I play for you?" he asked the Countess.

She thought for a moment. Musicians were notoriously vain, and the best way to get him into a flattered and compliant mood would be to ask for one of his own compositions —he was sure to have written some himself.

"Best of all we'd be after liking a tune you've made up yourself," she told him.

Mr. Bond beamed. Here was a true music-lover without a doubt—a very rare thing in this wilderness.

"I'll play you my new fantasia and fugue in the whole-tone scale," he said happily, delighted at a chance to get away from the folk-songs and country dances which he was obliged to play for the children.

He brought his hands down on the keys in a prolonged, crashing and discordant chord. The leprechauns shuddered from top to toe, the maidens clenched their teeth, and the Wicked Countess had to grip her hands on to the arms of her chair.

Then Mr. Bond really started to play, and the noise was so awful that the whole enchanted tower simply disintegrated, brick by brick. The Countess and her maidens vanished away moaning into the forest, the leprechauns retired grumbling into their bushes again, and when the schoolmaster finished his piece and looked round, he was astonished to find himself seated at the piano in the middle of a forest glade. He had to ask the people from the village to help him back with the piano, and was at great pains to try and think up some explanation for its presence in the forest.

They took no notice of what he said, however.

"Ah, sure, 'tis only some whimsy of the Countess's, the creature, bless her. What would the man expect, and he wandering about the forest on a May evening?"

After that, if by any chance Mr. Bond and the Wicked Countess met each other while walking in the forest, they said nothing at all, and each pretended that the other was not there.

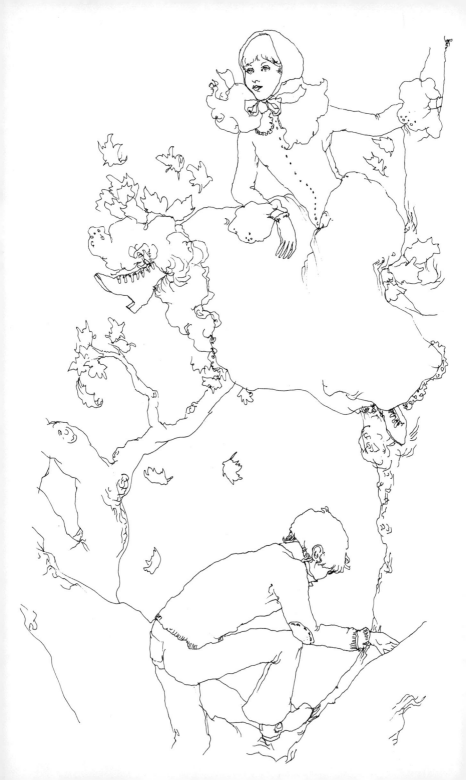

A Room Full of Leaves

Once there was a poor little boy who lived with a lot of his relatives in an enormous house called Troy. The relatives were rich, but they were so nasty that they might just as well have been poor, for all the good their money did them. The worst of them all was Aunt Agatha, who was thin and sharp, and the next worst was Uncle Umbert, who was stout and prosperous. We shall return to them later. There was also a fierce old nurse called Squabb, and a tutor, Mr. Buckle, who helped to make the little boy's life a burden. His name was Wilfred, which was a family name, but he was so tired of hearing them all say: "You must live up to your name, child," that in his own mind he called himself Wil. It had to be in his mind, for he had no playmates—other children were declared to be common, and probably dangerous and infectious too.

One rainy Saturday afternoon Wil sat in his schoolroom finishing some Latin parsing for Mr. Buckle before being taken for his walk, which was always in one of two directions. If Squabb took him they went downtown "to look at the shops" in a suburb of London which was sprawling out its claws towards the big house; but the shops were never the ones Wil would have chosen to look at. If he went with Mr. Buckle they crossed the Common diagonally (avoiding the pond where rude little boys sailed their boats) and came back along the white-railed ride while Mr. Buckle talked about plant life.

So Wil was not looking forward with great enthusiasm to his walk, and when Squabb came in and told him that it was too wet to go out and he must amuse himself quietly with his transfers, he was delighted. He sat gazing dreamily at the transfers for a while, not getting on with them, while Squabb did some ironing. It was nearly dark, although the time was only three. Squabb switched on the light and picked a fresh heap of ironing off the fender.

All of a sudden there was a blue flash and a report from the iron; a strong smell of burnt rubber filled the room and all the lights went out.

"Now I suppose the perishing thing's fused all this floor," exclaimed Squabb and she hurried out of the room, muttering something under her breath about newfangled gadgets.

Wil did not waste a second. Before the door had closed after her he was tiptoeing across the room and out of the other door. In the darkness and confusion no one would miss him for quite a considerable time, and he would have a rare opportunity to be on his own for a bit.

The house in which he lived was very huge. Nobody knew exactly how many rooms there were—but there was one for each day of the year and plenty left over. Innumerable little courtyards, each with its own patch of green velvet grass, had passages leading away in all directions to different blocks and wings. Towards the back of the house there were fewer courtyards; it drew itself together into a solid mass which touched the forest behind. The most important rooms were open to the public on four days a week; Mr. Buckle and a skinny lady from the town showed visitors round, and all the relics and heirlooms were carefully locked up inside glass cases where they could be gazed at—the silver wash-basin used by James II, a dirty old exercise book belonging to the poet Pope, the little pot of neat's foot ointment left by Henry VIII and all the other tiny bits of history. Even in those days visitors were careless about leaving things behind.

Wil was indifferent to the public rooms, though his relatives were not. They spent their lives polishing and furbishing and when everything was polished they went on endless grubbing searches through the unused rooms looking for more relics which could be cleaned up and sold to the British Museum.

Wil stood outside the schoolroom door listening. Down below he could hear the murmur of voices. Saturday was cheap visiting day—only two and six instead of five shillings—so there were twice as many people, and both Mr. Buckle and the skinny lady were at work escorting their little groups. Wil nodded to himself and slipped away, softly as a mouse, towards the back of the house where the tourists were never taken. Here it became darker and dustier, the windows were small, heavily leaded, and never cleaned. Little passages, unexpected stairways and landings wound about past innumerable doors, many of which had not been opened since Anne Boleyn popped her head round to say goodbye to some bedridden old retainer before taking horse to London. Tapestries hung thick with velvet dust—had Wil touched them they would have crumbled to pieces but he slid past them like a shadow.

He was already lost, but he meant to be; he stood listening to the old house creaking and rustling round him like a forest. He had a fancy that if he penetrated far enough he would find himself in the forest without having noticed the transition. He was following a particularly crooked and winding passage, leading to a kind of cross-roads or cross-passages from which other alleys led away, mostly dark, some with a faint gleam from a rain-streaked window far away down their length, and all lined with doors.

He paused, wondering which to choose, and then heard something which might have been the faintest of whispers— but it was enough to decide him on taking the passage directly fronting him. He went slowly to a door some twelve feet along it, rather a low, small door on his right.

After pushing he discovered that it opened outwards towards him. He pulled it back, stepped around, and gazed in bewilderment at what he saw. It was like a curtain, of a silvery, faded brown, which hung across the doorway. Then looking closer he saw that it was really *leaves*—piled high and drifted one on another, lying so heaped up that the entrance was filled with them, and if the door had swung inwards he could never have pushed it open. Wil felt them with his hand; they were not brittle like dead beech-leaves, but soft and supple, making only the faintest rustle when he touched them. He took one and looked at it in the palm of his hand. It was almost a skeleton, covered with faint silvery marks like letters. As he stood looking at it he heard a little voice whisper from inside the room:

"Well, boy, aren't you coming in?"

Much excited, he stared once more at the apparently impenetrable wall of leaves in front of him, and said softly:

"How do I get through?"

"Burrow, of course," whispered the voice impatiently.

He obeyed, and stooping a little plunged his head and arms among the leaves and began working his way into them like a mole. When he was entirely inside the doorway he wriggled round and pulled the door shut behind him. The leaves made hardly any noise as he inched through them. There was just enough air to breathe, and a dryish aromatic scent. His progress was slow, and it seemed to take about ten minutes before the leaves began to thin out, and striking upwards like a diver he finally came to the surface.

He was in a room, or so he supposed, having come into it through an ordinary door in a corridor, but the walls could not be seen at all on account of the rampart of leaves piled up all round him. Towards the centre there was a clear space on the ground, and in this grew a mighty trunk, as large round as a table, covered with roughish silver bark, all protrusions and knobs. The branches began above his head, thrusting out laterally like those of an oak or beech, but very little could be seen of them on account of the leaves which grew everywhere in thick clusters, and the upper reaches of the tree were not visible at all. The growing leaves were yellow—not the faded yellow of autumn but a brilliant gold which illuminated the room. At least there was no other source of light, and it was not dark.

There appeared to be no one else under the tree and Wil wondered who had spoken to him and where they could be.

As if in answer to his thoughts the voice spoke again:

"Can't you climb up?"

"Yes, of course I can," he said, annoyed with himself for not thinking of this, and he began setting his feet on the rough ledges of bark and pulling himself up. Soon he could not see the floor below, and was in a cage of leaves which fluttered all round him, dazzling his eyes. The scent in the tree was like thyme on the downs on a hot summer's day.

"Where are you?" he asked in bewilderment.

He heard a giggle.

"I'm here," said the voice, and he saw an agitation among the leaves at the end of a branch, and worked his way out to it. He found a little girl—a rather plain little girl with freckles and reddish hair hidden under some kind of cap. She wore a long green velvet dress and a ruff, and she was seated comfortably swinging herself up and down in a natural hammock of small branches.

"Really I thought you'd *never* find your way here," she said, giving him a derisive welcoming grin.

"I'm not used to climbing trees," he excused himself.

"I know, poor wretch. Never mind, this one's easy enough. What's your name? Mine's Em."

"Mine's Wil. Do you live here?"

"Of course. This isn't really my branch—some of them are

very severe about staying on their own branches—look at
him." She indicated a very Puritanical-looking gentleman in
black knee-breeches who appeared for a moment and then
vanished again as a cluster of leaves swayed. "*I* go where I
like, though. My branch isn't respectable—we were on the
wrong side in every war from Matilda and Stephen on. As
soon as the colonies were invented they shipped a lot of us out
there, but it was no use, they left a lot behind. They always
hope that we'll die out, but of course we don't. Shall I show
you some of the tree?"

"Yes, please."

"Come along then. Don't be frightened, you can hold my
hand a lot of the time. It's almost as easy as stairs."

When she began leading him about he realized that the
tree was much more enormous than he had supposed; in fact
he did not understand how it could be growing in a room inside a house. The branches curved about making platforms,
caves, spiral staircases, seats, cupboards and cages. Em led
him through the maze, which she seemed to know by heart,
pushing past the clusters of yellow leaves. She showed him
how to swing from one branch to another, how to slide down
the slopes and wriggle through the crevices and how to lie
back in a network of boughs and rest his head on a thick pillow of leaves.

They made quite a lot of noise and several disapproving
old faces peered at them from the ends of branches, though
one crusader smiled faintly and his dog wagged its tail.

"Have you anything to eat?" asked Em presently, mopping
her brow with her kerchief.

"Yes, I've got some biscuits I didn't eat at break this morning. I'm not allowed to keep them of course, they'd be cross
if they knew."

"Of course," nodded Em, taking a biscuit. "Thanks. Dryish, your comfits, aren't they—but welcome. Wait a minute
and I'll bring you a drink." She disappeared among the

boughs and came back in a few moments with two little greenish crystal cups full of a golden liquid.

"It's sap," she said, passing one over. "It has a sort of forest taste, hasn't it; makes you think of horns. Now I'll give you a present."

She took the cups away and he heard her rummaging somewhere down by the trunk of the tree.

"There's all sorts of odds and ends down there. This is the first thing I could find. Do you like it?"

"Yes, very much," he said, handling the slender silver thing with interest. "What is it?"

She looked at it critically. "I think it's the shoehorn that Queen Elizabeth used (she always had trouble with wearing too tight shoes). She must have left it behind here some time. You can have it anyway—you might find a use for it. You'd better be going now or you'll be in trouble and then it won't be so easy for you to come here another time."

"How shall I ever find my way back here?"

"You must stand quite still and listen. You'll hear me whisper, and the leaves rustling. Goodbye." She suddenly put a skinny little arm round his neck and gave him a hug. "It's nice having someone to play with; I've been a bit bored sometimes."

Wil squirmed out through the leaves again and shut the door, turning to look at it as he did so. There was nothing in the least unusual about its appearance.

When he arrived back in the schoolroom (after some false turnings) he found his Aunt Agatha waiting for him. Squabb and Buckle were hovering on the threshold, but she dismissed them with a wave of her hand. The occasion was too serious for underlings.

"Wilfred," she said, in a very awful tone.

"Yes, Aunt Agatha."

"Where have you been?"

"Playing in the back part of the house."

"Playing! A child of your standing and responsibilities playing? Instead of getting on with your transfers? What is that?" She pounced on him and dragged out the shoehorn which was protruding from his pocket.

"Concealment! I suppose you found this and intended to creep out and sell it to some museum. You are an exceedingly wicked, disobedient boy, and as punishment for running away and hiding in this manner you will go to bed as soon as I have finished with you, you will have nothing to eat but toast-gruel, and you will have to take off your clothes *yourself,* and feed *yourself,* like a common child."

"Yes, Aunt."

"You know that you are the Heir to this noble house (when your great-uncle Winthrop dies)?"

"Yes, Aunt."

"Do you know anything about your parents?"

"No."

"It is as well. Look at this." She pulled out a little case, containing two miniatures of perfectly ordinary people. Wil studied them.

"That is your father—our brother. He disgraced the family —he sullied the scutcheon—by becoming—*a writer,* and worse—he married a *female writer,* your mother. Mercifully for the family reputation they were both drowned in the *Oranjeboot* disaster, before anything worse could happen. You were rescued, floating in a pickle barrel. *Now* do you see why we all take such pains with your education? It is to save you from the taint of your unfortunate parentage."

Wil was still digesting this when there came a knock at the door and Mr. Buckle put his head round.

"There is a Mr. Slockenheimer demanding to see you, Lady Agatha," he said. "Apparently he will not take No for an answer. Shall I continue with the reprimand?"

"No, Buckle—you presume," said Aunt Agatha coldly. "I have finished."

Wil put himself to bed, watched minutely by Buckle to see that he did not omit to brush his teeth with the silver brush or comb his eyebrows with King Alfred's comb in the manner befitting an heir of Troy. The toast and water was brought in a gold porringer. Wil ate it absently; it was very nasty, but he was so overcome by the luck of not having been found out, and wondering how he could get back to see Em another time, that he hardly noticed it.

Next morning at breakfast (which he had with his relatives) he expected to be in disgrace, but curiously enough they paid no attention to him. They were all taking about Mr. Slockenheimer.

"Such a piece of luck," said Cousin Cedric. "Just as the tourist season is ending."

"Who is this man?" creaked Great-Aunt Gertrude.

"He is a film director, from Hollywood," explained Aunt Agatha, loudly and patiently. "He is making a film about Robin Hood and he has asked permission to shoot some of the indoor scenes in Troy—for which we shall all be handsomely paid, naturally."

"Naturally, naturally," croaked the old ravens, all round the table.

Wil pricked up his ears, and then an anxious thought struck him. Supposing Mr. Slockenheimer's people discovered the room with the tree?

"They are coming today," Uncle Umbert was shrieking into Great-Uncle Ulric's ear trumpet.

Mr. Slockenheimer's outfit arrived after breakfast while Wil was doing his daily run—a hundred times round the triangle of grass in front of the house, while Mr. Buckle timed him with a stop-watch.

A lovely lady shot out of a huge green motor car, shrieked:

"Oh, you cute darling! Now you must tell me the way to the nearest milk-bar," and whisked him back into the car with her. Out of the corner of his eye he saw that Mr. Buckle had been commandeered to show somebody the spiral staircase.

Wil ate his raspberry sundae in a daze. He had never been in the milk-bar before, never eaten ice-cream, never ridden in a car. To have it all following on his discovery of the day before was almost too much for him.

"Gracious!" exclaimed his new friend, looking at her wristwatch. "I must be on the set! I'm Maid Marian you know. Tarzan, I mean Robin, has to rescue me from the wicked baron at eleven in the Great Hall."

"I'll show you where it is," said Wil.

He expected more trouble when he reached home, but the whole household was disorganized; Mr. Buckle was showing Robin Hood how to put on the Black Prince's casque (which was too big) and Aunt Agatha was having a long business conversation with Mr. Slockenheimer, so his arrival passed unnoticed.

He was relieved to find that the film was only going to be shot in the main public rooms, so there did not seem to be much risk of the tree being discovered.

After lunch Mr. Buckle was called on again to demonstrate the firing of the 9th Earl's crossbow (he shot an extra) and Wil was able to escape once more and reach in safety the regions at the back.

He stood on a dark landing for what seemed like hours, listening to the patter of his own heart. Then, tickling his ear like a thread of cobweb he heard Em's whisper:

"Wil! Here I am! This way!" and below it he heard the rustle of the tree, as if it too were whispering: "Here I am."

It did not take him long to find the room, but his progress through the leaves was slightly impeded by the things he was carrying. When he emerged at the foot of the tree he found Em waiting there. The hug she gave him nearly throttled him.

"I've been thinking of some more places to show you. And all sorts of games to play!"

"I've brought you a present," he said emptying his pockets.

"Oh! What's in those little tubs?"

"Ice-cream. The chief electrician gave them to me."

"What a strange confection," she said, tasting it. "It is smooth and sweet but it makes my teeth chatter."

"And here's your present." It was a gold Mickey Mouse with ruby eyes which Maid Marian had given him. Em handled it with respect and presently stored it away in one of her hidey-holes in the trunk. Then they played follow-my-leader until they were so tired that they had to lie back on thick beds of leaves and rest.

"I did not expect to see you again so soon," said Em as they lay picking the aromatic leaves and chewing them, while a prim Jacobean lady shook her head at them.

Wil explained about the invasion of the film company and she listened with interest.

"A sort of strolling players," she commented. "My father was one—flat contrary to the family's commands, of course. I saw many pieces performed before I was rescued from the life by my respected grandmother to be brought up as befitted one of our name." She sighed.

For the next two months Wil found many opportunities to slip off and visit Em, for Mr. Buckle became greatly in demand as an adviser on matters of costume, and even Squabb was pressed into service ironing doublets and mending hose.

But one day Wil saw his relatives at breakfast with long faces, and he learned that the company had finished shooting the inside scenes and were about to move to Florida to take the Sherwood Forest sequences. The handsome additional income which the family had been making was about to cease, and Wil realized with dismay that the old life would begin again.

Later when he was starting off to visit Em he found a little group, consisting of Aunt Agatha, Uncle Umbert, Mr. Slock-enheimer and his secretary, Mr. Jakes, on one of the back landings. Wil shrank into the shadows and listened to their conversation with alarm.

"One million," Mr. Slockenheimer was saying. "Yes, sir, one million's my last word. But I'll ship the house over to Hollywood myself, as carefully as if it was a new-laid egg. You may be sure of that Ma'am, I appreciate your feelings, and you and all your family may go on living in it for the rest of your days. Every brick will be numbered and every floor-board will be lettered so that they'll go back in their exact places. This house certainly will be a gold-mine to me—it'll save its value twice over in a year as sets for different films. There's Tudor, Gothic, Norman, Saxon, Georgian, Decorated, all under one roof."

"But we shall have to have salaries too, mind," said Uncle Umbert greedily. "We can't be expected to uproot ourselves like this and move to Hollywood all for nothing."

Mr. Slockenheimer raised his eyebrows at this, but said agreeably:

"Okay, I'll sign you on as extras." He pulled out a fistful of forms, scribbled his signature on them and handed them to Aunt Agatha. "There you are, Ma'am, twenty-year contracts for the whole bunch."

"Dirt cheap at the price, even so," Wil heard him whisper to the secretary.

"Now as we've finished shooting I'll have the masons in tomorrow and start chipping the old place to bits. Hangings and furniture will be crated separately. It'll take quite a time, of course; shouldn't think we'll get it done under three weeks." He looked with respect over his shoulder at a vista of dark corridor which stretched away for half a mile.

Wil stole away with his heart thudding. Were they actually proposing to pull down the house, *this* house, and ship it to

Hollywood for film sets? What about the tree? Would they hack it down, or dig it up and transport it, leaves and all?

"What's the matter, boy?" asked Em, her cheek bulging with the giant humbug he had brought her.

"The film company's moving away, and they're going to take Troy with them for using as backgrounds for films."

"The whole house?"

"Yes."

"Oh," said Em, and became very thoughtful.

"Em."

"Yes?"

"What—I mean, what would happen to you if they found this room and cut the tree down, or dug it up?"

"I'm not sure," she said, pondering. "I shouldn't go *on* after that—none of us would in here—but as to exactly *what* would happen—; I don't expect it would be bad. Perhaps we should just go out like lamps."

"Well then it must be stopped," said Wil so firmly that he surprised himself.

"Can you forbid it? You're the Heir, aren't you?"

"Not till old Uncle Winthrop dies. We'll have to think of some other plan."

"I have an idea," said Em, wrinkling her brow with effort. "In my days, producers would do much for a well-written new play, one that had never been seen before. Is it still like that nowadays?"

"Yes I think so, but we don't know anyone who writes plays," Wil pointed out.

"I have a play laid by somewhere," she explained. "The writer was a friend of my father—he asked my father to take it up to London to have it printed. My father bade me take care of it and I put it in my bundle of clothes. It was on that journey, as we were passing through Oxford, that I was seen and carried off by my respected grandmother, and I never saw my father or Mr. Shakespeere again, so the poor man lost his play."

"Mr. Shakespeere, did you say?" asked Wil, stuttering slightly. "What was the name of the play?"

"I forget. I have it here somewhere." She began delving about in a cranny between two branches and presently drew out a dirty old manuscript. Wil stared at it with popping eyes.

The Tragicall Historie of Robin Hoode
A play by Wm. Shakespeere
Act I, Scene I. Sherwood Forest. Enter John Lackland,
De Bracy, Sheriff of Nottingham, Knights, Lackeys and
attendants.

JOHN L.   Good sirs, the occasion of our coming hither
Is, since our worthy brother Cœur de Lion
far from our isle now wars on Paynim soil,
The apprehension of that recreant knave
Most caitiff outlaw who is known by some
As Robin Locksley; by others Robin Hood;
More, since our coffers gape with idle locks
The forfeiture of his ill-gotten gains.
Thus Locksley's stocks will stock our locks enow
While he treads air beneath the forest bough.

"Golly," said Wil. "Shakespeere's Robin Hood. I wonder what Mr. Slockenheimer would say to this?"

"Well don't wait. *Go and ask him.* It's yours—I'll make you a present of it."

He wriggled back through the leaves with frantic speed, slammed the door, and raced down the passage towards the Great Hall. Mr. Slockenheimer was there superintending the packing of some expensive and elaborate apparatus.

"Hello, Junior. Haven't seen you in days. Well, how d'you like the thought of moving to Hollywood eh?"

"Not very much," said Wil frankly. "You see I'm used to it

here, and—and the house is too; I don't think the move would be good for it."

"Think the dry air would crumble it, mebbe? Well, there's something to what you say. I'll put in air-conditioning apparatus the other end. I'm sorry you don't take to the idea, though. Hollywood's a swell place."

"Mr. Slockenheimer," said Wil. "I've got something here which is rather valuable. It's mine—somebody gave it to me. And it's genuine. I was wondering if I could do a sort of swap —exchange it for the house, you know."

"It would have to be mighty valuable," replied Mr. Slockenheimer cautiously. "Think it's worth a million, son? What is it?"

"It's a play by Mr. Shakespeere—a new play that no one's seen before."

"Eh?"

"I'll show you," said Wil confidently, pulling out the MS.

"The Tragicall Historie of Robin Hoode," read Mr. Slockenheimer slowly. "By Wm. Shakespeere. Well I'll be gosh-darned. Just when I'd finished the indoor scenes. Isn't that just my luck. Hey, Junior—are you sure this is genuine?— Well, Jakes will know, he knows everything; hey," he called to his secretary, "come and have a look at this."

The dry Mr. Jakes let out a whistle when he saw the signature.

"That's genuine all right," he said. "It's quite something you've got there. First production of the original Shakespeare play by Q. P. Slockenheimer."

"Well, will you swap?" asked Wil once more.

"I'll say I will," exclaimed Mr. Slockenheimer slapping him thunderously on the back. "You can keep your mouldering old barracks. I'll send you twenty stalls for the premiere. *Robin Hoode by Wm. Shakespeere.* Well, what do you know!"

"There's just one thing," said Wil pausing.

"Yes, Bud?"

"These contracts you gave my uncle and aunt and the others. Are they still binding?"

"Not if you don't want."

"Oh, but I do—I'd much rather they went to Hollywood."

Mr. Slockenheimer burst out laughing.

"Oh, I get the drift. Okay, Junior, I daresay they won't bother me as much as they do you. I'll hold them to those contracts as tight as glue. Twenty years eh? You'll be of age by then, I guess? Your Uncle Umbert can be the Sheriff of Nottingham, he's about the build for the part. And we'll fit your Aunt Aggie in somewhere."

"And Buckle and Squabb?"

"Yes, yes," said Mr. Slockenheimer, much tickled. "Though what you'll do here all on your own—however, that's your affair. Right, boys, pack up those cameras next."

Three days later the whole outfit was gone, and with them, swept away among the flash bulbs, cameras, extras, crates, props and costumes, went Squabb, Buckle, Aunt Agatha, Uncle Umbert, Cousin Cedric and all the rest.

Empty and peaceful the old house dreamed, with sunlight shifting from room to room and no sound to break the silence, save in one place, where the voices of children could be heard faintly above the rustling of a tree.

Mrs Nutti's Fireplace

Mark, who wished to get rid of the space-gun his great-uncle had sent him, and acquire something more useful, had brought home a copy of *Exchange and Mart.*

" 'Princess-type boiler fireplace exchanged for gent's bicycle,' " he read aloud consideringly.

"But we don't want a fireplace," Harriet pointed out. "And we haven't a bicycle."

"Or there's five gross jazz-coloured balloons, a tiger's head, and two whale teeth. Offered in exchange for go-kart or griffin's eggs."

"The balloons would be nice." Harriet swallowed her last bite of cake—they were having Friday tea—and came to hang over his shoulder. "If we had a go-kart."

" 'Sale or exchange road-breaker tools interested arc welder, spray plant, w.h.y. Buyer collects.' I do wonder w.h.y.? They seem queer things to collect."

" 'Pocket Gym, judo suit, height increaser, neck developer, strength course, weights, and Dynamic Tension course.' *That* seems a bargain. Only three pounds."

"No height increasers in this family, thanks," said Mr Armitage, without looking up from his evening paper. "Or weight increasers. Kindly remember the house is three hundred years old."

" 'A hundredweight of green garnishing in 10-inch sections, de-rinder and sausage-spooling machinery'; they might come in handy for Christmas decorations," Harriet said thoughtfully.

" 'One million toys at 65p per 100, including Woo-Woos, Jumping Shrimp, et cetera.' "

"Mother wouldn't like the Jumping Shrimp."

"I would not," agreed Mrs Armitage, pouring herself another cup of tea.

"*Gosh!* '7 in. span baboon spider with ½ in. fangs, £5.' "

"*No.*"

"I don't really want it," Harriet said hastily. "But—listen —'2½-year-old Himalayan bears, only £42'—oh, Mother, *they'd* be lovely. 'Or would exchange griffin's eggs.' What a pity we haven't any of those. Lots of people seem to want them."

"*Forty-two pounds?* You can't be serious. Besides, it would be too warm for Himalayan bears here."

" 'Various rattlesnakes, 6ft Mangrove snake, £8' "

"Shall we get away from this section?" Mr Armitage suggested, lowering his paper. "Anyway, isn't it time for your music lesson, Mark?"

"Yes, in just a minute. Here's something that might interest Mr Johansen," Mark said. " 'Would exchange room in town for room in country; pleasant outlook required. View by appointment.' Mr Johansen was saying only last week that he wished he had a bedsit in London so that he could go to concerts and not always have to miss the last movements to catch the ten-fifteen. I'll take this along to show him."

"Bring it back, though," said Harriet, who did not want to lose track of the Himalayan bears.

Mark was very fond of Mr Johansen his music teacher, a sad, gentle man who, as well as teaching the piano and violin, had for many years run a dogs' weekend guest house. Lately, however, he had given up the dogs because he said he was growing too old to exercise them properly. When young, he had been in love with a German princess who had been lost to him by an unfortunate bit of amateur magic. He had never married. Everybody in the village liked him very much.

"Look, Mr Johansen," said Mark, before settling down to his five-finger exercises. "You were saying only the other day that it was a pity not to use your spare room; here's somebody who wants to exchange a room in town for one in the country. Don't you think that would do for you?"

"Ach, so?" Mr Johansen carefully scanned the advertisement. "Why yes, ziss might certainly be useful. I wvonder wvere ziss room is? I will write off to ze box number." He made a note of it.

A week passed. Harriet, who had developed a passionate wish for a Himalayan bear, was hardly seen; she spent every evening making very beautiful dolls' furniture out of egg-shells, plastic egg-boxes, yoghurt pots, snail shells, and shampoo containers; when she had a hamper full of furniture she hoped to sell it all to a London toyshop for the price of a bear. She had not mentioned this plan to Mrs Armitage, who thought that a cat and a unicorn were sufficient pets for one family.

"Candleberry's lovely to ride on," Harriet said to Mark, "but you can't bring him indoors. And Walrus is always out catching mice. A bear would be cosy."

Mark was in the middle of his lesson with Mr Johansen the following week when there came a brisk peal at the front-door bell. The music master opened the door and let in an uncommon-looking old lady, very short, very wrinkled, rather like a tortoise with a disagreeable expression, wearing rimless glasses and a raincoat and sou'wester which might have been made of alligator-skin. She limped, and walked with a stick, and carried a carpet-bag which seemed to be quite heavy.

"Answer to advertisement," she said in a businesslike manner. "Name, Mrs Nutti. Room in town exchange room in country. Which room? This one?"

She stumped into the music-room. Mark twirled round on his music-stool to look at her.

"No, no. Upstairs," said Mr Johansen. "Ziss way, if you please."

"Good. Upstairs better. Much better. Better outlook. Air fresher. Burglars not so likely. Can't do with burglars— Well, show way, then!"

Mr Johansen went ahead, she followed, Mark came too.

The music teacher's house was really a bungalow, and the spare room was really an attic-loft, with sloping ceilings. But it had big dormer windows with a pleasant view of fields and woods; Mr Johansen had painted the walls (or ceiling) sky blue, so that you could imagine you were out on the roof, rather than inside a room; there was blue linoleum on the floor, an old-fashioned bed with brass knobs and a patchwork quilt, and an even older-fashioned wash-stand with a jug and basin covered in pink roses.

"Very nice," said Mrs Nutti looking round. "Very nice view. Take it for three months. Beginning now."

"But wait," objected Mark, seeing that Mr Johansen was rather dazed by this rapid dealing. *"He* hasn't seen *your* room yet. And shouldn't you exchange references or something? I'm sure people always do that."

"References?" snapped Mrs Nutti. "No point. Not exchanging references—exchanging rooms! You'll find my room satisfactory. Excellent room. Show now."

She snapped her fingers. Mark and Mr Johansen both lost their balance, as people do in a fairground trick room with a tilting floor, and fell heavily.

Mark thought as he fell,

"That's funny, I'd have said there was lino on this floor, not carpet."

"Donnerwetter!" gasped Mr Johansen (Mark had fallen on top of him). They clambered to their feet, rather embarrassed.

"It is zose heavy lorries," the music master began explaining apologetically. "Zey do shake ze house so when zey pass; but is not so very often—"

Then he stopped, staring about him in bewilderment, for Mrs Nutti was nowhere to be seen.

Nor, for that matter, was the brass-headed bed, the patchwork quilt, the wash-stand with jug and roses, the blue ceiling—

"Gosh," said Mark. He crossed to one of two high, latticed casement windows, treading noiselessly on the thick carpet, which was intricately patterned in red, blue, rose-colour, black, and gold. *"Gosh,* Mr Johansen, do come and look out."

The music master joined him at the window and they gazed together into a city filled with dusk, whose lights were beginning to twinkle out under a deep-blue, clear sky with a few matching stars. Below them, a street ran downhill to a wide river or canal; a number of slender towers, crowned with onion-shaped domes, rose in every direction; there were masts of ships on the water and the cries of gulls could be heard.

Immediately below there was a small cobbled square and, on the opposite side of it, a café with tables set under a big leafy tree which had lights strung from its branches. A group of men with odd instruments—long curving pipes, bulb-shaped drums, outsize jews' harps—were playing a plaintive tune, while another man went round among the tables, holding out a wooden bowl.

"I do not understand," muttered Mr Johansen. "Wvat has happened? Wvere are we? Wvere is Mrs Nutti? *Wvere is my room?"*

"Why, don't you see, sir," said Mark, who, more accustomed to this kind of thing, was beginning to guess what had happened. "This must be Mrs Nutti's room that she said she'd show you. I thought she meant in London but of course in the advertisement it didn't actually say London it just said 'room in town'—I wonder what town this is?"

"But—ach, himmel—zen wvere is *my* room?"

"Well, I suppose Mrs Nutti has got it. This seems quite a nice room, though, don't you think?"

Mr Johansen gazed about it rather wildly, pushing long thin hands through his white hair until the strands were all standing on end and he looked like a gibbon.

Mrs Nutti's room was furnished in a much more stately way than the humble attic bedroom. For a start, there was a massive four-poster bed with crimson damask hangings. The walls, also, were covered with some kind of damask, which made the room rather dark. Two tall black polished cabinets on claw feet stood against the wall facing the windows. A lamp in a boat-shaped gilt container hung suspended by a chain from the ceiling and threw a dim light. A velvet curtain, held back by a tasselled cord, partly covered the doorway; a small organ stood to the right of the door. Strangest of all, opposite the doorway there was a fireplace with a large heavy pair of polished metal andirons and a massive white marble mantelpiece which appeared to have suffered from some accident. The right side of the mantel was supported by a large carved marble heraldic beast with a collar round its neck, but the beast that should have supported the left-hand side was missing; it had apparently been dragged out of the wall, like a decoration from an iced cake, leaving nothing but a jagged hole.

"That's a bit of a mess," Mark said. "I do think Mrs Nutti should have put it right for you before she lent you her room. It's rather a shame; the monster on the other side is awfully nice. A kind of furry eagle."

"A griffin," corrected Mr Johansen absently. "Ze legs, you see, are zose of a lion. Head, zat of an eagle, also wvings. But wvere *is* zis Mrs Nutti?"

"Wherever she is, she's left her carpet-bag behind," said Mark, picking it off the floor. "Blimey, what a weight. Hey, Mrs Nutti? Are you downstairs?"

He put the bag down again, walked through the open door, and stuck his head back through again to say, "She really has done a neat job, Mr Johansen, it's still your landing outside."

Bemusedly, Mr Johansen followed him out and discovered that, as Mark had said, the transformation of the loft-room went no farther than the door; outside were Mr Johansen's tidy bare landing, his coconut-matted stairs, and his prints of Alpine flora.

They went down, expecting to find Mrs Nutti in the music room. But she had gone.

"Back to wherever she came from, I suppose," Mark said.

"Taking my room wizz her," Mr Johansen murmured plaintively.

"But really, sir, hers is quite a nice room, don't you think? And it has a smashing view. I know it's not London, which was what you wanted, but maybe they have concerts in this town too. Where do you suppose it is?"

"How should I know?" said poor Mr Johansen, twisting his hair some more.

"Do let's go back upstairs and have another look."

But by the time they had gone back, full dark had fallen on the town outside the window of the new room, and not much could be seen except a wide prospect of twinkling lights. They could hear music from across the square, and smell delicious smells of herbs and grilled meat.

"We'll have to come back in daylight," Mark suggested. "Tell you one thing, though, this place must be east of England; it gets dark sooner."

"Zat is so," agreed Mr Johansen. "In any case, I suppose zose towers are minarets; zis town is perhaps in Turkey or Persia."

"What's Turkish music like, is it nice? Shall we have a wander round the streets and ask where the place is?"

Mr Johansen was somewhat hesitant about this; it took Mark a while to persuade him.

But now they came up against a difficulty: they could see the town, but there seemed to be no way of getting into it. If they went downstairs and out through Mr Johansen's front door, they merely found themselves in his ordinary garden, walking between neat rows of Canterbury bells towards the commonplace village street.

"We'll have to jump out of the window," Mark said.

But it was a very much higher drop from Mrs Nutti's window—and on to a cobbled street at that—than from Mr Johansen's attic. Mr Johansen demurred.

"Never should I be able to face your dear muzzer if you wvere to break your leg. Besides, how should wve get back?"

Mark had not considered this problem.

"I'll bring our fruit-ladder from home tomorrow morning," he said. "Perhaps I'd better be off now; Mother gets worried if I'm more than three-quarters of an hour late for supper, and thinks I've fallen in a river or something."

Harriet was greatly interested in the story of Mr Johansen's room-exchange.

"I wonder *why* Mrs Nutti wanted to swap?" she pondered, and made Mark tell her over and over the few not particularly enlightening things the old lady had said.

"She seemed worried about burglars? And part of the fireplace was missing? Perhaps burglars had gone off with it?"

"You'd hardly think anyone would pinch half a fireplace," Mark objected. "Still, it was gone, that's true. Maybe she wanted to make sure no one could go off with the other half."

"What was in the carpet-bag she left behind? Did you look? Do you think she left it by mistake or on purpose?"

"I didn't look. It was jolly heavy, whatever it was. Maybe she got fed up with carrying it about."

"When you go down tomorrow I'm coming too," Harriet said firmly.

"Good, then you can help carry the ladder."

Taking the ladder was a waste of time, however, as they soon discovered. They leaned it up against the front of the house, so that its narrow top was wedged firmly against what appeared to be the window of Mr Johansen's attic.

Then they rang the door bell and the music master let them in.

"Is the room still there, sir? Has Mrs Nutti been back? Did she fetch her bag? Can you still see the city?"

"Ja—ja—ze room is still zere, and ze bag also. But Frau Nutti has not returned. You wvish to see it?" he asked Harriet kindly.

"Oh yes, please!"

Mark and Harriet ran eagerly upstairs, Mr Johansen following more slowly.

"There!" said Mark with pride, pointing to the view.

"Coo!" breathed Harriet, taking it all in.

It was blazing daylight now, and obviously hot, hot weather, most unlike the grey chilly June day they had left behind downstairs. Dogs lay panting in the shade under the big tree. Men in caps like chopped-off cones sat sipping coffee and cool drinks. Boats with coloured sails plied to and fro across the river.

"What a gorgeous place," said Harriet. "Do let's go down. *Oh*—where's the ladder?"

"Not there," said Mark sadly.

"What a swindle. I've an idea though—next time we come we'll bring a rope. Then we can tie it to the window-catch and climb down."

Mark cheered up at this practical plan. "It's bad luck about your concerts, though, sir; still, I suppose it's only for three months."

"Is no matter. I can listen to zose men across ze square; zeir music is most uncommon. Also I have ze organ to play on."

He sat down at the little organ, fiddled around with bellows and pedals, and suddenly produced a short, sweet, powerful snatch of melody.

"Oh, do go on!" cried Harriet, as he stopped.

But he, looking round, said, "Wvat wvas zat noise?"

A kind of crack or tap had come from the other side of the four-poster. Harriet ran round.

"It sounded like an electric bulb going. Oh, is this Mrs Nutti's bag? Heavens, it's heavy—whatever can there be in it?"

Harriet parted the flaps of the bag, which was not fastened, and began lifting out masses of empty paper bags, crumpled old magazines, chocolate wrappers, squashed cereal packets, newspapers, tissues, paper napkins, and other wadding.

"What a lot of junk. There's something hard and heavy right at the bottom though—quite big, too. Oh, it's an egg."

Mr Johansen got up from the organ-stool and came to look over their shoulders at the contents of the carpet-bag.

An egg it certainly was, and no common egg either. It was a good deal bigger than a rugby ball; it might just have fitted into the oval kind of washing-up bowl. It was plain white, but veined over with faint greenish-blue lines. Egg-shaped.

"How queer that Mrs Nutti should have forgotten about it—" Harriet was beginning, when the sound came from the egg again—crack!

"It's hatching!"

At this, Mr Johansen suddenly became very upset.

"No, no, zis I cannot have. Zis is too much! Her room, yes I do not object, provided she take goot care of my room, I wvill do ze same for hers. But to have care of an egg, no, no, zat is ze outside, das tut mir zehr leid, I am not an incubator! Ze doggies I haf give up, because I can no longer take sufficient care—"

"I'll hatch it, I'll look after it!" said Harriet eagerly. "I've hatched lots of owls' eggs, I'll put it in our airing-cupboard, I'll really look after it carefully, Mr Johansen. I'm sure Mother won't mind. Oh, do you suppose it could be a roc?"

"Not big enough," said Mark.

Mr Johansen looked doubtful and distressed. "Suppose Frau Nutti come back? It is, after all, her egg?"

"Then you tell her to come up the road to us," Mark said. "My sister really knows a lot about eggs, sir, she's an expert chick-raiser."

"In zat case, best to get it home before it hatches quite out, nicht wahr?"

This proved a difficult task. The carpet-bag was so heavy that it took all their united strength to get it down the stairs.

"And you say Mrs Nutti was a little old lady?" said Harriet, scarlet with effort. "How can she ever have carried it all the way from—"

"All the way from wherever she came from?"

"Well, *we* certainly can't carry it from here to home. Mr Johansen, could we possibly borrow your wheelbarrow?"

"Jawohl, yes indeed," said Mr Johansen, only too glad to be rid of the responsibility of the egg before it hatched. They balanced the fruit-ladder across the barrow and put the carpet-bag on top of the ladder, and so set off for home. Mr Johansen watched them anxiously until they were out of sight; then he started upstairs, going slowly at first but faster and faster. He entered Mrs Nutti's room, sat down at the organ, and was soon lost, deaf, and regardless of anything but the beautiful music he was making.

When Harriet and Mark reached the Armitage house and unloaded the carpet-bag, they were disconcerted to find that the egg's weight had bent the ladder into a V like a hockey-stick.

"Oh, dear," Harriet said. "I'm afraid Father's not going to be very pleased."

Luckily their parents were out, so they were able to man-handle the egg upstairs without interference. A cast-iron cannon ball would not have been much harder to deal with.

"What kind of bird can it possibly be?" panted Harriet.

Mark had a theory, but he wasn't going to commit himself just yet.

"Maybe it comes from some planet where the atmosphere

is less dense. Anyway, whatever it is, it seemed to enjoy Mr Johansen's music. Perhaps we ought to play to it, to help it hatch."

"No organ, though; it'll have to be satisfied with recorders."

The egg took longer to hatch than they had expected; perhaps the recorder music was not so stimulating. A couple of weeks went by. Occasional cracking noises came from the airing-cupboard, but Harriet had carefully swathed the egg in winter blankets, so that it was not visible; Mrs Armitage said absently, "I do hope the immersion heater isn't going to blow up again," but she was busy making strawberry jam and did not investigate the noises. "Why have you children taken to playing your recorders on the upstairs landing all day long? Can't you find anything better to do?"

"Rehearsing for the fête," Harriet said promptly.

"It seems a funny place to rehearse."

"Well, it's warm, you see—just by the airing-cupboard."

At last the egg burst.

"Good god, what's that?" said Mr Armitage, rushing in from the garden, where he had been thinning out lettuces.

"Oh my gracious, do you think someone's planted a bomb on us?" exclaimed his wife, dropping a pot of jam on the kitchen floor.

"More likely something those children have been up to," said their loving father.

Mark and Harriet had been eating their elevenses—apples and cheese—in the play-room.

At the tremendous bang they looked at each other with instantaneous comprehension of what had happened, and raced upstairs.

"Heavens! The smell!" gasped Harriet.

It was very strong.

"Sulphur," said Mark knowledgeably.

There was a good deal of mess about, too. The airing-cupboard door was a splintered wreck, and the floor and walls for some distance round were splashed with yellow goo, like egg-yolk, only more so. Several windows were cracked.

A tangle of damp and soggy blankets and towels on the upstairs landing made it difficult to get to the airing-cupboard.

Mr and Mrs Armitage arrived.

"What *happened?*" cried Mrs Armitage.

"Harriet put an egg to hatch in the airing-cupboard," Mark explained.

"An egg? What kind of an egg, would you be so kind as to explain?"

"Well, we don't know yet—somebody left it with Mr Johansen, you see, and he didn't feel quite equal to the worry—"

"Oh, delightful," said Mr Armitage. "So he just passed it on to us. Mr Johansen is an excellent music teacher but I really—"

"Listen!" said Harriet.

From the sodden mass of household linen still inside the cupboard came a plaintive sound.

It was a little like the call of a curlew—a kind of thin, bubbling, rising, sorrowful cry.

"It's the chick!" exclaimed Harriet joyfully, and she began pulling out pillowcases and tablecloths. Out with them came the lower half of Mrs Nutti's egg, and, still crouched in it, filling it and bulging over the broken edges, they saw a bedraggled, crumpled, damp, dejected creature that seemed all bony joints and big eyes and limp horny claws.

"Well—it's rather a poppet," Harriet said, after a pause.

Mr Armitage stared at it and made a thoughtful comment. "I'm not a one for rash statements, but I don't think I *ever,* in all my born days, laid eyes on an uglier, scrawnier, soggier, more repulsive-looking chick. In the north country they'd call it a bare golly. What's it supposed to be, tell me that?"

"And for this hideous monster," wailed Mrs Armitage, "all our sheets and blankets and tablecloths and the best monogrammed towels have to be ruined?"

"Honestly, Ma, don't worry," Harriet said. "Mark and I will take everything down to the coin-op dry-clean after lunch, I promise. I must just give the chick a rinse first, and set him on the play-room radiator to dry. You'll see, when he's cleaned up and fluffed out he'll look quite different."

"He can look a whole lot different and still be as ugly as sin," prophesied Mr Armitage.

"And what's he going to eat?" demanded Mrs Armitage, as Harriet lifted up the chick, egg-shell and all, and carried him away, staggering under his weight, to the play-room, calling to Mark over her shoulder as she did so to fetch a bucket of warm water and some soapless shampoo.

While they were cleaning and disinfecting the sheets and blankets at the laundromat (it took three trips and the whole afternoon and all next month's allowance) Mark said to Harriet,

"Now do you know what the chick is?"

"No, but he's a very queer shape, I must say. His back end isn't a bit like a bird, and he's got a funny straggly tail with a tassel at the end. How big do you think he's likely to grow?"

"I should think he's about a fifth of his full size now."

"How do you reckon that?"

"I think he's a griffin-chick."

"A griffin?" said Harriet, dismayed. "Are you sure?"

"Well, he's just like the one carved on Mrs Nutti's mantelpiece."

"Oh my goodness," Harriet said sadly. "If only we'd known when he was in the egg, we could have exchanged him for a Himalayan bear."

"No we couldn't," said Mark primly. "He's not ours to swap. He's Mrs Nutti's. I suppose she sent him to the country to hatch out."

"Well, *I* think it was very neglectful of her to go off and just *leave* him."

When they finally tottered home with the last piles of clean laundry ("Honestly," grumbled Mark, "we shall have biceps like boa-constrictors after all the lifting we've done lately.") Harriet's disappointment over the loss of the Himalayan bear was greatly reduced.

"Oh, I say!" she exclaimed, lifting a fold of newspaper in the laundry basket which they had left propped against the warm radiator. "Do look! He's dried off and he's *furry!*"

At the sound of her voice the griffin-chick woke up, sleepily uncurled, and staggered out from among the crumpled newspapers.

His appearance was now quite different. The dark damp tendrils all over his back, sides, hind legs and tail were fluffed out into soft, thick grey fur, like that of a short-haired Persian cat. His stumpy little wings and head were covered with pale grey eiderdown. His beak, brown before, had turned red, and it was wide open.

"Gleep. Gleep. Thrackle, thrackle, thrackle. Gleep. GLEEP!"

"Oh, heavens, he's starving! Just a minute, Furry, hang on a tick, and we'll get you something to eat. Do you suppose he'll eat bread-and-milk?"

"We can try," said Mark.

Bread-and-milk went down splendidly, when dolloped into the gaping red beak with a dessert-spoon. One basinful was not enough. Nor were two. Nor were seven. But after the ninth bowlful the baby griffin gave a great happy yawn, closed his beak and eyes simultaneously, clambered on to the lap of Harriet, who was kneeling on the floor beside him, tucked his head under a wing (from where it immediately slipped out again as the wing was not nearly big enough to cover it) and fell asleep.

After about three minutes Harriet said,

"It's like having a cart-horse on one's lap. I'll have to shift him."

Struggling like a coal-heaver she shifted the chick on to the hearthrug. He did not even blink.

Harriet and Mark sat thoughtfully regarding their new acquisition.

"He's going to be expensive to feed," Mark said.

This proved an understatement.

After three weeks Mrs Armitage said, "Look, I don't want to seem mean, and I must admit your Furry does look better now he isn't so bony and goose-pimply but—thirty-six bowls of bread-and-milk a day!"

"Yes, it is a lot," agreed Harriet sadly.

"Maybe Mr Johansen could contribute towards his support?"

"Oh, no, he's awfully hard up," Mark said. "I'll pay for the bread and Harriet can pay for the milk. I've some money saved from apple-picking."

"That still leaves the sugar and raisins."

Harriet decided that she would have to dispose of her dolls' furniture.

Unfortunately that was the day when Furry, tired of his newspaper nest, looked round for somewhere new to roost, and noticed the wicker hamper in which Harriet stored her finished products. He flapped his little wings, jumped up on top, turned round two or three times, digging his claws into the wicker, until he was comfortable, stuck his head under his wing (where it now fitted better; his wings were growing fast) and went to sleep. Slowly the hamper sagged beneath his weight; by the time Harriet found him it was completely flattened, like a wafer-ice that has been left in the sun.

"Oh, *Furry! Look* what you've done!"

"Gleep," replied the baby griffin mournfully, stretching out first one hind leg and then the other.

He was hungry again.

"It's no use blaming him," Harriet said, inspecting her ruined work. "He just doesn't know his own weight."

The next night was a chilly one, and in the middle of it

Furry, becoming fretful and shivery and lonesome, clambered on to Harriet's bed for warmth and company. Harriet, fast asleep, began to have strange dreams of avalanches and earthquakes; by the morning three legs of her bed had buckled under Furry's weight; Furry and Harriet were huddled in a heap down at the south-west corner.

"It's queer," said Mark, "considering how fast he's putting on weight, that he doesn't grow very much bigger."

"He's more condensed than we are," Harriet said.

"Condensed!" said Mrs Armitage. "From now on, that creature has got to live out of doors. Any day now he'll go right through the floorboards. And your father says the same."

"Oh, Mother!"

"It's no use looking at *me* like that. Look at the play-room floor! It's sagging, and dented all over with claw-marks; it looks like Southend beach."

"I suppose he'll have to roost in the woodshed," Harriet said sadly."

They fetched a load of hay and made him a snug nest. While he was investigating it, and burying himself up to his beak, they crept indoors and went to bed, feeling like the parents of Hansel and Gretel.

Next morning Furry was up on the woodshed roof, gleeping anxiously. The woodshed had tilted over at a forty-five-degree angle.

"Oh, Furry! How did you ever get up there?"

"He must have flown," said Mark.

"But he can't fly!"

"He was bound to start soon; his wings are nearly full-grown. And proper feathers are sprouting all over them, and on his head too."

If Furry had flown up to the roof of the shed, however, he showed no signs of remembering how to set about flying down again. He teetered about on the sloping roof, gleeping more and more desperately. At last, just in time, he managed to fly a few hasty, panic-stricken flaps, and coasted to earth as the shed collapsed behind him.

"You *clever* baby," said Harriet, giving him a hug to show that nobody blamed him.

"Thrackle, thrackle. Gleep, cooroocooroo, gleep." Furry leaned lovingly against Harriet. She managed to leap aside just before he flattened her; he now weighed as much as a well-nourished grizzly.

Harriet and Mark were extremely busy. In order to earn Furry's keep they had taken jobs, delivering papers, selling petrol at the garage, and washing up at the Two-Door Café, but they were in a constant state of anxiety all the time as to what he might be doing while they were away from home.

"Do you think we ought to mention to Mr Johansen that it's rather difficult with Furry?" Harriet suggested one day. "It isn't that I'm not *fond* of him—"

"It's rather difficult to get him to pay attention these days; Mr Johansen, I mean."

Indeed, the music master seemed to be in a dream most of the time.

"Never haf I played such an instrument, never!" he declared. When he was not playing Mrs Nutti's organ he was leaning out of the spare-room window, gazing at the view, listening to the music across the square, rapt in a kind of trance. Mark was a little worried about him.

"Honestly, sir, don't you think you ought to get out for a bit of fresh air sometimes?"

"But you see I haf ze feeling zat from zis window I might some day see my lost Sophie."

"But even if you did, we still don't know how to get into the town."

Their experiment with rope had proved a failure. The rope had simply disappeared, as fast as they paid it out of the window. Nor was it possible to attract the attention of the people down below and persuade them to fetch a ladder (which had been another of Harriet's suggestions). Neither shouts nor waves had the slightest effect. And Mr Johansen had vetoed any notion of either Mark or Harriet climbing out.

"For you might disappear like ze rope, and zen what should I tell your dear muzzer?"

"So even if you did see your lost Sophie from the window it wouldn't do you much good; it would be more of a worry than anything else," Mark said with ruthless practicality.

"Ach—who knows—who knows?" sighed Mr Johansen.

Several more weeks passed. Furry, measured by Mark, was now nearly as big as the marble griffin under the mantelpiece.

Then, one evening, when Mark was in the midst of his piano lesson, Harriet burst in.

"Oh—Mr Johansen—I'm most terribly sorry to interrupt— but it's Furry! He's flown up on top of the water-tower, and he's dreadfully scared and gleeping away like mad, I'm so afraid he might damage the tower—*do* come, Mark, and see if you can talk him down, you're the one he trusts most. I've brought a pail of bread-and-milk."

They ran outside, Mr Johansen following. It was the first time he had been out for days.

The village water-tower stood a couple of fields away from the music master's bungalow. It was a large metal cylinder supported on four metal legs which looked slender to support the weight of goodness knows how many thousand gallons of water, but were apparently equal to the job. It did not, however, seem likely that they were equal to supporting a full-grown griffin as well, particularly since he was running back and forth on top of the cylinder, gleeping distractedly, opening and shutting his wings, leaning to look over the edge, and then jumping back with a tremendous clatter and scrape of toenails on galvanized iron.

"Furry!" shouted Mark. "Keep calm! Keep calm!"

"Gleep! Thrackle, thrackle, thrackle."

"Shut your wings and stand still," ordered Mark.

With his eyes starting out as he looked at the awful drop below him, the griffin obeyed.

"Now, Harriet, swing the bucket of bread-and-milk round a bit, so the smell rises up."

Harriet did so. Some bread-and-milk slopped out on the grass. The sweet and haunting fragrance steamed up through the evening air.

"Gleeeeeep!"

A famished wail came from the tip of the water-tower.

"You're very silly!" Harriet shouted scoldingly. "If you hadn't got yourself up there you could be eating this nice bread-and-milk now."

"Furry," called Mark, "watch me. Are you watching?"

Silence from up above. Then a faint thrackle.

"Right! Now, open your wings."

Mark had his arms by his sides; he now raised them to shoulder height.

Furry, after a moment or two, hesitantly did the same.

"Now lower them again. Do as I do. Just keep raising and lowering."

Following Mark's example, Furry did this half a dozen times. The tower shook a bit.

"Right, faster and faster. Faster still! Now—*Jump!* KEEP FLAPPING!"

Furry jumped, and forgot to flap; he started falling like a stone.

"Gleep!"

"*Flap*, you fool!"

The onlookers leapt away; just in time, Furry began flapping again and, when he was within eight feet of the ground, suddenly soared upwards once more.

"*Don't* land on the tower again. Flap with *both* wings—not just one. You're going ROUND AND ROUND," Mark shouted, cupping hands about his mouth. "That's better. Don't flap so fast. Slower! Like this!"

He demonstrated.

Furry hurtled past, eyes tight shut, claws clenched, wings nothing but a blur. Then back again. It was like the progress of a balloon with the string taken off.

"Make your strokes *slower*."

"It's as bad as learning to swim," Harriet said. "People get quick and frantic in just the same way. Still, he is doing better now. Just so long as he doesn't hit the tower. Or Mr Johansen's roof."

Several times Furry had only just cleared the bungalow. At last, more or less in control, he flapped himself down to Mr Johansen's front garden, shaving off all the front hedge on his way, and flattening a bed of Canterbury bells.

Mark and Harriet arrived at top speed, with the half-full bucket slopping between them, and set it down on the path. Furry, gleeping between mouthfuls, began frantically gobbling.

At this rather distracted moment, Mrs Nutti arrived.

"What's this, then, what's this?" she snapped angrily, taking in the scene at a glance. "Who let him out? Should be *up*-stairs, in room, not in garden. Burglars, burglars might come, might see him."

"Out?" said Harriet. "He's too heavy to keep indoors these days."

"All wrong—very bad," said Mrs Nutti furiously. "Why did I take room in country? To keep him out of way of griffin collectors. Town full of them. Come along, you!" she bawled at Furry. Before Mark or Harriet could protest she had snapped a collar on his neck and dragged him indoors, up Mr Johansen's staircase.

They ran after her.

"Hey, stop!" shouted Mark. "What are you doing with him?"

Arriving in the spare room, they found Mrs Nutti struggling to push Furry into the ragged hole under the mantel-piece.

"You don't mean," gasped Harriet, outraged, "that you intend him to spend the rest of his life *there,* holding up that shelf?"

"Why else leave egg here to hatch?" panted Mrs Nutti angrily. dragging on the collar.

But Furry, reared on freedom and bread-and-milk, was too strong for Mrs Nutti.

With a loud snap the collar parted as he strained away from her, and he shot across the room, breaking one of the bedposts like a stick of celery. The window splintered as he struck it, and then he was out and away, flapping strongly up into the blue, blue star-sprinkled sky over the foreign city.

One gleep came back to them, then a joyful burst of the full, glorious song of an adult griffin.

Then he dwindled to a speck and was gone.

"There!" said Harriet. "That just serves you right, Mrs Nutti. Why, you hadn't even looked after him and you expected him to hold up your fireplace!"

She was almost crying with indignation.

Mrs Nutti spoke to no one. With her lips angrily compressed she snatched up the carpet-bag, cast a furious look round the room, and marched out, pulling the room together behind her as one might drag along a counterpane.

By the time they heard the front door slam, they were back in Mr Johansen's attic, with its brass bedstead and patch-work quilt.

Mr Johansen walked slowly to the window and looked out, at the trampled garden and the empty bread-and-milk bucket, which still lay on the path.

"I suppose we'll never see Furry again," Mark said, clearing his throat.

"Or I, my Sophie," sighed Mr Johansen.

"Oh, I don't know," Harriet said. "I wouldn't be surprised if Furry found his way back sometime. He's awfully fond of us. And I'm *sure* you'll find your Sophie some day, Mr Johansen. I really am sure you will."

"We'll start looking for another room in town for you right away!" Mark called back, as they walked out through the battered gate.

"It really is lucky Furry didn't hit the water-tower," Harriet said. "I should think it would have taken years of pocket-money to pay for *that* damage. Now—as soon as we've fixed up the airing-cupboard door—"

"—And the fruit-ladder—"

"And the woodshed and the legs of my bed and Mr Johansen's front gate—I can start saving up for a Himalayan bear."

Humblepuppy

Our house was furnished mainly from auction sales. When you buy furniture that way you get a lot of extra things besides the particular piece that you were after, since the stuff is sold in lots: Lot 13, two Persian rugs, a set of golf-clubs, a sewing-machine, a walnut radio-cabinet, and a plinth.

It was in this way that I acquired a tin deedbox, which came with two coal-scuttles and a broom cupboard. The deedbox is solid metal, painted black, big as a medium-sized suitcase. When I first brought it home I put it in my study, planning to use it as a kind of filing-cabinet for old typescripts. I had gone into the kitchen, and was busy arranging the brooms in their new home, when I heard a loud thumping coming from the direction of the study.

I went back, thinking that a bird must have flown through the window; no bird, but the banging seemed to be inside the deedbox. I had already opened it as soon as it was in my possession, to see if there were any diamonds or bearer bonds worth thousands of pounds inside (there weren't), but I opened it again. The key was attached to the handle by a thin chain. There was nothing inside. I shut it. The banging started again. I opened it.

Still nothing inside.

Well, this was broad daylight, two o'clock on Thursday afternoon, people going past in the road outside and a radio

schools programme chatting away to itself in the next room.
It was not a ghostly kind of time, so I put my hand into the
empty box and moved it about.

Something shrank away from my hand. I heard a faint,
scared whimper. It could almost have been my own, but
wasn't. Knowing that someone—something?—else was afraid
too put heart into me. Exploring carefully and gently around
the interior of the box I felt the contour of a small, bony,
warm, trembling body with big awkward feet, and silky dangling ears, and a cold nose that, when I found it, nudged for
a moment anxiously but trustingly into the palm of my hand.
So I knelt down, put the other hand into the box as well,
cupped them under a thin little ribby chest, and lifted out
Humblepuppy.

He was quite light.

I couldn't see him, but I could hear his faint inquiring
whimper, and I could hear his toenails scratch on the floorboards.

Just at that moment the cat, Taffy, came in.

Taffy has a lot of character. Every cat has a lot of character,
but Taffy has more than most, all of it inconvenient. For
instance, although he is very sociable, and longs for company,
he just despises company in the form of dogs. The mere
sound of a dog barking two streets away is enough to make
his fur stand up like a porcupine's quills and his tail swell
like a mushroom cloud.

Which it did the instant he saw Humblepuppy.

Now here is the interesting thing. I could feel and hear
Humblepuppy, but couldn't see him; Taffy apparently,
could see and smell him, but couldn't feel him. We soon
discovered this. For Taffy, sinking into a low, gladiator's
crouch, letting out all the time a fearsome throaty wauling
like a bagpipe revving up its drone, inched his way along to
where Humblepuppy huddled trembling by my left foot,
and then dealt him what ought to have been a swinging right-

handed clip on the ear. "Get out of my house, you filthy little canine scum!" was what he was plainly intending to convey.

But the swipe failed to connect; instead it landed on my shin. I've never seen a cat so astonished. It was like watching a kitten meet itself for the first time in a looking-glass. Taffy ran round to the back of where Humblepuppy was sitting; felt; smelt; poked gingerly with a paw; leapt back nervously; crept forward again. All the time Humblepuppy just sat, trembling a little, giving out this faint beseeching sound that meant: "I'm only a poor little mongrel without a smidgeon of harm in me. *Please* don't do anything nasty! I don't even know how I came here."

It certainly was a puzzle how he had come. I rang the auctioneers (after shutting Taffy *out* and Humblepuppy *in* to the study with a bowl of water and a handful of Boniebisk, Taffy's favourite breakfast food).

The auctioneers told me that Lot 12, Deedbox, coal-scuttles and broom cupboard, had come from Riverland Rectory, where Mr Smythe, the old rector, had lately died aged ninety. Had he ever possessed a dog, or a puppy? They couldn't say; they had merely received instructions from a firm of lawyers to sell the furniture.

I never did discover how poor little Humblepuppy's ghost got into the deedbox. Maybe he was shut in by mistake, long ago, and suffocated; maybe some callous Victorian gardener dropped him, box and all, into a river, and the box was later found and fished out.

Anyway, and whatever had happened in the past, now that Humblepuppy had come out of his box, he was very pleased with the turn his affairs had taken, ready to be grateful and affectionate. As I sat typing I'd often hear a patter-patter, and feel his small chin fit itself comfortably over my foot, ears dangling. Goodness knows what kind of a mixture he was; something between a spaniel and a terrier, I'd guess. In the evening, watching television or sitting by the fire, one would suddenly find his warm weight leaning against one's leg. (He didn't put on a lot of weight while he was with us, but his bony little ribs filled out a bit.)

For the first few weeks we had a lot of trouble with Taffy, who was very surly over the whole business and blamed me bitterly for not getting rid of this low-class intruder. But Humblepuppy was extremely placating, got back into his deedbox whenever the atmosphere became too volcanic, and did his very best not to be a nuisance.

By and by Taffy thawed. As I've said, he is really a very sociable cat. Although quite old, seventy cat years, he dearly likes cheerful company, and generally has some young cat friend who comes to play with him, either in the house or the garden. In the last few years we've had Whisky, the black-and-white pub cat, who used to sit washing the smell of fish-and-chips off his fur under the dripping tap in our kitchen sink; Tetanus, the hairdresser's thick-set black, who took a fancy to sleep on top of our china-cupboard every night all one winter, and used to startle me very much by jumping down heavily on to my shoulder as I made the breakfast coffee; Sweet Charity, a little grey Persian who came to a sad end under the wheels of a police-car; Charity's grey-and-white stripey cousin Fred, whose owners presently moved from next door to another part of the town.

It was soon after Fred's departure that Humblepuppy arrived, and from my point of view he couldn't have been more welcome. Taffy missed Fred badly, and expected *me* to play with him instead; it was sad to see this large elderly tabby rushing hopefully up and down the stairs after breakfast, or hiding behind the armchair and jumping out on to nobody; or howling, howling, howling at me until I escorted him out into the garden, where he'd rush to the lavender-bush which had been the traditional hiding-place of Whisky, Tetanus, Charity, and Fred in succession. Cats have their habits and histories, just the same as humans.

So sometimes, on a working morning, I'd be at my wits' end, almost on the point of going across the town to our ex-neighbours, ringing their bell, and saying, "Please can Fred come and play?" Specially on a rainy, uninviting day when Taffy was pacing gloomily about the house with drooping head and switching tail, grumbling about the weather and the lack of company, and blaming me for both.

Humblepuppy's arrival changed all that.

At first Taffy considered it necessary to police him, and that kept him fully occupied for hours. He'd sit on guard by the deedbox till Humblepuppy woke up in the morning, and then he'd follow officiously all over the house, wherever the visitor went. Humblepuppy was slow and cautious in his explorations, but by degrees he picked up courage and found his way into every corner. He never once made a puddle; he learned to use Taffy's cat-flap and go out into the garden, though he was always more timid outside and would scamper for home at any loud noise. Planes and cars terrified him, he never became used to them; which made me still more certain that he had been in that deedbox for a long, long time, since before such things were invented.

Presently he learned, or Taffy taught him, to hide in the lavender-bush like Whisky, Charity, Tetanus, and Fred; and the two of them used to play their own ghostly version of touch-last for hours on end while I got on with my typing.

When visitors came, Humblepuppy always retired to his deedbox; he was decidedly scared of strangers; which made his behaviour with Mr Manningham, the new rector of River-land, all the more surprising.

I was dying to learn anything I could of the old rectory's history, so I'd invited Mr Manningham to tea.

He was a thin, gentle, quiet man, who had done missionary work in the Far East and fell ill and had to come back to England. He seemed a little sad and lonely; said he still missed his Far East friends and work. I liked him. He told

me that for a large part of the nineteenth century the
Riverland living had belonged to a parson called Swannett,
the Reverend Timothy Swannett, who lived to a great age
and had ten children.

"He was a great-uncle of mine, as a matter of fact. But
why do you want to know all this?" Mr Manningham asked.
His long thin arm hung over the side of his chair; absently
he moved his hand sideways and remarked, "I didn't notice
that you had a puppy." Then he looked down and said,
"Oh!"

"He's never come out for a stranger before," I said.

Taffy, who maintains a civil reserve with visitors, sat
motionless on the nightstore heater, eyes slitted, sphinxlike.

Humblepuppy climbed invisibly on to Mr Manningham's
lap.

We agreed that the new rector probably carried a familiar
smell of his rectory with him; or possibly he reminded
Humblepuppy of his great-uncle, the Rev. Swannett.

Anyway, after that, Humblepuppy always came scampering
joyfully out if Mr Manningham dropped in to tea, so of course
I thought of the rector when summer holiday time came
round.

During the summer holidays we lend our house and cat
to a lady publisher and her mother who are devoted to cats
and think it a privilege to look after Taffy and spoil him.
He is always amazingly overweight when we get back. But
the old lady has an allergy to dogs, and is frightened of them
too; it was plainly out of the question that she should be
expected to share her summer holiday with the ghost of a
puppy.

So I asked Mr Manningham if he'd be prepared to take
Humblepuppy as a boarder, since it didn't seem a case for
the usual kind of boarding-kennels; he said he'd be delighted.

I drove Humblepuppy out to Riverland in his deedbox;
he was rather miserable on the drive, but luckily it is not far.

Mr Manningham came out into the garden to meet us. We put the box down on the lawn and opened it.

I've never heard a puppy so wildly excited. Often I'd been sorry that I couldn't see Humblepuppy, but I was never sorrier than on that afternoon, as we heard him rushing from tree to familiar tree, barking joyously, dashing through the orchard grass—you could see it divide as he whizzed along—coming back to bounce up against us, all damp and earthy and smelling of leaves.

"He's going to be happy with you, all right," I said, and Mr Manningham's grey, lined face crinkled into its thoughtful smile as he said, "It's the place more than me, I think."

Well, it was both of them, really.

After the holiday, I went to collect Humblepuppy, leaving Taffy haughty and standoffish, sniffing our cases. It always takes him a long time to forgive us for going away.

Mr Manningham had a bit of a cold and was sitting by the fire in his study, wrapped in a shetland rug. Humblepuppy was on his knee. I could hear the little dog's tail thump against the arm of the chair when I walked in, but he didn't get down to greet me. He stayed in Mr Manningham's lap.

"So you've come to take back my boarder," Mr Manningham said.

There was nothing in the least strained about his voice or smile but—I just hadn't the heart to take back Humblepuppy. I put my hand down, found his soft wrinkly forehead, rumpled it a bit, and said,

"Well—I was sort of wondering: our spoilt old cat seems to have got used to being on his own again; I was wondering whether—by any chance—you'd feel like keeping him?"

Mr Manningham's face lit up. He didn't speak for a minute; then he put a gentle hand down to find the small head, and rubbed a finger along Humblepuppy's chin.

"Well," he said. He cleared his throat. "Of course, if you're *quite* sure—"

"Quite sure." My throat needed clearing too.

"I hope you won't catch my cold," Mr Manningham said. I shook my head and said, "I'll drop in to see if you're better in a day or two," and went off and left them together.

Poor Taffy was pretty glum over the loss of his playmate for several weeks; we had two hours' purgatory every morning after breakfast while he hunted for Humblepuppy high and low. But gradually the memory faded and, thank goodness, now he has found a new friend, Little Grey Furry, a nephew, cousin or other relative of Charity and Fred. Little Grey Furry has learned to play hide-and-seek in the lavender-bush, and to use our cat-flap, and clean up whatever's in Taffy's food bowl, so all is well in that department.

But I still miss Humblepuppy. I miss his cold nose exploring the palm of my hand, as I sit thinking, in the middle of a page, and his warm weight leaning against my knee as he watches the commercials. And the scritch-scratch of his toe-nails on the dining-room floor and the flump, flump, as he comes downstairs, and the small hollow in a cushion as he settles down with a sigh.

Oh well. I'll get over it, just as Taffy has. But I was wondering about putting an ad. into *Our Dogs* or *Pets' Monthly:* Wanted, ghost of mongrel puppy. Warm welcome, loving home. Any reasonable price paid.

It might be worth a try.